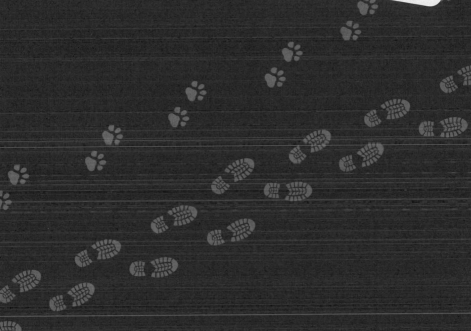

W9-BQZ-974

THE
LOVELY
AND THE
LOST

ALSO BY JENNIFER LYNN BARNES
The Naturals
Killer Instinct
All In
Bad Blood
Little White Lies

THE
LOVELY
AND THE
LOST

JENNIFER LYNN BARNES

 FREEFORM BOOKS

Los Angeles   New York

Copyright © 2019 by Jennifer Lynn Barnes

All rights reserved. Published by Freeform Books, an imprint of Disney Book
Group. No part of this book may be reproduced or transmitted in any form or
by any means, electronic or mechanical, including photocopying, recording,
or by any information storage and retrieval system, without written permission
from the publisher. For information address Freeform Books, 125 West End
Avenue, New York, New York 10023.

First Edition, May 2019
10 9 8 7 6 5 4 3 2 1
FAC-020093-19081
Printed in the United States of America

This book is set in Fairfield LH/Monotype
Designed by Marci Senders

Library of Congress Cataloging-in-Publication Data
Names: Barnes, Jennifer (Jennifer Lynn), author.
Title: The lovely and the lost / Jennifer Lynn Barnes.
Description: First edition. • Los Angeles ; New York : Freeform Books, 2019. •
    Summary: When a little girl is lost in a 750,000-acre national park, a family
    of search-and-rescue professionals reunites and three generations of secrets
    are uncovered.
Identifiers: LCCN 2017015165 (print) • LCCN 2017050054 (ebook) •
    ISBN 9781484785867 (e-book) • ISBN 9781484776209 (hardcover)
Subjects: • CYAC: Rescue work—Fiction. • Lost children—Fiction. •
    Search dogs—Fiction. • Rescue dogs—Fiction. • Dogs—Fiction. •
    Families—Fiction. • Secrets—Fiction. • Survival—Fiction. • Wilderness
    areas—Fiction.
Classification: LCC PZ7.B26225 (ebook) • LCC PZ7.B26225 Los 2019 (print)
    • DDC [Fic]—dc23
LC record available at https://lccn.loc.gov/2017015165

Reinforced binding
Visit www.freeform.com/books

SUSTAINABLE
FORESTRY
INITIATIVE

Certified Sourcing
www.sfiprogram.org
SFI-00993

THIS LABEL APPLIES TO TEXT STOCK

For Daniel, Matthew, Georgianna,
and Joseph (and their dog, Ginger),
Dominic and Julian (and their dog, Hazel),
and Connor and Colin (and their dog, Remy),
with love from Aunt Jen

THE
LOVELY
AND THE
LOST

CHAPTER 1

Saint Jude was the patron saint of impossible causes. My foster brother took his namesake very seriously. In the eleven years since his mother had found me, half-wild and dying in a ravine, I had never once known Jude to throw in the towel when the odds were stacked against him. Jude Bennett had never met a lost cause he did not immediately embrace with the whole of his overly optimistic soul.

I was a testament to that sometimes endearing, sometimes frustrating aspect of Jude's personality—and so was the fact that he was currently standing in the middle of a party at Hangman's Ridge, holding an old-school boom box over his head, and blasting eighties music in the direction of a girl who literally did not know his name. As in, I had *literally* heard her call him Kyle.

Twice.

"Boy still insisting that Kyle is a nickname for Jude?" Free came to stand beside me, leaning back against the truck. She shook her long blond hair back over her shoulder and crossed one ankle over the other as she hooked her thumbs through the belt loops on her faded jeans.

"He's moved on from *nickname* to *term of endearment*," I said, watching as Jude punched a fist into the sky. "Remind me to limit his consumption of eighties movies going forward."

"Won't help," Free opined, reaching up to swat at a mosquito on her arm. "Cady say anything to you about whether or not she's going to let the military have Pad?"

Free didn't believe in segues between one subject and the next.

"Not a word," I said, taking my eyes off Jude long enough to get a better look at Free. "Why? Did she say something to you?"

Pad, short for Padawan—Jude's choice of name, not mine—was a fourteen-month-old golden retriever and quicker on the uptake than any other dog we'd trained. Jude and Free were holding out hope that Cady—Jude's mother and my foster mother—would keep our star pupil, but every time I took Pad out, I could feel her energy, her determination. She needed to run, to track, to find.

She needed more than we could give her.

"I am not Cady's favorite person at the moment," Free admitted, "on account of the fact that we had a fundamental disagreement."

Free was as prone to disagreement as Jude was to optimism. She was the most stubborn person I'd ever met—and the woman who'd raised me was number two. Jude insisted that crossing horns was their way of expressing affection.

"Was this disagreement about the fact that you haven't been to school in over a week?" I asked Free.

Free shrugged. She was infamous in the Chester Falls public school system for two things: her perfect test scores and her less-than-perfect attendance. Free had a system. She aced every single test given during the semester, then skipped finals altogether, ultimately pulling home C's in every class. Free's parents, when this was first brought to their attention, had declared that they "respected their daughter's individuality and right to make her own decisions."

Cady, needless to say, did not. Our property backed up to the Morrows', and Free had spent as much time at our place growing up as she had at her own. Cady didn't treat her any differently than she treated Jude and me—and that meant that she and Free had their share of *fundamental disagreements*.

"You could just ask the teachers to let you take makeup tests," I pointed out. "Then you wouldn't need to ask *me* whether or not Cady was selling Pad to an army search and rescue unit. You could ask her yourself."

Free did not dignify that comment with a response. Instead, she nodded her head toward Jude. "It appears our boy has drawn the attention of some unsavory types."

It took me two seconds to analyze the situation. Jude was

standing in the midst of three very large, very angry townies. And being Jude, he appeared to be challenging them to a dance-off.

I pushed off the truck and headed for trouble. Free followed at a lazy pace.

"I assure you, gentlemen, proving yourselves to be better dancers than me would stick it to me far worse than any act of physical violence possibly could." My foster brother offered his would-be assailants a conspiratorial smile. "I'm not saying that I'm the second coming of Fred Astaire, but I'm also not denying it."

One of the townies reached for Jude. I got there first, stepping between them. The townie—twenty-one or twenty-two, too old to be at a high school party and too stupid to know it—barely managed to stop himself from ramming his knuckles into my face. Jude was a head and a half taller than me, six foot two to my five foot nothing. He was gangly.

I was small and dangerous.

"Well, well, well," the townie said, looking back at his friends, bleary-eyed and clearly amused. "What do we have here?"

I said nothing, but I could feel a familiar emotion unwinding inside of me, an old friend come out to play. These idiot boys didn't know what it was like to fight tooth and nail for survival. They didn't know what happened when you cornered an animal in its lair.

They didn't know that the biggest dog wasn't always the one in charge.

"Man," one of the other townies said, laughing, "I'd watch out for this one, Dave. She has the crazy eyes."

I didn't move, didn't stop staring at the lot of them, didn't so much as blink. All around us, the other partygoers began to realize what was going on. If Jude's assailants had been a few years younger, they might have realized, too.

I had a bit of a reputation.

"Gentlemen," Jude said behind me, "this is what is known as a *situation*. I would suggest that you take a step or two back, and then I can assure you with an entirely moderate degree of accuracy that this will probably not get ugly."

The party had gone completely silent, except for the music and the distant sound of the river down below. We were maybe ten feet from the edge of the ridge, a hundred feet above the river, 9.6 miles as the crow flew away from the ravine where Cady had found me eleven years before.

"And if we don't step back?" one of the boys taunted.

My upper lip wanted to pull back. Only years of social conditioning let me push down the urge to growl.

"Seriously," one of the townies said to Jude, a note of nervousness creeping into his tone at the expression on my face. "What's wrong with her?"

"Nothing's wrong with Kira," Jude said cheerfully. "I mean, who among us *doesn't* have anger management issues and difficulty socializing in the human world, am I right?" He laid his hand on my shoulder, a warm and steady weight. *Familiar. Home.* And just like that, I was five years old again and six and seven, and Jude was the one person in this world that I trusted. Back then, I wouldn't have stared down the bullies. Back then, I would have attacked.

"Dude," one of the townies said under his breath, "is she the one who . . ."

The one they found in the forest all those years ago. The one who'd forgotten how to speak. The one who'd fended for herself for who knows how long.

"And on that note," Free said, stepping forward, "let's break this little lovefest up." Even clad in Levi's and a ratty blue T-shirt, Free was the kind of girl that guys looked at and then looked at again. It wasn't the thick blond hair, falling in carefree waves past her chest. It wasn't her full lips or deep brown eyes. It wasn't even the hips beneath the jeans.

It was her confidence. It was the fact that Free Morrow walked through life knowing that she could ace any test it threw at her—and didn't much care either way.

She bent down and picked up Jude's boom box. "Who wants to dance?"

CHAPTER 2

The next morning, I was up with the dawn. The party had left me restless. If I'd thought there was any chance that I could have gotten away with it, I would have spent the night outside, but Cady would have noticed, and she would have pressed Jude for answers.

Jude did not hold up well under questioning.

So I'd lain in my bed all night, trying not to feel boxed in. When the first hint of sun hit my window, springing me from my seemingly endless sentence, I was up and digging through the pile of clean laundry on my desk in seconds. As I donned a pair of running shorts and looped my hair back into a ponytail, Silver stirred on the end of my bed. She lifted her head, liquid brown eyes meeting mine.

"Go back to sleep," I told her.

Silver made a huffing sound and jumped down to the floor. She was almost thirteen—old for a German shepherd—and didn't move as easily as she had in her youth. Still, she was spry enough to block me from exiting the room. Her head butted gently—and reproachfully—against my thigh.

No matter how old I got, Silver would never see me as more than a pup.

"I'm fine," I told her, sinking down to let her see for herself as I ran my right hand over her coarse fur. "I just need to run."

Silver was Cady's dog, but I was Silver's human. She'd been the one to find me all those years ago. Since then, she'd stood guard over me through much worse than a restless night's sleep. The stubborn look on her face now made it clear that she was *not* getting out of my way until she was certain I was okay.

"You're impossible," I commented.

Silver rested her head on my shoulder and huffed again. For a few seconds, I let my arms curve around her. *Silver's heartbeat. Silver's warmth.* Long before I'd stopped shrinking back from human hands, this had been *contact, safety, touch.*

I gave myself another instant, then stood. After a long moment, Silver exhaled loudly and stepped aside.

Humans, I could almost hear her saying. *They're so much work.*

"You're telling me," I muttered as I made my way down the stairs. I was halfway out the back door before I sensed eyes on the back of my head.

Busted. I turned around. A ghost-white dog with ice-blue eyes sat three feet away, watching me with an intensity that would have set most people's hearts to thundering in their chests. On paper, Saskia was a husky, but there was something wholly wolflike about her features that would have made most people think twice before holding out a hand.

I wasn't most people.

I snapped my fingers, and the husky sprang forward. She came to a standstill at the door's threshold, looking at me. I held up my right hand, accompanying the gesture with a verbal command. "Stay."

Saskia stayed where she was, but her blue eyes tracked me as I began walking backward. When I got ten feet away, I began bouncing on the balls of my feet. Saskia's ears flicked forward, but no matter how badly she wanted to give chase, she didn't move.

Stay. I let the command stand as I dodged back and forth and began moving backward once more. *Stay. Stay. Stay . . .*

"Come!" I lowered my hand. Saskia bolted from the doorway, and the moment she did, I turned and ran, as hard and fast as I could. I made it to the edge of the woods before she caught me. She circled me and barked, and I bent down to play, rough-and-tumble.

Most people thought that training animals was about obedience and control. But in reality, the center of any search and rescue training program was *play.* For the dog, searching was a game. Animals who had a strong play drive would keep playing indefinitely—through ice and snow, over hard terrain, for hours upon hours—until the game was won.

Until they found their target.

That Saskia was playing with me now—that she would do anything to *keep* playing with me—was a minor miracle, given the way we'd found her. She'd mistrusted humans, and she'd had reason to.

"That's my girl." I stepped back from the game, and Saskia went eerily still, waiting for instructions. Waiting for round two.

"Feel like some exercise?" I asked her.

She let out one loud, sharp bark.

The tension that had been building inside me since the night before began to dissolve. I gave Saskia a wolfish grin. "Let's run."

The deeper we ran into the woods, the rougher the terrain got, and the rougher the terrain, the harder we ran. My body was coated in sweat by the time we finally stopped. The burn in my muscles had gone from pleasant to verging on real pain. I bent over at the waist. My heart was racing in my chest. My skin tingled, a surefire sign that I'd come close to pushing myself too hard.

Everything in me wanted to go harder.

"Cady's already going to tear a strip off of me for skipping breakfast," I told Saskia, who wasn't even winded. "If I don't stop and rest, things could get ugly."

My canine companion eyed me for a moment and then lowered her front half toward the ground, silent and ready.

"I see how it is," I murmured. Saskia had an uncanny way

of looking at people, her gaze almost human and borderline predatory all at once. Cady had been against my training her.

My girl didn't play well with others.

I signaled, and Saskia pounced. After wrestling with her for a minute or two, I lowered myself to the ground. If anyone had seen us from a distance, they might have thought I was in danger—a small, fragile teenage girl with a fifty-pound animal looming over her.

Feeling more at peace than I had in weeks, I closed my eyes, and for the first time in twenty-four hours, I slept. When I opened my eyes again, Saskia was nestled beside me, and the sun was high enough in the sky that I was fairly certain the two of us weren't the only ones out and about. I reached into my pocket and pulled out a plastic bag. Inside was a rag—one I'd swiped out of Cady's room the day before.

I let Saskia get the scent, and then I climbed to my feet. "Shall we see what the boss is up to?" I asked the dog. Saskia's whole body was taut with the effort of staying in place until I gave her the command. "Find her."

CHAPTER 3

A single search and rescue dog could cover as much ground as fifty or more human searchers. It didn't take long for Saskia to find her target and come looping back to me. She gave three authoritative barks—sharp, loud, clear, just like she'd been trained to do.

Find. Recall. Re-find.

"Show me," I said. Saskia took off, slowing her pace just enough for me to follow. She led me over rocks and a small stream, straight to Cady, who greeted Saskia with a quick tussle.

Find. Play. Find. Play.

Years of training had tied these two things together in the dog's mind. I'd taught Saskia how to play—with me, with Jude, with Cady, with Free.

Her attitude toward the rest of the world was still a work in progress.

"You're up early," I greeted Cady before she could aim those same words at me. "One last training session?"

Cady had Pad on a lead, which I took to mean that my foster mother had already laid a scent path that our resident overachiever was following. Most dogs were either trained in air scenting, like Saskia, or in a method that focused more directly on retracing the target's progression. Pad could switch back and forth between air scenting to cover a large area, and trailing, following a specific scent path across any and all terrain.

The army would have uses for both.

"You eat anything this morning?" Cady finished playing with Saskia and turned her eagle-eyed attention to me.

I shrugged.

"That would be a no, then." Cady produced a PowerBar seemingly out of thin air and tossed it to me.

My hand whipped up to catch it. "Eat," I ordered in unison with Cady, mimicking her no-nonsense tone almost exactly.

The edges of Cady's lips twitched as she stifled a smile. "Is that your way of telling me I'm predictable?"

I shrugged again, but I didn't bother biting back my own grin.

"I'm your mother," Cady retorted. "I'm allowed to feed you. I'm *also* allowed," she emphasized, "to tell you that I heard there was a party last night up on Hangman's Ridge."

Cady had a sixth sense that let her read animals with

impressive accuracy. Unfortunately for Jude and me, that knack seemed to extend to her children as well.

Luckily, I had a better poker face than Jude did. "We went. We partied. We came home." I preempted Cady's next question. "We behaved ourselves, and Free left when Jude and I did. Happy?"

Cady reached out to push a piece of flyaway hair back from my face. "Ecstatic."

I leaned into her touch for a moment before pulling back, and Cady let me eat the rest of my PowerBar in peace. Some people found my capacity for silence off-putting, like the act of not chitchatting was the equivalent of spitting in another person's face. Cady never seemed to mind. She'd fought long and hard to give me back my voice, but she never acted entitled to my words.

If I'd stood there in silence for ten minutes, she would have stood there with me.

"Free was asking me if you'd decided to let the military have Pad," I said as I swallowed the rest of the PowerBar and let Saskia lick my fingers for crumbs.

"Free can woman up and ask me herself," Cady responded, in a tone that made it crystal clear that our neighbor wasn't off the hook for skipping finals yet.

"What if I'm not asking for Free?" I bent down and greeted Pad, who'd been sitting patiently at Cady's side. Saskia wasn't pleased to be sharing my attention, but she tolerated Pad the way a person might tolerate a coworker with particularly bad breath.

"If you're the one asking," Cady replied, "then my answer is that it depends."

"On what?" I straightened. Cady had about eight inches on me. Jude might have gotten some of his height from his mystery father, but at least part of it had come from her.

"On you," Cady replied. She held Pad's lead loosely in her left hand. The golden retriever sat with her haunches on the ground, ready and alert. "You'll be seventeen next month, Kira. Only one more year until you can get certified. Pad would be a good partner for that. For you."

A lump rose in my throat. With the price the military had offered for Pad, we were talking about a substantial sum of money. As much as it meant to me that Cady was willing to make the offer, it hurt, too.

"I already have a partner," I said.

"Don't take this personally. I have no doubt that Saskia will be able to blow through most of the exam," Cady said carefully.

Saskia's not sociable enough. She'll never be sociable enough. That was what Cady was saying. No matter how good my girl was at finding lost people, if she couldn't play well with others—other handlers, other dogs—it wouldn't matter.

How could I *not* take that personally?

"Saskia will be ready," I replied, my voice lower in pitch than it had been a moment before.

Cady knew better than to argue. "In that case, then yes, I intend to accept the military's offer for Pad. I know the team she'll be working with. They'll take good care of our little prodigy."

Fully aware that we were talking about her, Pad began wagging her tail.

"You want to take her out, one last time?" Cady asked me. "I can finish up with Saskia."

That wasn't really a question—or a request. Saskia needed to be able to work with other handlers, and Cady knew that if I was left to my own devices, I wouldn't take Pad out again.

I'd never excelled at *good-bye*.

There were two basic methods for directly following a scent path. A tracking dog worked with its nose to the ground. A trailing dog worked with her nose in the air. In addition to air-scenting to cover large areas, Pad was trained for the latter. She could follow a scent wherever she found it, take shortcuts, track a person from one environment to the next.

She blew through every challenge I laid out for her.

"I'm not going to miss you," I told our resident wunderkind. She responded to the warmth in my voice as I jostled her from one side to the other. When I signaled to allow it, she jumped up, putting her paws on my thighs. I buried my hands in her downy fur and scratched under her collar. "I'm not going to miss you at all, you awful dog."

Pad tilted her head to the side. Her ears went up.

She hears something, I thought. Unlike most dogs, Pad was unlikely to be distracted by small animals. A squirrel could have danced across the path, and she wouldn't have batted an eye.

The only thing that Pad was trained to pay attention to was humans.

A muscle in my jaw ticced. The boundaries of Cady's property were clearly marked. So was the fact that trespassers were not welcome. *Our territory. Not yours.* I kept a check on the part of my brain that whispered those words, but I didn't take Pad and head back to the house. Instead, the two of us went for a little walk. Being the human half of a SAR team required more than just training the dog and giving the appropriate commands. You had to be able to traverse all kinds of terrain. You had to know advanced first aid. You had to be able to navigate. You had to be able to strategize.

You had to have at least rudimentary tracking skills yourself.

It took me five or six minutes to find a sign that Pad hadn't been hearing things. A broken twig, a quarter of a footprint, if that. The size and shape indicated the owner was male and walked lightly. Whoever our visitor was, he knew how to hide his tracks.

"You ready for some fun?" I asked the golden.

In answer, Pad got a good whiff of the intruder's scent. The human body shed roughly forty thousand skin cells per minute. With a trail this fresh, those cells would be a beacon for the dog's nose, leading us straight to the trespasser.

Pad looked up at me, waiting for the command. "Find him."

Pad took off running. I gave her plenty of slack on the lead—thirty or forty feet—and jogged to keep up with her. She led me up and over rocks, twisting and turning deeper and deeper into the forest. I wasn't sure how long we'd been on the trail when Pad stopped. She stood perfectly still for a moment, then took off running with joyful abandon.

Find. Play. Find. Play.

I could feel the energy thrumming through her as she took us down a hill and into a clearing. To my surprise, our quarry was sitting on a rock, waiting for us. The intruder was older than I'd expected, and his suntanned, weather-worn face registered exactly zero surprise when we came tearing through the clearing.

When Pad plopped down in front of him and started barking, the old man held out a worn piece of rope. Instantly, she latched her teeth around it. I waited for the man to say something to me, but he was too busy playing tug-of-war with my partner to do it.

He knows she's a search and rescue dog, I thought. *She found him. She barked to indicate her find. They're playing.*

Another part of my brain focused on his posture, his size, any hint of movement in my direction.

"Would I be right in assuming you belong to Cady Bennett?" The man's gaze flicked up to meet mine. I focused on thinking in words, not feelings, not colors, not *heat*. I wondered if he was with the army, if he was here for Pad.

As long as I was wondering, I had everything under control.

"Cady Bennett," I repeated, the feel of the name familiar in my mouth—another safeguard, another anchor. "She's my mom."

I'd never called Cady by anything but her first name. Even after she'd adopted me, I'd still referred to her as my *foster* mother. Something inside me wouldn't let me do anything else, but here, now, with this man looking at me like he knew something I didn't, the words slipped out.

I was Cady Bennett's daughter, and every instinct I had was telling me two things. First, that she knew this man, and second, that she didn't know he was here.

Our territory. Not yours. The muscles on the back of my neck tightened. I wasn't conscious of taking a step toward him until he held up a hand—the gesture for *stay*.

"I'm not an animal," I gritted out, my throat tightening around the words.

"No," the man said gruffly. "You're my granddaughter. And from the looks of that glare on your face, you are very much your mother's daughter."

CHAPTER 4

"I feel this bodes well."

Jude and I were sitting at the top of the stairs, listening as best we could to the conversation that was going on in the kitchen. Cady had gone ashen the moment she'd seen her father. I hadn't wanted to leave her alone with the man, but the look on my foster mother's face had promised retribution if I didn't.

With most people, I wasn't capable of backing down. But every pack had its alpha—and Cady was ours.

"You think everything bodes well," I told Jude. "We didn't even know that Cady *had* a father. You really think she would have kept his existence a secret without a reason?"

Jude dismissed my objection with a wave of his hand. "He's our *grandfather*, Kira. By definition, that entitles us to certain grandchildly privileges."

Jude had a habit of making up words. Being Jude, he was

also optimistic that each and every one would be added to the dictionary, if only he used them regularly enough.

"I have to say, sister mine," Jude continued seriously, "I think this is shaping up to be the best summer of our lives."

"You say that every summer."

"And every summer," Jude countered, "I am correct!"

The sound of the hushed conversation in the kitchen gave way to silence. I tensed, preparing myself for an explosion. With Cady, it was always calmest right before the storm.

"How *dare* you come here, unannounced and asking for favors?" Cady's voice cut through the silence, rising in volume and pitch. Her tone was sharp enough to draw blood, but beneath the anger, I could hear something dark and cavernous. She wasn't just furious. Inside, *she* was bleeding. "I came to you," Cady said roughly. "Do you remember that? Do you remember me begging you to help us find Ash? I would have done anything to get him back, and you wouldn't even pick up a phone."

"I loved that boy, same as you did, Cadence, but there are some doors better left closed."

What doors? I thought. *What boy?*

For once, Jude didn't immediately pipe up to put some ridiculously positive spin on the situation. Cady had told us very little about Jude's father, other than the fact that she'd loved him. Jude had come up with a thousand theories about his "mysterious sire," each more elaborate than the last, but we'd never heard so much as a name.

I loved that boy, same as you did.

Without meaning to, I leaned my body into Jude's. He rested his forehead against mine.

"That wasn't your decision to make," Cady said down below, and somehow, even though her voice had gotten quiet again, I could hear every word. "It was my life, and my choice, and Ash was worth it to me."

Another silence stretched out between father and daughter. My body tensed, the way Saskia's had when I'd given her the command to stay. I knew, logically, that I couldn't physically protect Cady from an emotional onslaught, but there were some parts of my brain where logic meant nothing.

Cady was *mine*. Jude was *mine*. I'd tear this man apart before I let him hurt them.

The touch of something cold and wet on the back of my elbow was the only warning I got before Silver wedged herself between Jude and me. Her ears flicked forward, on high alert.

"Now, ladies," Jude said, casting a stern glance at both the German shepherd and me. "Physically attacking our mother's father would be a grandchildly and grandpuppy no-no."

Jude had gone from shell-shocked to convinced that a group hug was inevitable in under ten seconds. Sometimes, I questioned how hard he had to work to have that much hope—no matter how effortless he made it seem, no matter how calming just being near him was.

Jude chose that moment to press the tip of his index finger lightly to the end of my nose. "Boop."

Down below, the front door slammed open, then shut. "Marco!"

Cady never locked the house, and Free never knocked. Jude and I met eyes and then scrambled down the stairs in an effort to reach Free before she stumbled into World War III.

"Polo!" Jude yelled. "Polo! Polo! Po—"

We made it to the landing just in time to see Free's blond ponytail disappearing into the kitchen. Silver surged ahead to follow, and I took that as a sign that Jude and I should as well.

"Polo," Jude finished weakly as we skidded into the kitchen. I grabbed Silver's collar, but in reality, she was holding me back as much as the reverse.

Free looked at Cady, looked at the old man, looked at Jude, and looked at me.

Then she sauntered over to the stove and snagged a piece of bacon out of the skillet. "Can we agree," she said, taking a bite, "that my C average isn't looking like *that* big a deal in the grand scheme of things?"

Free might not have known what she'd just stumbled into, but she was as good at sniffing out people's hot buttons as she was at taking tests. She didn't need to know the particulars of a situation to know that there *was* a situation.

And she wasn't above defusing the tension *and* making a point.

"We can agree that you"—Cady narrowed her eyes at Free, then shifted the glare to Jude and me—"all of you, can take a lap around the perimeter and then try your hand at giving the bloodhounds a bath."

Free took another bite of bacon. I studied the interloper. Jude offered him a loopy smile.

"*Now,*" Cady snapped.

Her father chuckled. "You reap what you sow, Cady-girl, and this lot looks like they're about as good at following directions as you were."

Free tossed a glance at Jude and me. "I'll take old guys with boundary issues for two thousand, Alex," she said.

"Long-lost grandfather," Jude informed her, "no longer estranged and come to bring adventure into our otherwise ordinary lives!"

Cady kneaded her temple. Clearly, the situation had spiraled out of her control. Free was enjoying this a little too much. Jude wasn't leaving until he got an introduction, and I wasn't capable of turning my back on the same threat twice. After a long moment, Cady gave in to the inevitable.

"This is Jude," she told her father, her voice tight and controlled. "You've already met Kira. And the miscreant stealing my bacon is our neighbor Free. They were just on their way out."

"In terms of grandfather names," Jude asked the old man, "would you say you're more of a Granddad or a Papaw?"

The edges of the old man's lips ticked slightly upward. "You can call me Bales. That's my name, and if I know my daughter half as well as I think I do, that'll have to do." He stood with his hands by his side, nonthreatening, nonconfrontational, but ready to move. "Now, as much as I would like to continue this conversation, son, your mother and I have something to settle."

"No," Cady said. "We don't. What part of *no* don't you understand?"

Bales Bennett didn't bat an eye, didn't so much as raise his voice. I got the sense that he was the kind of man who never had to. "The part," he said, "where your issues with me are making you turn your back on a missing child."

CHAPTER 5

After that, Cady really did kick us out of the house. I barely noticed. The words *missing* and *child* would always take me to places in my memory that I didn't want to go—*the smell of wet dirt, gnawing hunger.* I remembered blood beneath my fingernails. In flashes, I could feel myself, *crouching, cowering, growling.* I could see my tiny body lying in the ravine.

I remembered the exact moment that Silver leapt down beside me.

But whenever I tried to picture what had come before—the weeks in the forest, how I'd survived, the events that had led me out there?

Nothing.

"Some people might say our grandfather is manipulative," Jude commented, preparing to lather up one of the bloodhounds. "I prefer to think that he is offering our family an opportunity for emotional advancement."

Jude never left me stranded in the dark for long. With a wink in my direction, he turned his attention to his K9 partner. NATO, a three-year-old bloodhound, was the peacekeeper of our makeshift pack—and every bit the optimist that Jude was.

"Come on, bucko," Jude crooned, patting the inside of the tub. NATO looked up at Jude adoringly and jumped haplessly in.

"Poor sap," Free commented. "Doesn't matter how many times we play this game, he never sees the betrayal coming."

"I am going to assume," Jude replied austerely as he turned on the hose, "that you are talking about the dog."

It was another few seconds before NATO realized, belatedly, that he was *being bathed*. He bayed mournfully.

"Whoever could have seen this coming?" Free asked the dog. "In related news, someone needs to help me with Her Ladyship."

NATO was Jude's dog. Duchess was Free's. Both were bloodhound mutts, but somehow, NATO had ended up with the temperament of a happy-go-lucky Lab, while Duchess was a bloodhound to her bones.

Her Ladyship was *not* getting in that tub.

"Cady would say," Free commented cheerfully as she tried—and failed—to grab hold of Duchess, "that this serves me right."

Everything else came easy to Free—school, people, boys. But she'd chosen the *one* dog that she could never outstubborn. She'd spent hundreds—maybe thousands—of hours training Duchess. Her Ladyship was an excellent tracker.

But baths were a different matter.

"Care to take a stab at this, K?" Free was the only one who ever shortened my name—the only one I *let* shorten it.

I crouched down to Duchess's level. For several seconds, we appraised each other. Duchess didn't *want* to be sweet-talked.

"That man is in there getting under Cady's skin," I told the dog, feeling about as agreeable as she did. "He's hurting her."

"Mom can take care of herself," Jude interjected. "She's the great Cady Bennett. She laughs in the face of danger and cantankerous relatives."

I kept my focus on Duchess, whose expression was mutinous. "Someone doesn't like being boxed in," I murmured. "Someone doesn't like surprises."

Free looked from Duchess to me. "Someone doesn't like changes that are out of her control."

Free's observation hit me harder than it should have. Pushing down the unexpected emotions roiling in my gut, I snagged the hose from Jude and tossed it to Free. "Splash around a little," I told her. "Let Duchess come to you."

Obligingly, Free ran her hand back and forth beneath the spray. Duchess cocked her head to the side, but Free knew better than to so much as look at the dog. Instead, she flicked a stream of water at me.

I jumped back, landing in a crouched position. A rumble made its way up my throat—a laugh. Free got a wicked gleam in her amber eyes and advanced on me slowly. Feeling like Saskia on the verge of a run, I dodged.

Play.

I needed this, and Free knew it. She feinted toward me, then, with an evil expression on her face, pivoted and turned the hose dramatically on Jude.

Full blast.

Jude shrieked like a banshee, sputtered, and fell smack on his haunches—in that order. "You know, of course," he said, soaking-wet hair drooping into his face, "that this means war."

An instant later, the three of us were grappling for the hose. I came out on top—but only for a second.

"Take that, you fiend!"

Jude wrapped his arms around my middle. Free went straight for the flying tackle. It didn't take Duchess long to decide she wanted in on the action. NATO jumped out of the tub to join in, and soon, all *five* of us were soaked through and soaped up.

Jude climbed to his feet, holding the hose high. "This will not stand!"

I'd just taken a spray straight in the face when I heard the sound of footsteps to our left. I went instantly silent, even as the human part of my brain overrode my instinctual response. I knew those footsteps—light and even, unafraid. There was no threat. No reason to stop playing.

But just like that, the day's events came roaring back.

I turned toward Cady, and she raised an eyebrow at the fact that Jude, Free, and I were all soaked to the bone.

"Good job," she told the bloodhounds as they bounded toward her. "You gave the miscreants a bath."

Part of me wanted to pick up the hose and aim it at Cady. I wanted to play. I wanted to give her what Free and Jude had just given me. But I couldn't banish the words *missing* and *child* any longer.

"One to ten?" I asked Cady. She was the one who'd invented the shorthand—for nightmares, for flashbacks, for times when I needed out. *How bad is it, one to ten?*

"I'd say I'm sitting at about a six." Cady shifted her attention from me to NATO, who was bounding toward her. "Don't even think about it, mister."

I squatted down and let NATO jump up on me. I was already soaked, and I deeply suspected that Cady's six was a normal person's nine.

"You're going, aren't you?" I asked. *Missing* and *child* were loaded words for Cady, just like they were for me.

My foster mother looked at me the way she had when I was small and angry and caught in a fight-or-flight cycle that neither of us could break.

"*I'm* not going," she said. "*We* are. Get packed."

CHAPTER 6

'd never been a person who cared much about material things. I didn't have prized possessions. I wouldn't have thought the idea of leaving home—the house, this room, my bed—would bother me.

A few hours ago, I'd been gnawing at the bit to get out.

But now that we were going someplace else, someplace new with new people and new rules that most humans never had to explicitly learn, I had the urge to put my back to the wall and hunker down. As I stared at my empty suitcase, I thought about the way Cady had said that Saskia would blow through *most* of her certification.

Not sociable enough. My fingers found their way to a patch of loose fabric on my bed. *Does not play well with others.* I stroked the threadbare cloth. Once upon a time, it had been a blanket. When Cady had first brought me home, the blanket had lived in Silver's crate. It had been years since Cady had stopped crate-training the dogs, years since I'd stopped spending my days holed up in Silver's crate while the German shepherd stood guard outside. The blanket wasn't just ratty now—it was shredded.

And it was mine.

I bunched the fabric in my hands. *Soft. Familiar.* I wanted to be happy that we were going. It was a *good* thing that Cady had agreed to join this search—and a better thing that she was taking us with her. This was what I'd been training for. It was my chance to show her that Saskia and I were ready.

I could do this, and Cady wouldn't have to face down her father alone.

"Hope I'm not interrupting anything."

I glanced up, not the least surprised to see Free sitting in my second-story window. The day Jude and I had met her, we were nine years old. Free had hopped the fence, walked right up to the two of us, and suggested that we join her in rigging up some handmade hang gliders. I'd been on guard. Jude had been ecstatic.

Cady had vetoed the hang gliders.

And Free had taken it all in stride. She'd never said a thing—not a single, throwaway comment—about the fact that I didn't speak in her presence for a year. She accepted Jude talking for me like it was normal.

The three of us had hang-glided off the roof the next year.

"You're not interrupting, Free." I let the fabric fall from my hands and back down onto the bed. Silver was asleep at my feet. Without even thinking about it, I burrowed my toes underneath her body. "I was just packing."

"Packing traditionally involves putting one or more items inside the bag," Free pointed out.

"Second-story windows," I countered, "are not traditionally considered doors."

That got me a smile. "Su casa es mi casa," Free said lazily. "And that bag is still empty."

I had a go-bag for search and rescue—we all did—crammed with the supplies we might need to meet whatever challenge Cady decided to lay out on any given day. But packing my personal suitcase was harder.

"It's not that I don't want to go." To anyone who didn't know me, my voice might have sounded flat. "I'm glad we're going. Cady will find this missing kid. Saskia and I will help."

It was easier, sometimes, to communicate things that I had already thought.

"Of course you'll help," Free replied. "You were born for search and rescue. And I . . ." Free let her legs dangle down toward the roof outside my window. "I'll be here all by my lonesome."

Cady had asked her to look after the place while we were gone. Free probably would have preferred looking after *us*.

Silver stirred at my feet. She stretched and made a loop around my legs. Finding me in one piece, she went to greet Free, then cycled back to my side. Free followed, and a moment later, she was sifting through the laundry on my desk.

"You'd tell me if these clothes weren't clean, right?"

"They're clean."

"Pack this." Free tossed a zip-up long-sleeved shirt in my general direction without so much as looking back. "And this." The sweatshirt hit me square in the face.

I dodged the next projectile and began wrangling the clothes Free had picked out into my bag.

"Cady should have invited you to come with us."

"Miscreants' Creed," Free countered. "Line seven. I solemnly vow to never say *should*."

Cady had referred to us as miscreants so often growing up that the name had stuck. The Creed was ever-evolving, and Free was its self-appointed keeper.

The words *ought* and *rule* were also verboten.

"It would be better if you came with us," I tried again.

Free spared me a brief but dazzling smile. "I happen to agree." She made a trip to my closet and returned with three pairs of cargo pants and twice that number of all-weather shirts. "But I think it's safe to say that Mama Bear has other things on her mind."

Cady had said she was at about a six. I didn't always get the full range of human emotion—especially other people's—but I did know *fear* and *anger* and *want* and *pain*.

Cady wasn't any better at admitting weakness than I was.

"No moping." Free pitched a balled-up pair of socks at my face. "Need I remind you of the Miscreants' Creed, line four?"

"Never look down?" I asked.

Free zipped the suitcase shut. "We were born ready," she corrected. "You're going to be just fine, Kira. And *I* . . ." She paused for dramatic effect. "Well, like a good and proper Miscreant, I have some trouble to stir up. Take care of yourself, K."

Free was already back out the window before I'd found the words to reply. "You too."

CHAPTER 7

Five hours later, I'd spent four hours too many in the car. I was restless, tense, and hungry—and we were almost there.

Not that *almost* or *there* meant a thing to the part of me that equated *car* with *cage*.

Breathe in. Breathe out. I counted back from one hundred, one number per breath. *One hundred. Ninety-nine.* I stared out the window as we drove up a winding mountain road. Spread out in the distance, I could see nothing but unvarnished wilderness. Something about the way the mountain range cut into the sky made *me* feel vast, like the green of the trees and the crisp white snowcaps—the stone and dirt and water and air—were part of me.

Like I could get lost out there without ever leaving this car.

"Sierra Glades National Park," Cady said. "Seven hundred and fifty thousand acres of mountains, foothills, canyons, and rivers—not to mention a forest that boasts some of the tallest, oldest trees on the continent."

"Or as I like to call it," Jude added from the passenger seat, "our new backyard!"

"Don't get too comfortable," Cady muttered as the town— what little there was of it—came into view. "We won't be here long."

Responding to Cady's muttering, Silver lifted her head from my lap. Behind us, Saskia prowled, making use of the space Cady had cleared when she'd removed the third row of seats from her SUV. Pad sat calmly at the back window, ready for action.

As Cady pulled off onto a gravel road, Silver laid her head back down on my lap and plopped one paw over my leg, a clear order that I should stay put.

"I take it that our beloved grandfather is greatly revered in the town of Hunter's Point?" Jude asked, continuing the steady stream of chatter he'd kept up for the whole drive. "For his wisdom. And his beard."

"Unless something's changed since I left, your grand-father doesn't mix much with the people in town." Cady didn't elaborate.

"You don't want to talk about him." I meant that as a statement, but a question burrowed its way into my tone. Cady hadn't told us anything about Bales Bennett. She had to have known that we'd overheard parts of their conversation, but she hadn't so much as mentioned it—not once.

"We're here to help with a search," my foster mother said,

her fingers tightening around the steering wheel for a split second before she forced them loose again. "That's all."

Cady was famous in search and rescue circles for training dogs, but as far as I knew, she hadn't participated in an active search in years. *Since she found me.*

"I sense that this is something of a bittersweet homecoming," Jude commented as Cady pulled in front of a cabin-style house and cut the engine. "Out of respect for the solemnity of the occasion, I shall refrain from confetti."

Why did I have a feeling literal confetti would be making an appearance before long?

Ignoring Jude, Cady opened the driver's-side door, and I took that as permission to open mine. Silver, determined to get the lay of the land, exited first. I tried not to notice the stiffness with which my aging companion jumped out of the car. It was ten or fifteen seconds before she turned back to me.

All safe, I could almost hear my self-appointed protector saying. *Kira get out of car now.*

I obliged. The second my shoes hit dirt, the tension that had been building inside me snapped like a rubber band. I closed my eyes and lifted my face toward the sky and listened. *Birds. Running water, somewhere nearby.*

I heard Jude let Saskia and Pad out of the back, and without turning toward them, I tracked their movements. Saskia stalked; Pad was more of a prancer, like a horse trained in dressage.

Another sound broke through. My eyes snapped open

as I angled my body toward the source. *Human.* A boy—eighteen or nineteen, dark hair, dark eyes, brown skin that glistened with a layer of sweat—drilled a soccer ball into the side of the house.

Again.

And again.

Maybe he was dangerous. Maybe he wasn't. When it came to strangers, my brain was wired to err on the side of caution.

Almost as if on cue, the stranger in question turned to look at us. Without missing a beat, he pounded the ball into the wall so hard that it rebounded over his head and into the woods.

I felt my nostrils flare but kept my lips pressed firmly together.

"I believe that is the traditional salutation of the Hunter's Point soccer enthusiast," Jude said, ambling to my side. Pad took up position just in front of us.

"Just curious," I said to Jude under my breath. "Are you two protecting me from the stranger or the stranger from me?"

Jude remained suspiciously silent.

"Hello," Cady called out.

As the boy began to make his way toward us, the tips of his fingers curled inward, a prelude to working themselves into fists, but his arms stayed dangling by his sides.

"Him from you," Jude murmured as he took in the expression on my face. "We're definitely protecting him from you."

Pad went out to greet the stranger.

"Hello," Cady repeated. "I'm—"

"You're the daughter." The boy bent to scratch Pad behind the ears, then rose again. "I'm supposed to be on my best behavior, so I suppose I should welcome you home."

I felt, as much as saw, him cross the invisible threshold that put him within two arm's lengths of my family. Saskia took a single, threatening step toward him.

"Easy, Sass," I murmured. I followed my own advice, right up until the boy bared his teeth at Cady in a smile that didn't strike me as *friendly* in the least.

"We heartily accept your dubious welcome!" Jude beamed at him. "I admire a man with pent-up anger and a casual disregard for even the most basic social norms! You do you, I always say."

The boy came to a stop. There was nothing overtly aggressive in his posture. But that didn't stop the part of my brain that had been on high alert since this interaction began from sizing up my opponent's weaknesses.

Worse came to worst, I could go for his throat.

"We're here for the search," Cady said.

"You don't want to be here at all." The boy rocked back on his heels. "Believe me, Ms. Bennett, that's perfectly, crystalline clear."

"Crystalline," Jude repeated. "An excellent vocabularical choice! I'm Jude. This is Kira. We will be your same-age peers today."

The boy flicked his gaze away from Cady, just briefly. But he didn't look at Jude. He looked at me.

"Gabriel."

The boy didn't introduce himself. An older woman, who'd just appeared on the cabin's front porch, did it for him. She wiped her hands on a faded blue apron as she strode toward us. She was tiny and bird-boned, but moved like she was used to people getting out of her way.

When she reached us, she gently lifted a wrinkled, sun-worn hand to cup Cady's face. "It's good to see you, Cady-girl."

For the first time since we'd entered Hunter's Point, Cady smiled. "Ness."

The older woman pulled Cady into a long, tight hug, then reverted to business mode. "Cadence Bennett," she said, pulling back, "meet Gabriel Cortez." She turned her eagle eyes to the boy next to her. "Gabriel," she said, her tone warning him to play nice, "has been helping your father run this place for the past year."

"An altruist if I've ever seen one!" Jude sidestepped Cady to get a better look at Ness. "I'm Jude, and the lovely lady glowering in your general direction is Kira. Glowering is Kira's way of showing love."

The older woman arched an eyebrow at Jude. "I take it you don't get your temperament from the Bennett side of your family tree."

"I am, in many ways, an enigma," Jude intoned. "At

the moment, I happen to be an enigma who is wondering whether or not there are any cookies to be had in the near vicinity?"

Ness snorted. "That's quite a nose, young man. I just finished baking a fresh batch. If you're lucky, your friend won't have devoured them all."

There was a moment of silence and then Jude tilted his head to the side, like NATO the moment someone so much as mentioned the word *t-r-e-a-t*.

"What friend?" Cady asked.

I knew the answer to that question *before* Free sauntered out onto the porch, a cookie in each hand. I should have guessed, when she was helping me pack, that Free wouldn't just roll belly-up and let us leave her behind.

"I brought the bloodhounds," she informed Cady. "In case you need them. Or, you know, in case you need me."

"Miscreants' Creed, line nine," Jude whispered in my ear. "It's better to ask forgiveness than permission."

"Do I want to know how you beat us here?" Cady gave Free what Jude liked to call *The Look*. "Or how you knew where exactly we were going?"

"I could invoke my constitutional right not to incriminate myself," Free mused. Being Free, she didn't stop there. "But for argument's sake, let's just say that Jude can't keep a secret, and once I knew where you guys were going, I might, hypothetically, have talked my way into a ride."

Cady's *Look* intensified. "Did you know the person who drove you here?"

Free shrugged. As protective as she was of us, she'd never had any particular talent for taking care of herself.

I could practically *see* Cady counting back from a hundred. "You and I are going to be having words, Free." Cady let that single sentence hang ominously in the air for a moment before she turned to Ness. "Where's my father?"

Gabriel took it upon himself to answer the question. "Exactly where you should be," he said. "At the rangers' station, joining the search for that girl."

CHAPTER 8

By the time we arrived, there were easily sixty people at the rangers' station, awaiting instructions. Jude, Free, and I weren't the only ones under the age of eighteen. With this much area to cover and a child's life at stake, the authorities needed every warm body they could get.

Beside me, Saskia strained slightly on her lead. She didn't like crowds. Neither did I, but search and rescue was a cooperative effort.

I forced my attention from the mass of people to my training. If I settled down, Saskia would follow suit. *A first-response team would have been deployed as soon as the child's family reported her missing*, I thought, willing the muscles in my neck to relax. *This will be the second wave, or the third—civilians, useful primarily for their numbers.*

I didn't need to get a good look at the local authorities to know that they would keep volunteers on a short leash. The last thing anyone needed was another missing person, and though I suspected most people in Hunter's Point knew a little something about wilderness survival, that wasn't a risk any reasonable leader would take.

Not even for a child.

"Thank you all for coming."

Those words were meant to silence the crowd, and they did. The lack of noise put my senses on high alert. *The sound of the man behind me breathing. The snap of a twig beneath a woman's feet, up and to the right*—I forced myself to look at Saskia, who was sitting as close to me as she could get without touching.

"Good girl," I said softly. The muscles in my chest loosened slightly, and I focused on the man whose voice had sent a hush through the crowd. Based on his uniform, he wasn't a park ranger.

He was the local sheriff.

"Bella Anthony disappeared from her family's campsite at the base of Bear Mountain sometime between ten p.m. on Thursday and six a.m. Friday morning." The sheriff had a visible sidearm and a voice that carried. "Bella is nine years old, four foot two inches tall, and has shoulder-length medium-brown hair. When last seen, she was wearing pale pink pajamas and a red windbreaker."

The sheriff nodded to one of his men, who began passing out flyers with the child's picture on them. When the stack came to me, my fingers locked around it with surprising force. I stared at the picture. There was nothing remarkable about the little girl in the black-and-white photo. She could have been any other child.

But she wasn't.

I knew better than anyone that if Bella Anthony was out there much longer, she wouldn't ever be *any other child* again.

A hand brushed the edge of mine. My head whipped up. A man—the heavy breather who'd been standing behind me—gestured to the flyers I was holding. "Take one and pass it on."

Breathe in. Breathe out. I managed not to recoil from the man's touch. I took a flyer and passed the stack on. No claws, no fangs, no fight, no flight. I was in control—and I was here for a reason.

"The park rangers are already out there, looking for Bella." The sheriff picked back up where he had left off, once the flyers had made the rounds. "Our job is to help comb the forest within the radius that Bella could have traveled. You will work in teams of two, walking straight lines no more than thirty feet apart. Call Bella's name. Look for any evidence of her presence—tracks, food wrappers, disturbed foliage. Once we've covered one section of the grid, we'll move to the next."

The strategy made sense—for civilians. But Bales Bennett hadn't brought Cady here to walk the woods.

As the sheriff dismissed us and the crowd began to disperse, snatches of conversation hit me like shrapnel. The quiet had sent my senses into overdrive, and now that quiet was gone.

Jude leaned toward me. "On a scale of yea to nay, how are we doing?"

I fixed my gaze at a point in the crowd—a child, maybe two or three years old. He had dark hair and chubby, sun-kissed cheeks, and he was staring, wide-eyed, at Saskia.

"Sass and I are fine," I said, keeping my eyes focused on the child and tuning everything else out. As if to prove my point, Saskia docilely observed a butterfly flutter by. The child watched, delighted

And then Saskia snapped her teeth and swallowed the butterfly in a single gulp.

The toddler threw back his head and howled.

Jude glanced at Free, then cleared his throat. "We shall speak of this no more."

Quite pleased with herself, Saskia cast triumphant looks at Duchess and NATO and settled back by my side. I watched as a woman about Cady's age bent to pick up the screaming toddler. Her arms curved around his sturdy little body, and he laid his chubby cheek against her chest. I ached, watching them. Not because I couldn't remember my own mother. Not even for little Bella, lost in the woods.

I ached because I didn't *want* to be held. Most of the time, I didn't want to be touched at all.

It was a minute or more before Bales Bennett made his way through the crowd toward us, a youngish woman I didn't recognize by his side. He introduced her as Angela

Anthony, Bella's mother. Dark smudges marred the skin under her gray eyes. She looked like a breeze could have blown her away, but the animal part of my brain said that Bella's mother could kill every person here—every single one—if it meant bringing Bella home.

"Mrs. Anthony." The sheriff intervened before she could say anything to us. "What are you doing here? You should be at the hotel. You need sleep."

The reply was immediate and guttural. "I need my baby."

I had no word for the shuddering emotion in her tone. *Like gnawing hunger. Like a jagged cut.* I couldn't label the feeling, but I knew it, viscerally.

"Cadence Bennett." The sheriff shifted his attention to Cady. "It's been a while."

"Brad." My foster mother returned his greeting. "Or should I say Sheriff?"

"I appreciate your coming all this way." The sheriff showed too much teeth for my liking as he spoke. "But the rangers have already been over the campsite."

"Not with these dogs," Bales interjected. "My daughter's the best in the world at training rescue animals. The rangers have already indicated that they'll welcome her help."

Subtext wasn't my forte, but I knew, in my gut, the importance of *hierarchy* and *competition* and *strength*.

Cady was joining this search—whether the sheriff liked it or not.

"We might find something." Cady addressed those words

equally to the sheriff and Bella's mother. "We might not. But I'd like to try."

After a long, tense moment, the sheriff gave a curt nod. His gaze traveled to Free and Jude and their K9 partners before landing on Saskia and me.

"Husky," I said, answering the question in his eyes. *Not a wolf.*

"Your children are welcome to join the other searchers," the sheriff told Cady, "but—"

"My children are less than a year away from being FEMA-certified in search and rescue." Cady let that sink in. "With all due respect, Brad, the three of them can cover more ground than the rest of your search party combined."

CHAPTER 9

When it came to wilderness searches, the first step was to locate and secure the PLS—point last seen. In this case, the rangers had set up a perimeter around the campsite where little Bella had last been seen snuggled down in her sleeping bag. Her family had gone to sleep that night. When they'd woken up the next morning, she was gone.

"It's different," Free said, coming up behind me, "when it's real."

I didn't tell her that it was always real for me—every training exercise, every scenario we'd worked our way through back home. For me, searching was always—*always*—about survival.

"Are we using the sleeping bag to get the girl's scent?" I asked Cady. "Or is there clothing?"

I needed to move. I needed to do something. I needed to stop standing here, doing *nothing*.

Cady lifted her hand to get the attention of the closest park ranger, but the ranger's attention was already occupied. He was talking to a stranger. Tall and broad through the shoulders, the newcomer had long blond hair tied into a ponytail at the nape of his neck. The dog by his side was indeterminate in breed, as large for its species as the man was for his.

"Mackinnon Wade." The sheriff cut across the campsite, his stride bigger with each step. "This is a crime scene, and as familiar as you are with all things criminal, Wade, I'm sorry to inform you that this particular scene is closed."

All missing-persons cases were treated as criminal, so the sheriff's use of the phrase *crime scene* was less concerning than the way he pushed back his shoulders and took a deliberate step into the other man's space. *Aggressive. Male.*

I couldn't have so much as inched forward or backward if I'd tried.

"Mr. Wade is here to help with the search," one of the rangers informed the sheriff. "He's military-trained search and rescue, the best in the world."

"Second best," Mackinnon Wade corrected the ranger, his eyes locked onto Cady's.

Jude leaned forward to whisper in my ear. "I believe the implication our very large new friend has just made is that *Mom* is number one. He's pleased to see her." Jude paused. "She is . . . err . . . less pleased to see him."

Cady crossed the campsite to stand toe to toe with Mackinnon Wade. "My father called you?" she demanded.

"Your father called me," Wade confirmed. He seemed . . . *calm*. Steady. Like he could walk through a war zone without batting an eye. "Cady." He inclined his head in greeting.

"Mac," she returned, echoing the calm in his voice with steel in her own.

"And the plot thickens," Jude whispered.

"By my count we have five K9s and five handlers here," the sheriff said loudly. I'd been so intent on watching Cady and the man she'd called Mac that I'd stopped tracking the sheriff's movements. "As far as I'm concerned, that's about four teams too many." The sheriff stared directly at Mac. "You all have ten minutes to get what you need and get yourselves out of my crime scene."

"I think he likes us," Jude told Free and me. "Deep down."

We got to work. Within ninety seconds, a plastic bag was being passed around so the dogs could get the girl's scent. I assumed it contained clothing, until it came to me.

Not clothing—a blanket, I realized, my stomach inexplicably heavy. *A baby blanket.*

The fabric might have been lavender once, but it was faded nearly to white now. It was threadbare and tattered, and the moment I saw it, I wondered if the little girl slept with it at night. When she was lonely, when she was scared, did she hold on to it? Did she press her face into it?

Did it help?

I will find you. The promise unfurled inside me, unexpected and with the strength of a creature with a life and will of its own. *I will bring you home.*

"Kira?" Cady's voice broke through the din in my mind.

I wasn't sure how long I'd been standing there, holding the bag. I went to offer the scent to Saskia, but Cady stopped me. "Hang back for now," she directed. "Let the bloodhounds find the trail, then we'll be able to let you and Saskia loose in the right direction."

I told myself that Cady didn't want us searching with the group because the bloodhounds were more suited to this task—not because of the way I'd reacted to Bella's blanket. Not because she didn't trust Saskia around strangers.

Less than sixty seconds later, Cady, Jude, and Free had cleared out. I could hear them plowing through brush, following the trail Bella had laid when she'd left the safety of her family's campsite in the middle of the night. I pictured Bella's face, drew it in my mind—each strand of hair, each happy crinkle at the corners of her eyes. I pictured her sleeping, the blanket tangled in her arms.

Why had she woken up? Why had she left the campsite? I wanted to stop there, but couldn't. I could see it happening in my mind. I could see small feet—*bare feet*—dirt-smeared and disappearing into the brush.

Bella's feet weren't bare, I reminded myself. *Her shoes are missing, too.* They'd told us that when they'd briefed us on the scene. But for some reason, the image of bare feet lingered in my mind. Somewhere, deep in my subconscious, another question reared its head. Not *Where did she go?* or *Why did she leave?* but *How long?*

How long before anyone bothered to look for her? I knew

55

that question wasn't about Bella. Bella had been gone for less than forty-eight hours, and park rangers, law enforcement, and dozens of volunteers were already combing the woods for her.

By the time anyone had come looking for me, I'd been on my own for weeks.

Forest. Dirt. Water. Blood. Threat—

My grip on Saskia's lead tightened as the images flashed through my head. I wanted to let go of the lead, to cut Saskia free.

I needed to run.

"Beautiful animal."

My eyes whipped toward Mackinnon Wade, who knelt next to his own K9 and held a hand out to mine.

"Careful," I started to warn him, but Saskia considered the out-held appendage with a calm she'd never before exhibited around an adult male, let alone one of his size. Her vigilant blue eyes on his, she stepped forward to get the man's scent.

She's not usually this friendly. I recognized that as the benign thing to say, the *normal* thing to say.

"Why are you still here?" I asked instead. "Don't you want to find Bella?"

Mac withdrew his hand from Saskia and ran it over his own K9's head and down the back of her neck. "I want that little girl found," he said quietly. "But I pray to God that I'm not the one to find her."

I heard something in his voice that Jude probably wouldn't

have recognized, or even heard. But part of me would never leave the forest. Part of me would always be wild and half-dying in that ravine.

"You never offered your dog the scent," I noted, my voice as soft as his. There was only one type of search dog that wouldn't need Bella's scent. The kind of dog that wasn't trained to search for Bella.

The kind that was trained to search for Bella's body.

CHAPTER 10

"She's a cadaver dog?" I asked, my gaze on Mac's K9 partner.

"We work mostly overseas." Mac took his time with his reply. "Disaster relief."

A well-trained cadaver dog could scent human remains beneath a mudslide, buried in rubble, or under running water. That was useful in criminal investigations, but also played a key role in bringing closure to the families of those killed in natural disasters.

"We find the bodies." Mac spoke in simple sentences. "Give the ones who remain something to bury. Help them say good-bye."

I appreciated someone who said exactly what he meant and didn't dress the truth up with frilly and unnecessary words. "The sheriff doesn't like you," I commented. Without Jude here, there was no one to tell Mac that this was my version of being friendly.

"I'm a Wade," Mac replied, unruffled. "There are a lot of people hereabouts who don't care too much for my kind."

I held my hand out to Mac's dog, the way he'd held his out to mine. Saskia allowed the massive animal to delicately sniff my fingers before flashing her teeth. The mutt returned to Mac's side.

Abruptly, Mac stood and turned toward the brush. His dog reoriented her body to match his, like they were a single unit, and I followed suit. The wind lifted my hair. The smell of the forest invaded my nostrils, damp and fresh and *alive*. In the distance, a K9 barked three times.

One of the dogs found something. Bittersweet hope and heavy dread battled it out in the pit of my stomach. Muscles clenching, I thought of the faded blanket in the plastic bag. I pictured a little girl in a bright red windbreaker. I let myself imagine a happy ending.

What I got was a phone call from Cady, informing me that Bella's scent had intensified, then dead-ended—in the river.

CHAPTER 11

The rangers' probable search area for Bella had been calculated assuming the little girl had been traveling on foot. The river changed things. When we found Bella—if we found her—we'd find her downstream.

We might not be looking for a little girl. We might be looking for a body. No one said those words, but Mac quietly joined the search, his dog running the riverbank, wading in and out as he followed her with surprising swiftness for a man his size.

I pray to God that I'm not the one to find her. Mac's prayer echoed in my mind as I was given my own assignment. Saskia and I would take the west side of the river. Cady and Pad would take the east. If Bella had made it out of the water—if she'd survived—she could have ended up on either shore, and that meant the forest was fair game on both sides of the water.

Now that I had something to focus on, the tightness in

my stomach slowly unwound. Saskia was a flash of white in the wilderness, running from the riverbank to the tree line, weaving in and out, over rocky ground. She looped back to me often enough to make sure that I was keeping up.

Nightfall drew closer.

Cady would never let me search on my own past dark—not in unfamiliar territory. Not in a 750,000-acre wilderness that could swallow an adult nearly as easily as it had devoured Bella.

As the countdown clock ticked down, Saskia and I pressed on. I made sure she stopped for water breaks and did my best to stay hydrated as well. Thirst was an old acquaintance—*dry lips, head pounding, each breath hot in my throat.* Pushing back against the memories, I let myself crouch down on the forest floor. Cady had said that Sierra Glades had some of the tallest trees on the continent, but this part of the forest wasn't filled with those giants. As I looked up into the branches, the dying sun caught the leaves just so. My fingers sank into the dirt, and I closed my eyes.

Bella was nine years old. She'd been missing for almost forty-eight hours. Her trail had dead-ended in the river. In all likelihood, she was dead. But that was what Cady had been told years ago when the authorities had asked her to help search for me.

I opened my eyes and took out my radio. In an area where cell phone reception was spotty—sometimes nonexistent—a two-way radio could be a lifesaver. For a moment, my dirt-smudged fingers hovered over the power button. If I turned it off, I wouldn't hear them telling me to report back to base camp.

If I turned it off, the sun's descent didn't have to mean I'd failed.

Saskia ran toward me. She didn't bark, didn't indicate that she'd found any hint that Bella had made her way out of that river and into the woods. I pictured the current in my mind, the water, whitecapped against the rocks. I could *feel* the sharp bite of uneven stones tearing into tender flesh.

Bruises and blood. Lying on my back. Can't . . . can't . . .

Saskia bumped her nose against my hand. I stood. "Good girl," I told her, keeping the energy in my voice high. "Good girl, Sass."

Bad things happen to bad little girls, a voice whispered from the dark place.

I forced myself to breathe. *Ninety-nine. Ninety-eight. Ninety-seven.*

Almost as abruptly as the memory had come on, it was gone. I let my fingers curl into fists to keep my hands from shaking and led Saskia away from the river. I steered her toward the mountain, pushing the boundaries of the search area I had been assigned. Men like the park rangers looked at a picture of a lost little girl and saw an innocent, a victim, someone helpless and fragile and small.

They had no idea what a child was capable of—really capable of—when the civilized world melted away and nothing but instinct remained.

On some level, I was aware of a call coming in on my

radio. On some level, I was aware that darkness was falling, that I'd gone too far. But I just kept pushing. *Just a little farther up the mountain. Just a little farther off the path.*

I couldn't even see Saskia. She had to be getting tired, but like me, she wouldn't give up, wouldn't back down, wouldn't—

"Kira." Cady's voice on the radio cut through the laser focus that had driven me up this path. "Are you there?"

I hesitated, just for a second, before lifting the radio to my mouth. "I'm here," I said. "Saskia and I haven't found anything, but we're still looking."

Still climbing, still running, still going.

"Give me your coordinates, and I'll have someone meet you." Cady had to have known that every fiber of my being would fight coming in, but she'd painstakingly taught me that there was no room for *fight* or *flight* in SAR. Instincts were good—necessary, even—but the human partner had to work within certain parameters, by certain rules.

I could give Cady my coordinates now, or I could forget about continuing the search tomorrow.

"Coordinates," I said, my throat dry.

I will find you. That had been my silent promise to Bella. *I will bring you home.*

"Kira," Cady said. "You're cutting out."

I wasn't cutting out. I was stalling. A sound in the distance sliced through the mountain air. It took me a moment to realize what it was.

Three barks.

I was sure that I'd imagined it, willed it into being, heard it the way I sometimes *heard* or *saw* or *felt* things in a place in my mind that seemed real. My pulse pounding in my throat, I fixed my eyes on a clearing in the trees. If Saskia had found something, she'd circle back and give the signal a second time.

Find. Recall. Re-find.

A blur of white burst through the clearing. Saskia barreled toward me, and I knew, just from the way she was running, that I hadn't imagined anything. She bounded up to me—joyful, wild, free—and barked.

Three times.

CHAPTER 12

Saskia hadn't found Bella Anthony. She'd found a piece of Bella's windbreaker, caught in brambles. That piece of red cloth, uneven and torn, was like a shot of adrenaline, straight to my heart.

Bella had made it out of the river.

She'd made it this far.

She's alive. I knew, logically, that the river wasn't the only danger a child would face in these mountains. Based on the tracks I'd seen, it was home to mountain lions. In all likelihood, that wasn't all. *Black bears, rattlesnakes, foxes.* My brain began to rattle off what a child would face out here alone. *Dehydration. Hunger.*

"How did a little kid even make it this far?" one of the rangers asked as the sheriff marked off a perimeter around the scene. "Why would she keep going? Why head up the mountain at all?"

"Because," I said softly, "if you stop, it's over."

If you stop, you die. Bella might have been taught to stay in one place if she got lost, to wait for someone to find her. But there came a point when you realized that no one was coming. *Keep moving. Girl has to keep moving. Find water. Food. Run—*

Cady laid a hand on my shoulder, her touch light and fleeting. Once upon a time, I would have bristled at the contact. Instead, I reached out and caught her hand in mine. I brought it back to my shoulder.

"Pad and I will see if we can pick up the trail from here," Cady told me, rubbing her thumb gently over my arm. "You should head back to town, get some rest. Free and Jude went back hours ago."

I should stay. I thought the words, and then I said them. I said them so that Cady would know they mattered.

"Kira." Cady forced me to look at her. "I'll take one of the rangers with me. I won't be alone. And," she continued, preempting any argument, "*I* haven't run myself ragged. You have."

Getting into a staring contest with Cady was never a good idea.

"If you haven't found her by dawn, I'm coming back."

Cady gave a brisk nod, then turned and led Pad to the strip of red cloth, barely visible in the moonlight as it wafted in a wind too light to feel.

"Miss?" A park ranger came up behind me. *Directly* behind me.

I whirled, every muscle in my body tightening. The

ranger gave me a look I recognized all too well. Even a hundred miles away from home and whispered rumors about the feral girl from the forest, there was still something about me that told other people that I wasn't quite right.

"Come on," the ranger said, his voice quiet and kind. "Let's get you home."

Home was Bales Bennett's house, but Cady's father was nowhere to be seen. Ness was the one who met us at the door. She looked the ranger up and down, then thanked him for coming all this way. He was probably halfway to town before he realized how handily he'd been dismissed.

"You need food." Ness issued that statement like a woman declaring martial law. Without waiting for a reply, she turned and headed for what I could only presume was the kitchen.

Saskia stayed outside. I would have preferred to do the same. But people lived in houses, ate at tables. My lungs constricted as the front door closed behind me. I felt trapped. *Cornered, no way out—*

The smell of chili wafted in from the kitchen. I breathed in and breathed out and tried not to think about the fact that there had been a time when fresh meat had been the only way Cady could lure me indoors. Fighting the déjà vu, I walked slowly toward the kitchen. As I crossed the threshold, I wondered if Ness was the one who'd taught Cady to make chili.

I wondered if she was the one who'd taught my foster mother what it took to bring home a stray.

"Sit. Eat." Ness didn't even turn from the stove to see if her words were being obeyed. There was a bowl of chili waiting for me on the kitchen table, along with a double helping of corn bread.

I sat, suddenly aware of how long it had been since I'd had food. *Eat slowly,* I reminded myself as my fingers latched themselves around the spoon in a death grip. *The food is yours. No one is going to take it from you.*

"Kira. Sister mine." Jude appeared in the doorway. He lumbered over to the table and took the seat across from me, blocking my view of Ness and the stove. He was freshly showered and wearing flannel pajamas.

Clearly, he'd made himself right at home.

"The hero triumphant, returned to the fold," he pronounced, giving an artistic wave of his hand in my direction.

"Would 'the fold' like some more chili?" Ness asked wryly, setting a bowl down in front of Jude. Apparently, in the last few hours, she'd come to know him well.

"Where there is food," Jude declared solemnly, "so, too, there is Jude."

As he dug in, I felt my own grip on my spoon relax. There was a time when I'd refused to eat at a table—and Jude had eaten on the floor next to me.

"Where's Free?" I asked. I was fairly certain there was at least one line in the Miscreants' Creed devoted to the core value of never turning down a second helping.

"Upstairs," Jude replied, dabbing at his mouth with his napkin. Glancing at Ness to make sure she wasn't watching, he then pantomimed climbing out a window, which I took to mean that Free was probably already halfway to town. For someone who was awfully fond of skipping school, she didn't do "leisure time" well.

Not that I had any room to throw stones.

"Is this the part where you regale us with tales of your heroics and/or indicate that the case has moved in a more hopeful direction?" Jude asked. In preparation for my answer, he pulled a small packet of what I could only assume was confetti out of his pocket.

"Bella made it out of the river." My voice failed to convey even a fraction of the relief I'd felt at that discovery, but Jude had been fluent in Kira long before I'd spoken in actual words. "Saskia caught the scent again in the mountains," I continued. "We found a piece of Bella's windbreaker. Cady and Pad are still out there, searching."

"Given half the chance, your mother will run herself ragged." Ness clucked her tongue. "Never was a girl like that one for needing someone to take care of her, but thinking she could face down the big bad world alone."

"You don't say." Jude gave me a look. "Sounds like someone else I know." He paused. "Rhymes with Mira."

I would have flicked food at him, but I wasn't willing to give up a single bite.

"I assume you told Mom we'd be back in the morning?" Jude asked me once he'd realized no edible projectiles were forthcoming.

"Break of dawn," I confirmed. Technically, I'd told Cady

that *I* would be back, but now that we'd picked up the trail again, Jude and Free would be able to offer the bloodhounds a scent path to follow.

"I have a good feeling about this," Jude announced, jiggling the packet of confetti.

I didn't take the bait. How could I, when even the best-case scenario would leave its marks on that little girl?

"Saskia needs food," I said, finishing my chili.

"Gabriel will take care of that," Ness assured me. "He's already fed the others. If I know that boy half as well as I think I do, he's out there seeing to your pup right now."

I wasn't sure which was more notable: the fact that Ness had just referred to take-no-prisoners Saskia as a *pup* or the way she seemed to believe that Gabriel could feed Saskia without losing a hand.

"Mayhaps Kira should just *check* on them," Jude suggested delicately. "For funsies."

I took that as permission to bolt.

Darkness had fallen outside. The moon was a quarter moon, the stars hidden by a thick blanket of clouds. In a single, fluid motion, I brought my index fingers to my mouth and let out a loud and piercing whistle. Through the discordant buzz of bugs and the rustling of wind weaving through the grass, I listened for Saskia.

I heard human footsteps instead.

"You rang?" Gabriel said dryly. His white T-shirt caught the scant moonlight—bad camouflage for someone who liked sneaking up on people.

"I wasn't whistling for you," I emphasized.

"Well, that is a relief."

I did not, as a rule, always pick up on sarcasm—but Gabriel wasn't exactly subtle.

An instant later Saskia came tearing around the side of the house.

"Your dog doesn't trust me," Gabriel said, sounding almost amused. "She accepted my offering of food, but she wasn't happy about it. Probably a sign of discernment on her part. I'm not really the trustworthy type."

I had a way of looking at people that tended to unnerve most, but Gabriel was apparently an exception, because he didn't bat an eye when I turned to face him.

"Would it be inappropriate for me to ask if the great Cady Bennett has found anything yet?" he asked. "Because I would *hate* to be inappropriate."

The way he said Cady's name had my hackles rising. "We found the trail." I had nothing to prove to him. I knew that, *and yet* . . . "There's a chance the girl is alive."

"Maybe this kid's alive." Gabriel angled his face toward the night sky. "Maybe she isn't. Around here?" His face was shadowed in the moonlight. "People go missing all the time."

CHAPTER 13

Ness put me in a bedroom on the second floor. My first instinct would have been to open the window, but it was already open. That, along with the fact that Free's bag was sitting on the floor, told me that we'd be sharing.

As I took in the rest of the room—a double bed, a dresser, an antique mirror—I realized that it had once belonged to a teenage girl. The pictures tucked into the frame of the mirror told me who that girl was.

Cady. There was a snapshot of her as a preteen with her arm around a German shepherd with darker markings than Silver's. Another shot showed Cady on horseback, her dark hair flying in the wind behind her. But the picture that drew my gaze and held it was of three teenagers. Cady stood between two boys. One was tall and blond and didn't look happy to be having his picture taken. The other boy's lips were parted in what Jude would have called a devil-may-care grin. Mr. Devil-May-Care had thick honey-brown hair, lighter than Cady's, but darker than the other boy's. There was something about him that made it very hard to look away.

"Doesn't *he* look like trouble?" Free didn't bother to announce her presence before taking the picture from my hand. The fact that I hadn't heard her come in made me wonder how long I'd been staring at the picture. "The good kind," Free clarified.

"The good kind of trouble?" I repeated.

"My specialty." Free took in the rest of the photo. "And there's our overly large friend from the campsite," she continued. "Maybe Jude was right about the plot thickening."

I'd been so focused on Cady and the grinning boy that I hadn't paid much attention to the one who'd been glaring at the camera. *Mac.* As I stared at the three teenagers, I thought of the exchange Jude and I had overheard between Cady and Bales.

I loved that boy, same as you did, Cadence, Bales had told her. And Cady had snapped back that it was *her* life and *her* choice, and that Ash was worth it to *her.*

"Ash," I said, taking the picture back from Free and letting my finger hover over The Good Kind of Trouble.

"You got something you want to share with the class there, K?"

I looked up from the photo. "I think the smiling boy might be Ash. Cady and Bales argued about him." I paused, remembering the way Jude had gone quiet the moment we'd heard Cady say the name. "Cady said she loved him."

"Think he's Jude's father?" Free had an almost religious objection to beating around the bush. She stared at the picture for several seconds. "I could see that." She leaned back at the dresser. "Cady's always been good at loving trouble."

I wasn't sure if Free was referring to herself or to me.

"How was town?" I asked. I tucked the photo back into the mirror's frame. It felt important somehow, to leave this room exactly as I'd found it.

"Town was barely a town," Free replied. "Not much to see, but I think I left an impression." Coming from Free, that was somewhat concerning. "In related news: I'm adding a couple of new lines to the Creed." She glanced over at my suitcase. "Want me to unpack for you?"

"No." My response was instantaneous. Understanding my own reasoning took longer. "If I unpack, that means we're staying."

Free waited.

"If we're staying, that means that we haven't found Bella yet."

I caught Free up on the evidence Saskia and I had uncovered, but the entire time, I kept thinking that I hadn't done enough. I'd *let* Cady send me packing. I'd let her tell me that I needed rest.

I should have fought harder.

Free didn't let me wallow for long. "Flip you for the bed?" she said. She glanced meaningfully at the double. "Unless you'd prefer to cuddle."

I walked over to the still-open window. The breeze was

cool, the mountain temperature falling steeply. Cady was out there, searching.

Bella was out there.

And I'm not.

"Bed's all yours," I told Free.

On nights like these, I preferred the floor.

CHAPTER 14

irl shouldn't have eaten the berries. She lurches forward, stomach on fire. Hurts. It hurts. Everything inside her comes up.

Again. And again.

Finally, she collapses. She can smell the sick—smell it everywhere. Girl trembles, tries to push herself to all fours.

Bad things.

Bad things happen with that smell. She has to get away before—

I woke crouched in the corner, my hair stuck to my face with sweat. Moonlight kept the room from utter darkness. I could make out the outline of Free's form on the bed. Slowly, I remembered where I was, *when* I was.

"Kira." I whispered my own name under my breath. Over and over, I said it, an audible reminder of who I was—and who I wasn't. Slowly, I came back to myself.

One to ten? I could hear Cady asking. *Eight.* It had been months since the last nightmare, years since I'd had one that vivid. *That real.* I didn't need any of the specialists I'd seen as a child to tell me that the hunt for Bella had triggered something in me.

The last psychologist Cady had taken me to—the only one who hadn't made me feel like an animal trapped in a hole—had told me that she could help me remember, if that was what I wanted.

She'd also told me that the brain repressed memories for a reason.

I pushed myself off the floor, digging the heels of my hands into the wood floor harder than I had to. I stalked out of the room and down the stairs. I needed space. I needed air.

I needed to breathe.

But as my hand closed around the knob on the front door, I heard the murmur of voices coming from the kitchen and turned toward them.

"You won't sleep tonight." Ness's voice was matter-of-fact. Without meaning to, I crept toward it, in time to hear the reply.

"Cady knows her way around the wilderness."

"Of course she does," Ness replied evenly. "And of course that doesn't matter. You're her father. Worrying is what you do."

I came to a stop just outside the kitchen door. The light was on inside, but the hallway was dark—better to mask my presence.

"I've missed this," Ness commented after a long silence.

"Coffee you didn't have to make yourself?" Bales asked gruffly.

"Worrying about them," came the reply. "Knowing enough to know what we should be worrying about."

There was a long pause. "Cady's the one who chose to leave."

"The one who didn't even tell you she was pregnant," Ness said. "I know." She paused. "Would it have made a difference if she'd told you?"

I came to you, Cady had told her father. *Do you remember that? Do you remember me begging you to help us find Ash? I would have done anything to get him back, and you wouldn't even pick up a phone.*

I missed Bales's reply to his housekeeper's question—if he'd answered it at all. There was almost a minute of silence before he spoke again. "You never blamed me."

"Blame doesn't change things, Bales Bennett. You, of all people, should know that by now."

There was another pause, and I heard the light clink of a coffee mug being set down. "Mac came back to town," Bales commented. "For the search."

"For you," Ness corrected.

"Not for me."

There was *something* in the old man's tone when he said those words. I needed Jude here to translate.

"Did you tell Mac—"

"No." Bales clipped the word. "And you won't, either, Ness Ashby."

Tell him what? I wondered. My weight shifted from one foot to the other, and the floor creaked beneath me. *Did they hear that?* The sound of a chair scraping against the kitchen tile made a breath catch in my throat.

I went to retreat, but Ness's voice held me back. "Thirty-plus years, Bales Bennett, and you're still telling me what to do."

"Thirty-plus years," Bales replied, his voice rough and hoarse and oddly quiet, "and you still don't listen."

I felt suddenly like this wasn't something I should be eavesdropping on.

This—whatever *this* was—was private.

I backed away—from the door, from listening—but as I edged toward the exit, a final piece of their conversation made its way to my ears.

"Cady won't thank you for bringing Mac into this, Bales."

"Since Ash, Cady doesn't thank me for much."

CHAPTER 15

I spent the night outside, sleeping propped up against the base of a tree, Saskia and Silver curled by my sides for warmth. I woke the next morning to the sound of a low, warm chuckle. At first, I thought I'd been spotted, but then I tracked the laughter to its source.

A dozen yards away, Gabriel Cortez knelt on the ground, his body disappearing under an onslaught of wiggling, yipping little balls of fluff. The pups' mother—a golden retriever—watched, amused, as they mobbed Gabriel. A crooked smile on his face, he set down several bowls of food. The entire litter descended like a horde of locusts, except for the biggest puppy, who appeared quite satisfied rolling back and forth at Gabriel's feet, and the smallest, who couldn't seem to find a way around his siblings to the food. As I watched, Gabriel lifted the runt toward one of the bowls.

Beside me, Saskia stood and shook the morning dew off her fur, pelting me straight in the face.

That's what you get, her expression seemed to say, *for admiring puppies.*

I stood, and though I moved with near silence, Gabriel looked up. "I'm going to go out on a limb and assume you don't want me asking why you look like you slept on a tree."

I stared directly at him. "I slept on a tree."

"Never would have guessed."

Jude had once spent an entire day trying to teach me what a *smirk* looked like. It had ultimately been unsuccessful because Jude was as bad at smirking as I was at recognizing that particular expression.

But I was nearly certain that Gabriel was smirking now.

"Why do you keep talking to me?" The question came out lower in pitch and more intense than I'd intended.

"Because I don't know how to keep my mouth shut." Gabriel delivered that statement in a tone that matched his facial expression almost exactly.

Beside me, Silver huffed. She stood, pressing the front half of her body down toward the ground in a stretch. Within seconds, she'd made a loop around my feet. She sniffed me, then glanced at Saskia, as if expecting the younger dog to report.

"Don't take this the wrong way," Gabriel said, lowering his voice. "But I'm pretty sure they're talking about you."

I almost smiled, but Gabriel chose that moment to shift his weight—slightly, almost imperceptibly—and the reminder that he was a *stranger* and *unpredictable* and a *threat* thrummed through me.

I didn't put my guard down around threats.

He wants something. That's what people do. They want, and they take. They—

A door slammed behind me, muting the thought, but not the increase in adrenaline that had come with it.

"I mean this in the least confrontational way possible, Gabriel, my well-muscled, puppy-feeding friend, but if this devolves into a wrestling match, I do not like your odds." Jude knew how to make an entrance. He also knew how to take the attention unerringly off of me. "So let's keep this civilized," Jude continued. He gestured toward the puppies. "Think of the children!"

I managed a smile, and that let me refocus my thoughts. We were here for Bella. Everything else was noise.

"Grab breakfast and the bloodhounds—and Free, if you can find her," I told Jude, channeling the restless energy inside me toward a purpose. "We need to get back out there."

As long as I was doing something, I was in control.

"Technically," Free hollered in our general direction as she carried a plate piled high with bacon out of the house, "we need to get *up* there. Sheriff called. They found Bella's trail again, farther up the mountain. He's on his way here to personally deliver us to our new ground zero."

The moment Free mentioned the sheriff, Gabriel went very still. If I wasn't already on high alert, I might not have noticed, but there was something in that stillness that hit me like the sound of fingernails on a chalkboard, like a dog whistle, too high in pitch for normal people to hear.

A moment later, Gabriel, who claimed to be incapable of keeping his mouth shut, walked away without a word.

CHAPTER 16

When the sheriff arrived, Gabriel was nowhere to be seen. Bales beat us to answering the door. He looked the sheriff up and down. "Mind if I ask how you're planning to get the kids to Sorrow's Pass?"

"Airlift." The sheriff kept his reply brief. "The rangers will fly them out."

I didn't like the sheriff's tone—and I really didn't like the fact that it was at odds with the small, sharp-edged smile on his face.

Bales said something else. The sheriff replied. I lost track of what was being said. We didn't have time for this.

"Bella's out there." I looked past the sheriff—and past Bales—as I spoke. "Talk won't bring her home."

The sheriff shifted his gaze from Bales to me. "Then let's get you kids in the car."

His stare coated me like oil. The muscles in my stomach clenched, and before I knew what was happening, the sheriff was reaching for Saskia's collar. In a flash of motion, Bales stepped in between them to push the sheriff back. Saskia's teeth snapped together a fraction of a second later. A growl vibrated through her entire body, and she snapped again.

The sheriff shook off the old man's grip. He rounded on me. "You need to control that animal."

The way he said *animal* slithered under my skin. I stood there, nostrils flaring, caught between lunging forward and skittering back. My girl had come to us with scars—visible, human-inflicted scars. Saskia didn't like men, and she didn't like being touched.

I should have been the one to protect her.

"She doesn't know you," I told the sheriff, shifting my weight forward. "You can't just try to grab her like that."

"As a general rule," Free added, drawing the sheriff's attention away from me, "most dogs aren't terribly fond of being manhandled by total strangers."

There was a single beat of silence.

I didn't realize that I'd stopped breathing until the sheriff took a half step back, and my lungs started functioning again.

"It's a beautiful day to rescue lost children," Jude offered brightly. "Wouldn't you say, Sheriff?"

"Thinking this through a little," the sheriff said, turning back to Bales, "we really only need two of them." Something about his posture and the tone in his voice made me think of a house cat, batting a mouse between its paws. "Sorrow's

Pass is dangerous terrain. I want all our searchers working in pairs, and since there are three of them . . ." He paused and glanced back at Saskia—and at me. "Why don't we give Kira and her . . . *partner* . . . a little break. Seems like they could use some time to decompress."

I felt like he'd kicked me straight in the teeth.

"You need as many hands on deck as you can get," Bales replied before either Jude or Free could.

"Bringing any of them into this goes against my better judgment," the sheriff retorted. "I'm not opening this up for discussion, Bales. They search in pairs, or they don't search at all."

"Fair enough." Bales turned his attention from the sheriff to the three of us. "Jude, you're with Free. I have another partner for Kira. He knows the mountain better than anyone."

That got a response out of the sheriff, the way that a match gets a *response* from gunpowder. "You can't seriously think—"

"I think," Bales said, his voice quiet and low, "that I know things that you would prefer I not know." He gave the sheriff a moment to process that statement. "And I think Kira's right. Talk isn't going to bring that child home."

CHAPTER 17

The sheriff didn't drive us to the rangers' station. Bales did, and the *us* in question included Gabriel. *He knows the mountain better than anyone.*

In the old man's presence, Gabriel didn't poke and prod at me, but he did seem to get some pleasure out of watching me. No matter what I did or how hard I stared back, he didn't look away. I kept hoping Jude would explain to Bales that *Saskia* was my partner, that I didn't need Gabriel, and that if I had to work with another human, I would have preferred one I knew.

Instead, Jude decided to make conversation. "If you were a crustacean," he asked Gabriel, "what kind would you be?"

Gabriel blinked. Twice. "I'm going to pretend that's a rhetorical question."

Jude grinned. "But it's *not* a rhetorical question."

"For what it's worth," Free interjected, "the correct answer is usually lobster." Without waiting for a reply, she asked Bales about the specs of the helicopter awaiting us at the rangers' station.

"Two-blade, dual engine," Gabriel answered on the old man's behalf. "Military-grade."

I absorbed that information without joining in the conversation that followed. The helicopter was a means to an end.

A too-small, too-loud means to an end.

Knowing what to expect didn't keep my shoulders from squaring or my teeth from grinding against each other as the car came to a stop and I took in our ride. The deafening roar of the blades saved me from having to speak to Gabriel—or anyone else—as we loaded up. The helicopter was a seven-seater—bigger than most of what I'd encounter if I went into SAR.

Still not big enough.

I didn't let my heart race. I didn't let the tight quarters matter any more than the company. Fear was one thing. Adrenaline was another.

Adrenaline, I could do.

Focused and in control, I latched myself into the seat. Saskia sat at attention between my legs. I kept my hand on her collar, but she seemed to sense that there was no leeway here—if any of our K9s showed the least bit of anxiety at the noise or tight space, that was game over, before we'd even taken off.

After a safety check, the pilot nodded to Bales, who was observing from a distance, then coaxed the aircraft slowly off the ground. The front of the copter tilted forward, and my harness bit gently into my shoulders as the world below us got smaller and smaller. We cruised over the top of the tree line. From this vantage point, Bear Mountain didn't just look massive; it looked ancient and unmovable, beautiful, deadly.

I could feel my pulse thrumming in my wrists, my stomach, my neck. I concentrated on the feel of Saskia's fur beneath my fingers as the copter angled hard to the right. The mountain was a blur of colors—silver and white and green. The trees were dense enough on this side that I wasn't sure where—or if—we could touch down, but slowly, a flat brown area came into view.

"Sorrow's Pass is about a half-mile hike inward," our pilot informed us as we touched down. "This is as close as I can get you. Exact coordinates—"

"I know Sorrow's Pass," Gabriel said, and somehow, the words weren't lost under the sound of the slowing blades.

Thirty seconds later, we were feet-on-the-ground, and the helicopter was in the air again.

"I am only mostly as motion sick as anticipated," Jude said, looking distinctly paler than usual. "I count that as a win."

"This way." Gabriel barely looked back at the rest of us as he hoisted his pack onto his shoulders and headed across the packed dirt toward the tree line. For a good ten minutes, we followed him, Jude and Gabriel and Free taking turns filling the silence. The trek to the pass was steeper than

I'd expected—not for the faint of heart. Free, Jude, and I had trained for this. Endurance was almost as important in search and rescue as the ability to assess the terrain and know your limits—and your K9's.

"A little kid wouldn't have come this way," Gabriel commented as rocky forest flattened out in a clearing. "Obviously. If she was coming in from the southeast, there's a path."

"Path," Jude murmured. "What is this path you speak of? I am a *big* fan of paths."

Free tossed her blond ponytail over one shoulder. "I'm guessing the scenic route takes a bit longer and isn't helicopter accessible."

Gabriel glanced over at her. "Good guess."

Cady met us at ground zero. There were a half dozen rangers in the area, already combing through the surrounding woods and calling Bella's name. Instinctively, I began to scan the scene for the development in the case that had brought us here. I'd expected physical tracks, or another piece of our target's jacket.

I hadn't expected blood.

Gabriel knelt to the ground, touching the tips of his fingers to the dirt at his feet as he observed the trail. "Shallow wound." There was no emotion in his voice, no hint that he was talking about a little girl. "Blood's dripping, not pooling. And whatever happened, it didn't slow her down."

"That was my read as well." Mac approached. He introduced himself to Gabriel.

"Any reason you're standing around here instead of searching?" That was apparently Gabriel's version of an introduction. "I somehow doubt that 'wait for teenagers to arrive' is search and rescue SOP."

"Standard operating procedures," Jude translated, whispering in my left ear. "And in case you can't tell, our good friend Gabriel doesn't appear to deal well with authority figures, our own dear grandpapa excluded."

Mac didn't rise to the bait. "The dogs needed to rest. So did Cady."

"Cady can take care of herself." My foster mother strode past Mac to address Gabriel directly. "You know this mountain?"

"I spent a lot of time out here growing up," Gabriel stated. "Then again, from what I hear, so did you."

Free chose that moment to lean forward and pluck a stray leaf from Cady's hair. "Don't take this the wrong way, but you look like crap."

Now that Free had mentioned it, I could see the strain on Cady's face, the wear. She'd sent me home to sleep, but the dark circles under her eyes told me that she hadn't gotten any herself.

"Last I checked," Mac told Cady mildly, "pacing the scene, badgering the rangers, and waiting for your kids to arrive doesn't qualify as *resting*."

I expected Cady to put Mac in his place, but a flicker of emotion took hold of her features. "Mac? You don't need to tell me that when people get tired, they make mistakes."

What mistakes? I thought. *What people?*

Cady supplied zero context for her words. "One hour off," she told Mac. "For both of us. That's all we can afford. In the meantime . . ." She knelt down to greet the dogs. "Jude, Free: See if the bloodhounds can pick up the trail and follow it as far as you can. Kira, I want you and Saskia to give the hounds a wide berth. We've got weather headed in and need to cover as much ground as we can before it gets here."

If it rained, we were in trouble. Whatever evidence Bella had left in her wake could be washed away.

"I've got a ball of dollar bills in my sock drawer that says it won't rain until noon." Gabriel didn't wait for Cady's response before turning to me. "Sorrow's Pass and the surrounding woods are bounded by cliffs on one side and ninety-degree inclines on the other. We can beat a wide path around the perimeter and work our way in."

Our way, I thought, making my best attempt to swallow the implication there. *Because we're partners.*

"Sounds like a plan." Jude adopted a conspiratorial whisper and leaned toward Gabriel. "Good luck getting Kira to shut that ever-moving trap of hers. She's a talker, this one."

"I'll talk enough for both of us." Gabriel didn't miss a beat. "If you promise to search for my body when she kills me dead."

Very funny. The words were on the tip of my tongue, but they wouldn't come. I was used to Jude whispering conspiratorially to *me.* I wasn't used to my people opening the ranks to someone else.

"We'll cover as much area as we can," I said abruptly. I wasn't here to converse—or make friends. I turned my attention to Saskia, leading her to get the scent of Bella's blood.

"Kira?" Cady waited until I turned back to face her before parting with a final bit of instruction. Jude and Free had made me watch television frequently enough that I knew this was the part where most TV parents would have told us to be careful.

Cady had a different refrain. "Be smart."

CHAPTER 18

Despite his promise to talk enough for both of us, Gabriel gifted me with silence as we pushed through the woods. There was a chance he was hoping to prod me into speaking first.

Not going to happen. There had been a time in my life when people were convinced I *couldn't* talk. If Gabriel was waiting for me to break, he was going to be waiting for a very long time.

It took half an hour to reach the forest's edge. In that time, Saskia covered more ground than a human searcher could in an entire day—and found nothing. As the tree line broke and the three of us stepped out onto a rocky ledge, I realized that Gabriel hadn't been exaggerating when he said that the search area was bounded on one side by cliffs.

The drop-off wasn't just steep; it was deadly. Like the gods had sawed the edge of the mountain off with a knife. Rocks jutted out from the cliff's side, and a light fog rose up from the valley, obscuring my view of the bottom, a thousand feet below.

Without meaning to, I walked closer to the edge and looked down. My heart didn't beat faster. It didn't jump into my throat. I thought about Bella Anthony, about how her story could end with a drop-off like this.

Girl is running. She bolts through the forest. She's bleeding, stumbling. The memory hit me like a wave, but it was the undertow that pulled me down, down, down—

Can't look back. Can't stop. Girl is supposed to stay hidden. Brush bites at her face, arms, legs, but she can't stop. Girl can never stop.

And then she needs to, and it's too—

A sharp pain pulled me from the flashback. I looked down to see Saskia beside me, her teeth locked around my hand. She'd nipped once, hard enough to draw blood, but her grip was softer now—solid, implacable, but not painful as she pulled me back from the cliff's edge.

It wasn't until an instant later that I realized just how close I'd been standing, the tips of my toes hanging over the ledge. I took a step back, and gravel and dirt skittered over the side of the mountain, dropping soundlessly into the vast nothingness below.

A masochistic part of me held tight to the snatch of memory that had taken over my mind a moment before. I remembered running. I remembered the feel of a predator bearing down on me, the feel of being prey. I remembered skidding over uneven ground.

I remembered falling—and waking up in the ravine below.

Beside me, Saskia yipped sharply—just once, not an indication of anything other than her annoyance at my distraction.

Find. Play. That was what we were here to do. That was the mission.

"Yeah," a low voice said behind me. "What she said."

I turned to face Gabriel, ready and willing to make him back off if I had to. But for the first time since I'd met him, there wasn't a hint of challenge in his expression. I'd known his eyes were dark brown, but standing this close, I could see a lighter ring around the pupil.

"You okay?" he asked.

I wiped my sweating palms roughly over the fabric of my pants. "I'm fine."

As the morning wore on, the sky darkened overhead like a canvas painted in shades of black and blue and gray. Gabriel and I made our way from the cliffs inward toward the vertical incline of solid stone, stretching up in the direction of the mountain's peak.

The terrain under our feet got more uneven, but I didn't slow my pace, and Saskia didn't slow hers. I could hear the crunch of Gabriel's boot against gravel behind me, but I focused my senses outward and threw everything I had into forward momentum.

The rain was coming. It was only a matter of time.

Saskia looped back to check on me. She didn't need me to tell her to keep going. And *I* didn't need to stop for so much as a drink.

Chrrrrrk. Without warning, a rock shifted beneath my feet. I pitched forward. Fingers caught my arm and hauled me up. *Breath on my neck. No space. No room.* I heard noise but barely recognized that it was Gabriel talking. His grip on my arm wasn't tight, but it didn't matter.

My body was *mine*.

Instinct washed away everything else. I saw red. I *felt* my fingernails digging into the flesh of Gabriel's forearm, hard enough to draw blood. On some level, I was prepared for him to fight back. I was ready for it, but instead, he let go of me.

It was three seconds—*six heartbeats*—before I processed that there was no retaliation forthcoming. It was another two seconds—*three heartbeats*—before I pried my fingers loose from Gabriel's arm. My ears still roaring with white noise, I managed to focus on the outline of Saskia's form beside me.

One second. My breathing slowed, and the sounds of the real world came slowly back. *One heartbeat.*

Gabriel's gaze traveled down at the marks I'd left on his arm. I tried to find the words to ask him not to tell Cady. I was better than this. I had more control.

He found his voice before I found mine. To my surprise, he aimed his commentary to Saskia. "My apologies," he told her as my canine partner stared him down. "It is understood that if I touch your human again, you will have no choice but to eat my face."

Saskia seemed to find that acceptable.

"We good here?" Gabriel asked, finally glancing back at me.

My voice caught in my throat, but I pushed the words out. "We're good." I felt like I should say something else, but *I'm sorry* wouldn't come. Instead, I knelt to Saskia's level. "Find Bella."

Saskia took off again. Gabriel and I set off in the same direction.

"I'm game to ignore the drop of rain I just felt if you are," he informed me a few minutes later.

I upped my pace. "I'm game."

CHAPTER 19

The rain picked up. A clap of thunder sounded overhead, and I felt it, all the way to my bones.

"I don't like the look of those clouds," Gabriel told me. "I'm not saying we have to head back to base camp. I'm just saying that most people with smaller self-destructive streaks than mine would probably agree that we should."

I stopped listening to Gabriel and started listening for Saskia. Horizontal lightning cut across the darkened sky. I brought my index fingers to my mouth and let out a sharp whistle. I trained my gaze in the direction Saskia had gone, waiting.

Nothing.

"Saskia should have checked back by now," I said

Gabriel scanned our surroundings and diverted from the path we'd been on a moment before. "She came this way."

We moved fast and in tandem. The sky blackened, like

ink spilling onto a page. On the radio, the call came in for us to take shelter.

It's just rain, I told myself. But that *just rain* was suddenly pelting us hard enough to leave marks.

Gabriel pressed past me, taking the worst of it as the wind beat against us.

"I don't need you to protect me," I bit out.

Saskia was my responsibility. Not Gabriel's, not Cady's—*mine.* Four years earlier, someone had dumped a bone-thin and bleeding adolescent husky on our property. She'd bristled if you looked at her, skittered backward if you stepped forward, and snapped when you got too close. Cady had managed to treat her wounds but ordered Jude and me to stay away.

I hadn't. From the moment I'd seen her, from the moment she bared her teeth at me—Saskia was *mine.*

"Did you hear that?" Gabriel's face was lit by another bolt of lightning—closer this time.

I froze, listening. Second after second ticked by—long enough for me to think of all the predators who lived in the mountains. Long enough for me to remember what Saskia's coat had looked like, knotted with blood.

"I don't hear anything." The words felt rough against my throat.

Gabriel held up one hand. I stilled—and then I heard it. Faint but audible.

Saskia. Within the span of a heartbeat, I'd taken off

running toward the distant sound of barking, toward her. The closer I got, the harder I ran.

Be smart. Cady's admonition was there in my brain, but all I could think about was the fact that Saskia hadn't come back. I'd called, and I'd whistled, and she hadn't come back.

And that meant that she *couldn't.*

I called her name again, and Saskia's barking took on a more desperate quality. She wanted to get to me as badly as I wanted to get to her. Following the sound, vaguely aware that the rain was coming in sheets now, that I was bone-soaked, the ground beneath me was growing slicker by the second, I hauled myself up onto higher ground and found myself staring at rock—solid rock.

The mountain.

I could hear Saskia, but I couldn't see her. All around me, stony crags too steep to climb jutted out of the ground.

"Kira!"

I turned. Gabriel was standing maybe fifteen feet away from me. He knelt to the ground, his gaze locked onto . . . *something.* I started making my way toward him, but as I did, the sound of Saskia's barking grew fainter. Everything in me said to turn around, but I didn't. It wasn't until I was right on top of Gabriel that I saw what he'd seen—a break in the mountain, an opening large enough for a single person to squeeze through.

I crouched down to get a better look.

"Caves," Gabriel said. "My brother used to insist that they

were out here, but I spent an entire summer looking and never found one."

I braced my palms against the rocks on either side of the entrance. I couldn't see very far, but what I could see included a drop—a steep one. I stepped forward.

"Hold up there, princess." Gabriel moved to block me. "Let's not do anything rash."

I squeezed past him, through the opening in the rock, and jumped down. I could hear Gabriel cursing behind me as I landed roughly on the cave's floor. Lightning flashed behind me, allowing me to see—for an instant—that the cave stretched out for a dozen or so paces, then took a sharp turn to the right. I glanced back.

The entrance was a good seven or eight feet overhead. If Saskia had come this way, she wouldn't have been able to make it out.

I reached into my pack and took out a flashlight. By the time I'd turned it on, I wasn't the only one in the cave—and Gabriel wasn't what I'd call happy about it.

"Does insanity run in your family?" he asked me, his voice a little *too* pleasant and his jaw clenched.

I held up my flashlight, then jerked my head toward his pack. Before he had his own flashlight out, I was already off and around the corner.

"Saskia?" I called, my voice echoing through the space. I heard her before I saw her, nails against the stone as she came barreling toward me. I knelt, the flashlight falling from my hand as my arms locked around her.

"Good girl," I told her, my voice shaking as I ran my hands over her fur, assuring myself that she was all right. "That's a good girl. I'm here, Sass. *I'm here.*"

She snuffed once, shook me off, and then barked.

Once. Twice. Three times.

"She found something," Gabriel stated.

With barely a glance in his direction, I followed Saskia as she led the way deeper and deeper into the cave. I heard the sound of running water—*an underground river?*—but kept my focus on the here and now, the band of light cast by my flashlight illuminating the steel-gray ground beneath our feet.

The cave hit a dead end, and Saskia barked again, three times. *Find. Recall. Re-find.*

I knelt to jostle her back and forth, to scratch behind her ears, even as my left hand aimed the flashlight past her. There was a red windbreaker on the floor. I stood, angling the flashlight to get a better look as Gabriel did the same with his.

"Bella!" I called the little girl's name. If she'd found her way down here, like Saskia, she might not have been able to find her way out. "Bella? Can you hear me?"

Nothing.

The ground shook with a roll of thunder, close enough to set my teeth on edge. I turned back to Gabriel.

"She was here," I said.

Gabriel let his light roam over the area around us and stopped it on what appeared to be some kind of makeshift fire pit. He knelt next to it, dipping his fingers into the ash and studying the way the brush was scattered.

Then he looked back up at me. "Bella was here," he echoed. "And she wasn't alone."

CHAPTER 20

I tried to radio in what we'd found, but between the weather and the fact that we were *inside* the mountain, reception was shot.

We found Bella's windbreaker. I ignored the roiling emotions gnashing inside me and focused on rehearsing what I would say when we finally got through. *There are signs of a campsite. Bella isn't just lost. Someone took her.*

"You're pacing." Gabriel was leaning against the wall of the cave, standing guard over the evidence. Saskia lay at his feet, surprisingly docile. "Afraid that whoever has Bella might be coming back?"

Fear wasn't something I felt about *possible* threats. Fear was *here* and *now, fight* or *flight*. I wasn't afraid.

I was angry.

"Some crimes make sense." I didn't pause to think about how that comment might sound. "Taking what you need, even if it belongs to someone else. Striking hard and fast and *first.*"

But this? I stopped walking and stopped talking, because taking a child, hurting a child in any way?

"This doesn't make sense." Gabriel said the words for me.

Restless, I crouched, my weight on the balls of my feet and my fingertips braced against the cave floor. The scene looked no different from this angle. The harder I stared at the physical traces Bella had left behind, the further into my own mind I retreated.

Girl presses herself back into the darkness. Wet. Cold. Her throat burns. Can't move. Can't make a sound—

"Kira? Come in. Kira and Gabriel, come in."

My hand tightened around the radio as I fought my way through the flashback, lashing out against the memories, tearing at them in my mind. The real world came slowly into focus.

I lifted the radio to my mouth. "Bella was here." I'd practiced. I was ready. But somehow, the rest of what I needed to tell them wouldn't come.

Gabriel squatted beside me. "We'll give them directions," he said quietly.

"We'll give you directions," I repeated. My grip on the radio relaxed slightly, and I continued, my eyes on Gabriel. "We found a cave. There are signs of a campsite. . . ."

It was another half hour before the rescue crew reached us. In the last few moments of quiet before the chaos descended,

I made myself look at Gabriel. "Bales was right. You know this mountain."

That was the closest I could come to *thank you*.

Gabriel, apparently, wasn't a person who liked to be thanked. "We both know who the real hero here is, and it's not me. There's no trace of hero in my DNA." He nodded to Saskia. "All credit goes to her."

Saskia was the one who'd found this place. She'd gone in blind. She'd taken the risk. It meant something that Gabriel recognized that, when most people couldn't look past the wolf in her eyes.

"Kira!" Cady called my name from somewhere near the cave's entrance.

"Here," I called back, moving toward the sound of her voice. "Sass and Gabriel, too."

A beam of light, brighter by far than what my flashlight could offer, flooded the entrance. Cady's hair was soaked, her clothing dripping. Mackinnon Wade crouched beside her. With unnatural calm, he surveyed the situation, then dropped down into the cave himself. He let out a low, soothing whistle and held out a hand to Saskia.

My dog's blue eyes studied the large man intently. After several long seconds, she approached.

"What do you say, superstar—how about we get you out?"

Gabriel snorted. "Saskia has a counteroffer. She would like to eat your face."

To his credit, Mac didn't seem to take offense. "Will she

let me pick her up?" he asked me. "I can hoist her out without much fanfare."

"Will she let a large man wrap his arms around her and constrain her?" I rephrased Mac's question. The answer was obvious, but this was our chance to prove to Cady that my girl *and* I could work with a team.

"She trusts you," Mac responded. "You need to trust me."

"Kira has a counteroffer," Gabriel started to quip.

I shot him a disgruntled look. "Shut up, Gabriel."

Gabriel seemed to prefer being told to shut up to being thanked. As I turned my attention back to Mac, my pulse jumped slightly, and I tamped down on the part of me that had gone vigilant. *Cady trusts Mac,* I told myself. I pictured the photograph Free and I had found. *Cady knows him.*

My breathing evened out, and I knelt in front of Saskia. "Sit," I said. I gestured, palm to the ground. "Down."

Saskia went to the ground. I went with her. I pressed my belly to the cave floor, nose to nose with my K9 partner. It went against every instinct I had to stay there, with Gabriel and Mac standing over us, but I wouldn't ask Saskia to do something I couldn't.

"Stay," I said softly. I could do this. *She* could do this.

Mac slowly knelt and got into position beside her.

"Stay," I repeated, my eyes on Saskia's and hers on mine. The cave floor was damp. My heart was racing. Saskia didn't so much as look at Mac. She looked at me. She trusted *me.* I lay there, vulnerable with no line of defense. With liquid grace, Mac made his move. One second, Saskia was on the ground, and the next, he had the husky in his arms, over his head, and out.

Even once she was back on solid ground, Saskia held the down position. *For me.* I was on my own feet in an instant. Mac boosted me up. I barely even felt the contact.

The second I was on solid ground, I dropped the stay signal, and Saskia came barreling into my body.

"Are you hurt?" Cady asked me. "Is Saskia?"

I let her run her hands over me, assure herself I was okay—and then I shook off both her worry and her touch. "We're fine."

"You're better than fine." Cady looked down at Saskia. "I can't believe she let him do that."

"I can." I allowed myself one moment of victory, and then I got down to business. "Gabriel and I aren't sure how big the cave system is, but it wasn't on any of the maps. There could be other entrances, other exits. I'm fairly certain there's running water down there."

"And how exactly *did* you find this place?" The sheriff announced his presence. A half dozen deputies and rangers began making their way down into the cave as Mac boosted Gabriel out.

"I didn't find the cave," I said, unsure what exactly it was about the way the sheriff had spoken that set my teeth on edge. "Saskia did."

I prepared myself to recount the search, step-by-step, but the sheriff looked past me, toward Gabriel. "And I suppose," he said, drawing out the words in a way that made my stomach lurch, "that Gabriel will tell me that he had no idea this cave was here, either."

I shifted my weight forward without knowing why.

"I could confirm your assumptions," Gabriel replied contemplatively. "Or I could tell you that you have a tiny piece of kale caught in your teeth."

The space between the sheriff and Gabriel shrank to nothing so quickly that I wasn't even sure which one of them had closed the gap. Saskia moved lightning-quick to Gabriel's side.

I realized a moment later that I had done the same.

"Kira." Cady had to repeat my name once more before my eyes flickered from the sheriff's to hers. "You and Gabriel have done your part here. I'm sure one of the rangers would be glad to see you two home."

"I can't go," I said fiercely. *Can't*, not *won't*. I knew on some level that Cady was probably trying to defuse the situation. I just didn't know why—or what exactly this situation between Gabriel and the man opposite us entailed.

"I'm sure the sheriff will agree." Cady threw him a bone. "It was one thing letting you kids search when this was a missing persons case, but this isn't a missing persons case anymore. This is a kidnapping, Kira. And you—and Gabriel—are going home."

CHAPTER 21

"Tell me again about the part where Broody McSmirkpants called you 'princess' and you *didn't* rip out his throat."

The minute we'd been dropped off, Gabriel had pulled a disappearing act, and Free and Jude had descended on me. Now the three of us were sequestered in the room Free and I were sharing. Jude was lying upside down on the bed. In typical Jude style, he'd immediately zeroed in on the one thing— out of everything I'd caught them up on—that *didn't* have weighty implications.

"I'm guessing Kira would prefer to tell us again about the teeth-gnashing injustice of being kicked off this search." Free assumed her perch in the open window.

Being with the two of them should have loosened the knot in my stomach. It should have made me feel more like myself and less like the Girl in the Woods. But all I could think was that I'd shown Cady that I wasn't a liability, and she'd still sent me away.

Silver nudged the back of my knees, herding me toward Jude.

"I should be out there," I said. Cady might as well have tied me up. I *felt* like she had. "I should be looking for Bella and hunting this predator down."

Backing away from a challenge was never easy for me, but backing away when some sicko was out there dragging a child through the wilderness? When that child was bleeding and running and forced into the dark?

"Heads up!" That was only warning I got before a pillow hit me straight in the face. I narrowed my eyes at Jude.

"Miscreants' Creed, line twelve," he cited quickly, his sense of self-preservation clicking on. "Mild to moderate pillow violence is a sign of affection."

"Not an actual part of the Creed," Free commented. "But I'll take it under advisement."

An obstinate Silver nudged my legs again, then circled in front of me and gave me the canine version of Cady's *Look*. She wanted me to sit. She wanted me to breathe.

"The person who took Bella has seven hundred and fifty thousand acres of wilderness to hide in." I let that statement hang in the air, then forced myself to sit. It wasn't Silver's fault I'd been thrown off the search, any more than it was Jude's fault or Free's. With a self-satisfied bob of her head, Silver curled by my side, and the moment I felt the German shepherd's body next to mine, something inside me gave.

"I can't just sit here," I said, my voice threatening to break. "Bella Anthony sleeps with a blanket." I swallowed. "Or at least, she did. Now she's out there, sleeping who knows where, and she's scared and in danger, and she doesn't even have that pathetic scrap of fabric for comfort."

Free leaned back, her palms flat against the windowsill. "I'd suggest sneaking out and starting a search of our own, but barring extreme circumstances, even I don't think pushing Cady that far would be wise."

When I was a child, I'd learned to trust Cady the way that Jude had learned to read—slowly, painstakingly, painfully. That trust couldn't be undone overnight. Cady was protecting me the only way she knew how.

Girl doesn't need protection. My hand throbbed, and when I looked down, I saw that I'd dug my fingers into the carpet underneath me. I forced them loose, and Silver licked my palm.

Silver is here, I imagined her saying. *I'm here, Kira. I'm here. I'm here.*

Wasn't that what Jude and Free had been saying in their own ways since I got back?

"Distract me." My body physically shook with the effort of trying to take a mental step back from this case—from Bella. I bowed my head and let it rest against Silver's. Her fur was coarse, but it didn't feel rough against my skin. "Tell me something that has nothing to do with kidnapping or missing children or what might be happening to that little girl right now."

My fellow Miscreants obliged.

"Bales has officially banned the use of confetti," Jude said at the exact same time that Free opted for, "I might have made another trip to town. And I might have asked around about Ash. And Cady. And Mac."

Now *that* was a worthy distraction. Jude and I hadn't really talked about the argument we'd overheard between Cady and Bales. We hadn't discussed Ash—or what the fact that Cady had "loved" Ash might mean for Jude. I couldn't remember Cady ever dating. She'd had Jude young.

She'd known Ash when she was young.

Jude sat straight up on the bed and twirled toward the window. "And what, pray tell, might you have learned on this trip to town, Free Morrow?"

Free took her time responding. "Cady ever mention anything to either of you about spending her early twenties as part of an elite search and rescue team?"

I felt my eyebrows skyrocket.

"Traveling the world?" Free continued. "Partaking of death-defying adventures in some of the worst and scariest places this planet has to offer?"

"I would like to say that this sounds vaguely familiar," Jude replied. "However . . ."

However. That wasn't the beginning of a sentence. It was the end of one. Cady hadn't told us anything—not about her past, not about this SAR team, and not about Ash. For once, Jude did not offer up a maniacally optimistic view of the situation.

A protective instinct stirred inside me. If there was one thing that could distract me from the predator who had Bella, it was a threat to my family. Whatever secrets Cady had been keeping, whatever answers she'd withheld—they meant something to Jude.

"Did you find out anything else?" I asked Free, talking for Jude the way he'd always spoken for me. "Who Ash was? What happened to him?"

"Ash's full name," Free said after an appropriately dramatic pause, "was John Ashby."

"Ashby." Jude was the one who made the connection. "Isn't that Ness's last name?"

"I'm guessing Ash was either her nephew or her son." Free wound her blond hair around her fist. Even when it came to absentminded hair twirling, she did nothing halfway. "There's more of a story there," Free declared, "but dragging those particular skeletons out of the family closet might require venturing back to town and finding some chattier locals."

I didn't know what was going on inside Jude's head. I wasn't even sure if *he* thought that Ash was his father, or if Free and I were the only ones who'd gone there. But I had enough question marks in my own past to know how they could eat at you, tearing chunks out bit by bit.

Cady had leashed me for the remainder of the search. There was nothing more I could do for Bella right now. But Free and I? We could make another trip to town. We could find some chatty locals—for Jude.

CHAPTER 22

Jude wasn't about to sit out this particular adventure and neither was Silver. Given the German shepherd's history of keeping an eye on us in Cady's absence, that was hardly surprising.

Also unsurprising: the fact that it didn't take long for Jude to recover his voice. "It's a lovely day for being inexcusably nosy, is it not, ladies?"

"I believe the phrase you're looking for," Free put in as we hugged the side of the winding road that led into town, "is that it's a lovely day for mischief."

"Miscreants' Creed," I said, a small smile creeping over my lips. "Line one."

As we hit the outskirts of town, we drew a few looks from locals.

"I was thinking we'd head for the wilderness-supply store." Free chose that moment to saunter across the street, well aware that people were watching and completely unbothered by the attention. "It was closed earlier, but my little sojourn by the local pool hall last night led me to believe that Hunter's Point is the kind of place where people nickname their guns and keep their wilderness supplies well stocked. Ten-to-one odds say the place is a family business that's been here for years."

"Phoebe Eloise," Jude said fondly. "Have I ever told you that you're terrifyingly perceptive?"

Free lightly kicked a rock and watched it skid across the concrete. "Call me by my full name again, Saint Jude, and play Russian roulette with your chances of waking up tomorrow morning with only one eyebrow intact."

Jude meditated on that threat as we made our way to the supply store. The bell over the door alerted the shopkeeper to our arrival. Free went in first, and I went in last. The place seemed to be about one part hardware store, one part camping outlet, and one part armory.

"Can I help you kids with something?"

The man behind the counter was about seventy-five, dressed in flannel with a beard he kept shaved close to his face. There was nothing unwelcoming about his expression, but I wasn't sure it was welcoming, either.

"Jackpot," Free murmured to me. "I bet he's worked here for forty years. The older they are, the more they like to gossip."

"I am hopeful that you can help us, fine sir." Jude offered

the old man his most charming smile. "Do you have any thoughts on the kind of supplies one might need if one were hoping to spend some time in beautiful Sierra Glades National Park?"

"You're Cady Bennett's kids, aren't you?" The old man met Jude's question with a question. "Your mother was one of my best customers when she was growing up. If you asked her about supplies, I imagine she'd tell you that it depends on where you plan on heading. The Glades has nearly as many ecosystems as it has trees."

Near the door, Silver watched the old man for a moment, then settled down, laying her head on her front paws. I took that to mean that she'd decided that if push came to shove, we could take him.

"Some folks head out to the mountains," the shopkeeper continued, leaning forward, his elbows on the counter. "Others prefer the canyons or the foothills or making their way along one of the purest, cleanest rivers in the country."

I edged farther into the store, keeping half an ear on the shopkeeper and waiting for Jude to cut to the chase. A glass display case caught my attention. Inside, I counted a dozen knives. As the old man rattled off something about ancient forests and three-hundred-foot-tall trees, I couldn't help thinking that the blades in the case looked lifeless.

No matter how sharp its edges, no knife could hold a candle to fang and claw.

"Have you lived here long?" Jude fed the shopkeeper

another easy question, and I continued my circuit through the shop. The next case over held guns. *Rifle. Hunting rifle.* A tinny taste rose in the back of my mouth. By the door, Silver lifted her head slightly, knowing brown eyes meeting mine.

I'm fine, I told her silently. *It's nothing. It's just a gun.*

So why were the hairs on the back of my neck standing straight up?

"It's a beauty, isn't it?" The shopkeeper came out from behind the counter, and the muscles in my legs and torso instinctively tightened. "I probably don't need to tell you kids that Bales Bennett is the best shot on this side of the mountain."

"Tell," Jude encouraged him. "Tell like the wind."

I tried to push down the rush of red-tinged anger rising up inside me, the one that said that guns were *cheating.*

They were *death.*

"Word is that Bales is former military—either intelligence or special forces, depending on which set of rumors you believe." The old man winked at me. "He retired when his wife died and moved up here when Cady was a bitty thing."

I couldn't make myself turn my back on the gun case. But I *did* make myself speak. "You knew Cady when she was a kid?"

"I can assure you," Jude chimed in, "that any embarrassing stories you might feel compelled to share about Mom's misspent youth would be put to good and not at all self-serving use."

The old man smiled. "If such stories do exist—and I'm not saying they do—you'd have to hear them from a braver man than me."

Free strolled to my other side. "You wouldn't happen to know if Cady had a friend named Ash, would you?"

"John Ashby," the shop owner said immediately. "Ness Ashby's boy. I never could decide whether that kid was the second coming of Dennis the Menace or James Dean. He and your mother and one of the Wades—the quiet one, the one who made good they got up to all kinds of mischief in these parts growing up."

Cady. Ash. Mac. I pictured them, the way they'd looked in the photograph—barely any older than Free, Jude, and me.

"What happened when they left Hunter's Point?" I tried and failed—to sound casual.

Before the old man could reply—*if* he was going to reply—the door to the shop opened again. I registered the size and build of the person who stood there before I recognized her features. Bella's mother had pulled her hair back. I doubted she'd washed it recently. The day before, she'd looked exhausted. Today, she looked like everything inside her had been hollowed out.

"I'm sorry to interrupt, Mr. Ferris." Angela Anthony didn't sound sorry. As quiet as her voice was, she sounded the way

Saskia looked when you tried to put her in a crate. "I wanted to check to see if you needed any more flyers."

Everything in me had fought the idea of stepping back from the search. What was it like for Bella's mother to be here when Bella was out there? My mind went to the threadbare, well-loved blanket—and then to the red windbreaker, abandoned on the cave floor.

For the first time in years, I tried—*really tried*—to remember my own mother's face.

No. Girl can't. The memory came down on me, like a window being slammed shut. *Can't go home.* My stomach threatened to empty itself on the shop floor. I pressed my tongue to the roof of my mouth and gritted my teeth.

I'm in control, I thought. *I'm fine.*

Silver climbed to her feet. She came to check on me, then surprised me by padding across the shop toward Bella's mother. *Sad,* I could almost hear the dog say as she lay down at the woman's feet. I wanted to tell my canine guardian that she was right and that I could see it, too.

"I'll take more flyers if you've got them." The shopkeeper's voice was gruff but not unkind. "I'll keep handing them out to folks as they come through."

Bella's mother nodded, but she didn't move to take the flyers to him. "Do you get a lot of people through here?" There was something deep and cutting about the set of her features. "Families? Hikers? Survivalist types?" She pressed her lips together into a firm line. After a moment, that line wavered. "Drifters?"

Jude came to stand beside me. "She knows," he whispered in my left ear. "She knows that Bella was kidnapped."

I searched Angela Anthony's features for whatever clues Jude had seen. Had the sheriff been the one to break the news to her? If she knew, how could she possibly stomach being here, instead of out there?

"I've been talking to folks around town." Mrs. Anthony's voice quivered, but she thrust her chin out. "A couple of fellows in the bar said that Bella's not the first person around here to go missing."

"These fellows," the shopkeeper said, leaning forward as his eyebrows knit together. "They wouldn't happen to have the last name Wade, would they?"

No reply.

"Wades like to talk." The shopkeeper's tone reminded me that Mac had said that most people in Hunter's Point didn't care much for his kind. "And they like to drink."

We waited for Bella's mom to reply, but she didn't.

"Talking and drinking doesn't preclude the possibility that they could be telling the truth." Free never had trouble inserting herself into conversations. She rocked back on her heels slightly, her eyes eagle-sharp. "*Has* anyone else gone missing?"

I thought back to what Gabriel had said, his face moonlit and his tone impossible to decode. *Around here, people go missing all the time.*

Our trip to town was supposed to be a distraction, but all I could think, looking between the shopkeeper and Bella's mom, was that what Saskia and I had done, the evidence we'd found—it wasn't enough.

I needed to move. I couldn't bring myself to walk past Bella's mother, so instead of leaving the store, I stalked toward the back wall. *Pull it together, Kira.* This wasn't *my* tragedy. I wasn't Bella. The shell of a woman in the doorway wasn't my mother.

For all I knew, my mother hadn't looked for me at all.

I focused on the sound of my own breathing. I fixed my eyes on a point in front of me—and immediately wished that I hadn't. Sitting on the shelf, there was a large metal trap, the kind that didn't concern itself with being humane.

Meat smell. Food. Girl crouches, hunched on all fours. I shook, but couldn't fight it—and suddenly, I didn't want to. *Girl knows which berries to eat now, which berries not to, but this . . . this . . .*

Meat smells good.

She creeps closer, her eyes stinging, her hands aching to reach out, to bury themselves in the meat.

Eat it.

Eat it before someone can take it away.

A rustling sound stops her. She freezes, her head whipping around. Wolf. *She remembers the word. But words don't matter. Nothing matters but the creature stalking toward her meat.*

She darts forward, and the animal's hackles rise. It snaps its jaws, and Girl falls, scrambles backward.

Watches the wolf turn its attention from her to the meat.

Watches the wolf step forward.

Thunk. *The sound is sudden, bone-crunching. The wolf snarls and fights and bleeds, but it can't escape. The monster has it.*

The monster almost had Girl.

CHAPTER 23

The first thing I heard when I came back to myself was the sound of the shop door opening. I smelled fresh air and dirt.

Meat. The memory lingered longer than it should have, vivid enough that my nostrils flared.

"Mr. Ferris." It took me a moment to place the voice behind me as its owner greeted the shopkeeper and then continued, "Mrs. Anthony, I thought I might find you here."

I turned. There was nothing particularly aggressive in the sheriff's posture.

I still shifted to put my back to the wall.

"Please don't tell me to go back to the hotel, Sheriff." Bella's mother's voice was muted. "I can't just sit around waiting for updates. You can't expect me to."

The sheriff placed a comforting hand on her shoulder. "The FBI is sending a team to join the investigation. The rangers are calling in reinforcements. I assure you, ma'am, we are doing everything we possibly—"

"I'd like access to all your missing persons reports for the past five years." Mrs. Anthony was quiet but forceful. "I appreciate what you and your men are doing, but for my own peace of mind, Sheriff, I need to see those reports."

There is no peace, I found myself thinking as I wound my way back toward the two of them—and toward Free and Jude. *The human mind is not a peaceful place*

"You need to go back to your husband, Angela. Keep your phones charged. The feds will want to talk to you both."

Something about the sheriff's too-gentle tone hit me like a rusted knife to the gut. I knew what it was like to be handled with kid gloves, to be treated like a *victim* instead of a *person.*

"How many are there?" It took me a few seconds to realize that I was the one who'd asked the question. I forced myself to elaborate, each word hard-won. "How many people have gone missing from Hunter's Point?"

The shopkeeper must have seen something in the sheriff's face—or in Mrs. Anthony's or mine—because he intervened before the sheriff could answer. "I get people in here asking about missing loved ones from time to time," he said, taking control of the situation. "But that doesn't mean those people are really missing. If a person wants to start over, if they want to disappear—a national park isn't a bad place to do it."

The sheriff let the lot of us chew on that for several seconds. "Some people don't want to be found," he said evenly. "Others set off without a real idea of where they're going. A person who enters the park from Hunter's Point might not be planning to come back the same way. My office takes reports, but we're not responsible for every Tom, Dick, or Harry who passes through."

"And Bella?" Jude took the words straight from my pounding, bloody heart. "Are you responsible for her?"

Mrs. Anthony drew in a ragged breath.

"Does your grandfather know you're here?" the sheriff asked Jude pointedly. "Or, for that matter, your mother?"

Silver trotted over to Jude and plopped down at his feet, as if to declare that there *was* an adult keeping tabs on the three of us, thank you very much. I half expected the sheriff to reach for her, the way he'd tried to grab Saskia.

"Sheriff Rawlins is right." Mrs. Anthony straightened her spine and focused on the three of us. "I appreciate the moral support, but this isn't something I want kids mixed up in. Given the circumstances, I doubt your family would feel any different."

Our *family* was out there looking for her daughter right now.

"Would this be an appropriate time to mention the Freedom of Information Act?" Free adopted her most wide-eyed, innocent expression. "Because I'm pretty sure that as a law enforcement agency, the local sheriff's office can only withhold government records in accordance with a small number of exceptions that don't seem to apply to Mrs. Anthony's request."

If any of the adults in this room had known Free, they would have realized that telling her to stay out of something was as good as sending her an engraved invitation to dive right in.

"Is she right?" Mrs. Anthony turned back to the sheriff. "Do you have a legal obligation to give me those reports?"

"Not if disclosure would endanger the lives of civilians or interfere with enforcement proceedings."

"Which would only be the case," Free interjected sweetly, "if the files were part of an ongoing investigation. But since you can hardly be held responsible for every Tom, Dick, or Harry who passes through . . ."

A sixth sense warned me against pushing the sheriff further.

"Darn kids these days," Jude declared, diverting the man's attention from Free before I could. "With their internet access and detail-oriented interest in the criminal justice system!"

Take one step toward them, I told the sheriff silently, keyed in to his every move. *Just one step, and I'll—*

Jude bumped my hip with his own. I got a handle on myself, then bumped back.

"You're welcome to file a request for those records with my office," the sheriff told Bella's mother. When she excused herself to do just that, the sheriff zeroed in on Jude, Free, and me.

Just one step, Sheriff.

Fortunately, for his sake, he decided not to take his frustrations out on my friends. "Kira," he said pleasantly, "could I have a word?"

Jude cleared his throat to get my attention. When that didn't work, he bumped me again. I bumped back. If the sheriff had chosen to go after Free or Jude, I might have lost it. But he hadn't, and I didn't need Jude to spell out what my gut was already screaming: The sheriff had targeted me for a reason, like a predator picking off the weakest member of the herd.

Girl is not weak. I didn't push the thought away. I let the human part of my brain recede, until I could hear the part that was *other* loud and clear. *Girl doesn't need protection.*

Girl survives.

"Stay," I told Silver, knowing that my fellow Miscreants would realize I wasn't just talking to the dog.

I let the sheriff lead me away from the group and ended up with my back to the wall. Maybe I should have felt cornered—maybe he was hoping I would—but there was a comfort in knowing that I couldn't be attacked from behind.

Cady always said, if someone wanted to show you who they were—let them.

"Your adoptive mother is an incredible woman." The sheriff put emphasis on the word *adoptive*, but unfortunately for him, whatever point he was trying to make was lost on me. My instincts were more focused on the way he stood, the distribution of weight between his feet.

"Given what you did for Bella today, it appears that you and Cady have that much in common." He shifted his weight forward, toward me, into *my* space. "But if Gabriel Cortez is the one who put you and your friends up to that little stunt with Bella's mother just now, then you and Cady also have something else in common, and that's incredibly bad judgment in the opposite sex."

The ridiculousness of the sheriff's statement allowed me to tamp down on the desire to invade *his* space. Gabriel hadn't put me up to anything, and my judgment about the opposite sex wasn't good *or* bad. It was nonexistent.

In the wild, some animals puff themselves up to seem bigger, I thought. It was a defense mechanism, an attempt to fake strength. The sheriff was posturing.

I didn't particularly care why.

"You don't know me," I said. I had a tendency to fall on the wrong side of the line between looking at someone and staring them down. At the moment, I didn't fight it. "You don't get to talk about my judgment—or Cady's."

Despite his best efforts not to, the sheriff looked away first.

"Do you know how Gabriel Cortez came to work for your grandfather?" The question was aimed at a spot just over my left shoulder. "Bales Bennett trains animals—for law enforcement, personal security, general obedience. But for the past few years, his pet project has been a pilot program that uses juvenile delinquents to train service animals."

Service animals, as in Seeing Eye dogs, I thought, remembering the litter of rough-and-tumble golden retriever puppies. *And juvenile delinquents,* I continued silently, *as in Gabriel.*

"Why don't you ask Bales where he met Gabriel?" The sheriff took a generous step back and smiled in a way that made me wish he'd taken two. "Better yet, ask Bales why he trusts a kid who went to juvie for kidnapping and assault."

CHAPTER 24

Some words got a visceral reaction out of me. *Hunt. Threat. Hunger. Blood.* But *kidnapping* and *assault* were different. They didn't hit me the way they might have hit Jude or Free. I didn't recoil.

I *thought.*

I remembered Gabriel helping me find Saskia, the wounds I'd left in his arm, and the expression on his face when he'd shrugged them off.

When the sheriff made his exit, Jude and Free descended on me, but Silver was the one who gave me a piece of her mind: a high-pitched whine in the back of her throat, followed by a five-point check: *hand, hand, knee, knee, stomach.* She wasn't quite as gentle as she could have been.

"Somebody's in trouble," Free said tartly.

I'd allowed the sheriff to take me aside. I'd put myself in a vulnerable position, then chosen to let some fraction of my animal instincts out. Free probably wasn't any happier about that than Silver was.

"The sheriff said that Gabriel has a juvie record." I stuck to the bare-bones facts—and kept the words *kidnapping* and *assault* to myself.

"So he has a record." Free shrugged. "If I wasn't a blond-haired, light-eyed looker, so would I."

The shopkeeper came out from behind the counter. "I've known Bradley Rawlins since he was a kid. His bark is worse than his bite. He's a good sheriff, cares about the community, even coaches soccer at the local high school."

"I'm sensing a *but* coming here," Jude said hopefully.

The old man frowned at him, then sighed. "But when a Rawlins gets something in his teeth, he doesn't let go." He ran the back of his fingers over the underside of his chin. "As near as I can remember, the sheriff went to school with your mother. Cady had a bad habit of leaving broken hearts in her wake."

Free tossed her long blond ponytail over one shoulder. "It doesn't count as breaking someone's heart if they never had a piece of yours."

I could feel Girl stalking in the shadows of my mind. She hadn't forgotten about the knives or the guns in the cases. She hadn't forgotten the trap. I'd officially reached my limit on chitchat.

Ash, I reminded myself. We'd come here to ask about Ash.

"John Ashby," I said, knowing that I'd reached my capacity

for human interaction but pushing forward for Jude's sake. "Did Cady break *his* heart?"

It wasn't subtle, but it was the best I could do. I couldn't make eye contact, couldn't keep my teeth from gritting so hard that I could hear it in my ears.

Jude nudged me toward the door. "We'll take it from here."

He didn't have to tell me twice.

The rush of cool air that hit my face when I flew out the door calmed me. Maybe the sheriff had gotten under my skin, or maybe the events of the day were catching up with me. Either way, I fell back on habit and began counting down from one hundred.

By *seventy*, I'd quelled the desire to run.

By *fifty*, I'd managed to turn my mind to Free and Jude and the questions they were probably still asking inside.

One for all, and all for trouble. No matter how many lines Free added to the Miscreants' Creed, the last one was always the same.

Thirty. I could breathe. *Twenty.* The sound of the door opening behind me told me that I wasn't alone.

"Would now be a good time to share some excellent news?" Jude appeared beside me.

Nineteen. Eighteen. A breeze lifted my hair away from my face as I finished the countdown. I stared up at the mountain's peak. I could feel it, like a magnet or a black hole or a siren's song calling me home.

In. Out. In. Out. I breathed, and Jude timed his breaths to mine. "I sense that now would be a good time to share some excellent news!"

"You got the information you wanted?" I asked.

"No." Jude grinned. "The old man was remarkably silent on the topic of whether or not Mom and Ash were involved. However, he *did* share that John Ashby left town with Mom and Mac way back when."

"The difference is that Ash didn't come back," Free added.

"That's not the good news," Jude clarified archly. "The good news is that when the topic cycled back around to Bella Anthony, and our dear Phoebe Eloise *happened* to mention that it was a shame that the sheriff might eventually realize that the Freedom of Information Act only applies if you have enough specifics to zero in on the files you're requesting . . ."

Free swiped at Jude for using her full name, but matched his grin. "The old gossip couldn't help volunteering the information that someone else in town had already made some very specific FOIA requests."

"His great-niece!" Jude was practically vibrating. "She works at the local library. I gathered that she wants to be an investigative journalist and is generally considered the black sheep of the Ferris family."

"She requested copies of the missing persons reports?" I furrowed my brow. "Why?"

"To investigate!" Jude replied. "Journalistically."

If we hadn't run into Bella's mother, I might have been able to leave it at that.

"This was supposed to be a distraction," I pointed out.

"And what," Free replied wickedly, "could be more distracting than the library?"

The Hunter's Point library had, at one point in time, been a saloon. Old-fashioned doors still marked the entrance, and the checkout counter looked like it had once been a bar. The wood floors were scratched up enough that I deeply suspected Silver wasn't the first dog to pass through the swinging doors.

I scanned the area: only one woman working. She was at least six feet tall, broad through the shoulders and thin through the waist. Her blue eyes matched the pointed plastic rims of her glasses almost exactly. She smiled and handed a picture book to a little girl with dark-haired pigtails. When we approached the desk, she tapped on the edge of her glasses and made a show of studying the three of us.

"Nonfiction," she proclaimed, pointing her index finger at me before turning it on Free. "Something with explosions." She paused and considered Jude. "And . . ."

"Happy endings," he told her.

She nodded. "I can see it."

"Clearly, you are a woman of true discernment," Jude declared. "And hopefully one who might be willing to share any and all police reports she's obtained from the local sheriff's office?"

There was a single beat of silence.

"Who have you been talking to?" the librarian asked. Maybe her *journalistic* ambitions weren't well-known.

"Who *haven't* we been talking to?" Jude replied jubilantly.

From there, the conversation went exactly as one might have predicted. She wanted to know why teenagers were asking her for police reports. Jude mentioned that we'd been part of the search for Bella—though he may have conveniently left the past-tense aside.

The high-pitched sound of a child laughing, followed by the even-higher-pitched sound of one shrieking bloody murder, had the librarian whipping her head toward a colorful rug—and its many ankle-biting occupants.

"Story time," the librarian muttered, like it was a curse word. Belatedly, she realized we were still standing there and remembered why. "Right. The reports. If you think they'll help in the search for the missing girl, I *suppose* I can pull together some notes for you, once I avert the story-pocalypse over there."

The dark-haired girl with pigtails was the only one sitting quietly, the book the librarian had given her hugged tight to her chest. The rest of the children appeared to be planning a coup.

"When might we expect these 'notes'?" Jude asked, making liberal use of air quotes.

"Bright and early tomorrow morning," the librarian replied. "Promise. In the meantime . . ." She walked to a nearby shelf and fluttered her fingers along the spines of book after book until she found the one she was looking for and pulled it from the shelf.

"*A History of Hunter's Point?*" I read the book's title as she held it out to me.

"Written by yours truly," the librarian said. "Nonfiction. You should give it a try."

I closed my fingertips around the book an instant before one of the kids at story time threw up on the brightly colored carpet.

"Don't look now," Jude whispered as the librarian bolted toward the puking child, "but the cavalry has arrived." There was a slight pause. "The cavalry is Gabriel."

I turned my head, but kept my body still. Gabriel had entered through a side door. I expected him to be looking for us.

He wasn't.

Kidnapping, the sheriff had taunted me. *Assault.*

Gabriel walked with his head down and disappeared behind one of the shelves.

"That's not suspicious," Jude declared. "That's not suspicious at all!"

Jude and Free only knew that the sheriff had mentioned Gabriel having a criminal record. They didn't know what that record entailed. I wasn't used to keeping secrets from them, and I wasn't entirely sure why I had kept this one.

The sheriff might have been lying.

He might have been telling the truth. I reached out and laid a hand on Jude's arm before he could start strolling in Gabriel's direction.

"We should go," I said.

"Should we?" Free was clearly on the verge of whipping out the Creed. I knew that if I *had* told her what the sheriff had accused Gabriel of, dragging her away from a chance for answers would have been every bit as impossible as coercing Duchess into the bath. I wanted answers, too, but I doubted that Gabriel would respond any better than I did to being cornered. When I faced him down, when I asked my questions—I'd do it one-on-one.

I started for the exit, knowing that Jude would follow me and that, eventually, Free would follow Jude. But I couldn't help looking back over my shoulder. Gabriel was no longer hidden from view. He was doing a good job of acting like the contents of a nearby bookshelf had commanded his attention, but from this angle, I could see the way his dark eyes stared through a gap in the shelf.

At story time.

At the kids.

CHAPTER 25

After the library, we headed back to the house. Dinnertime came and went, and there was still no word from Cady. Jude and Free had uncovered a treasure trove of old board games and were currently trying to play three at once, but I didn't feel like *playing*.

Restlessness clawed at me. I'd never been the biggest or the strongest or smart in the way that tests captured, but I had a finely developed sense of when to fight and when to turn tail and run, and this time, I'd given up too soon.

I should have been out there looking for Bella.

When staying inside became impossible, I roamed. Pacing the Bennett land, I found two other houses inside the property line: one a cottage, the other closer to a shack. Burying myself in the woods near the latter, I sat with my legs stretched out along the base of a fallen tree. My right hand made its way to my ankle, feeling the coarse, scarred skin on my legs.

The monster almost had Girl.

The sky overhead might have looked clear, but a dull ache beneath the scars told me that there was weather headed in. *If they don't find Bella before the storm hits . . .*

Trying to ignore the constant, gnawing churn inside me, I turned my attention to the book in my lap. *A History of Hunter's Point* was, it turned out, less of a written history than a town scrapbook. It traced the town's development from its founding in the 1850s through modern-day. By the time I made it to the 1920s, when Sierra Glades was established as a national park, I'd noticed that the same names appeared over and over again in Hunter's Point history, across the generations. *Rawlins. Turner. Ferris. Ashby. Wade.* These were the founding families.

It wasn't until I made it to the last few chapters that I started seeing people I recognized. *Cady Bennett and John Ashby. Bales Bennett on horseback. Sheriff Bradley Rawlins, his first day on the job.*

"You're smarter than this." A sharp voice broke my concentration, and I looked up. There, through the trees, I could make out two figures. *Gabriel and Bales.*

"No one saw me." Gabriel stopped on the shack's makeshift porch. He was avoiding eye contact with Bales.

"The librarian did."

The sound of gentle padding alerted me to the fact that Silver had followed them out here. It was only a matter of time before she scented me, if she hadn't already.

I willed her to stay right where she was.

"Penelope's on my side," Gabriel was saying, his voice low.

Bales gave Gabriel a hard look. "Which is exactly why she called me to tell me where you'd been."

"She would have married my brother, if things had turned out differently. I doubt she's going to go opening her mouth to the sheriff."

I froze, all too aware of the sound of my own breathing. *What won't she open her mouth about? What don't you want the sheriff to know?*

Silver stayed by Cady's father's side for a moment longer, then began making her way to me. There was enough brush between the shack and my position that I wouldn't be easy to spot, but Bales and Gabriel were as familiar with the outdoors as I was.

I considered retreating, but my body refused to move.

"You're eighteen, Gabriel. Not a juvenile—not anymore."

Gabriel's head was bowed, but I knew, even from a distance, that it wasn't a gesture of submission.

"It won't happen again," he said.

"Are you lying to me, or to yourself?"

Silver butted my hand with her head. I curled my fingers silently into her fur, warm and steady beneath my touch.

"You're one to talk about lying," Gabriel muttered. "Have you told her yet? Your daughter?"

Silver chose that moment to lie down beside me. A twig snapped beneath her. Bales turned toward the forest. I pressed my body to the ground. Bales Bennett's eyes never found mine, but I couldn't shake the feeling, as he turned back to Gabriel, that the old man knew I was there.

That feeling was confirmed when Gabriel took refuge inside the shack, and Bales let out a low whistle. Silver padded toward him, and he bent down to her level. "Care to show me what you found?" he murmured.

I could have run, could have melted into the forest, but I didn't.

"I ought to say a thing or two about eavesdroppers." Bales came to stand in front of me, as Silver resumed her position at my side. His boots were flecked with mud. "But I'm guessing you were out here first, so maybe I should apologize for intruding on your quiet instead."

I wondered how different his tone would be if he knew that this wasn't the first time I'd listened in on one of his conversations.

"I saw Gabriel today. At the library." My mouth went dry around those words.

Bales settled down beside me, his back up against the tree trunk, same as mine. "And what were you doing at the library?"

He'd left space between us—enough that I could breathe and enough that not a single muscle in my neck tightened at the question.

Asking the librarian to give us copies of police reports. I wasn't about to offer up that explanation, so instead, I held out the book.

Bales raised an eyebrow. "And the supply store?" he asked. I must have looked surprised, because he elaborated. "Small town."

"Cady never said we couldn't explore."

The edges of the old man's lips curved ever so slightly. "Did *I* say you couldn't?"

He hadn't. Nothing he'd said to me so far had sounded even remotely like an order.

"If you take after my daughter as much as I think you do, I'd be a fool to try to tell you what you can and cannot do."

If anyone else had said those words, I would have sat there in silence, but I could see Cady in her father as easily as he could see her in me.

"Are you?" I asked him. "A fool?"

Bales chuckled and studied the backs of his hands, the skin worn by age and exposure. "I can be, when it's worth the cost."

I wasn't quite sure how to respond to that.

"What you overheard, with Gabriel—it's nothing you need to concern yourself with." Bales managed to sound like he hadn't just changed the subject. "And it's not something he'd thank you for overhearing."

I know. I didn't say that out loud. Instead, I opted for a different truth. "Jude, Free, and I ran into the sheriff at the supply store." I addressed the words to the back of my hands. "He said some things. About Gabriel."

The silence Bales offered in return didn't feel pointed. It felt like breathing room.

"The sheriff," I continued after a long pause, "told me to ask you about how you and Gabriel met."

If that statement took Bales off guard, he gave no sign of it that I could see. "That a question?" he asked.

Was it?

The night before, Gabriel had said that he wasn't the trustworthy type. But today, he'd knelt next to me in the cave. He hadn't tried to pry the radio from my hand. He'd fed me the words to say, until I could speak on my own.

"No," I found myself telling Bales. "That wasn't a question."

I wanted answers, but not from him.

"I would have liked to have known you," Bales commented, his eyes fixed on the horizon. "When you were young."

As seconds stretched into minutes, I expected Bales to get up and leave, but he didn't. As the sun set, and the wind began to whip, Cady's father kept his eyes locked on the Glades.

"You going to ask me what Gabriel meant when he said I was lying to Cady?"

I wasn't sure how long we'd sat in silence when that question finally broke it. "Would you tell me?"

Bales didn't answer.

"Why bring Cady back here?" I asked, climbing to my feet. "Why this search?"

I wasn't sure I'd get an answer. I wasn't entirely sure why I'd asked.

"Because," Bales replied gruffly, closing his eyes, "it's not the things you can't find that haunt you. It's when you choose not to look."

CHAPTER 26

What Bales had said nipped, needle-sharp, at the edges of my mind. The last thing I wanted to do was surround myself with walls, but when night fell and the storm rolled in off the mountain, I forced myself to take refuge inside.

It's not the things you can't find that haunt you. Bales hadn't been talking about me. I knew that, but as the hours wore on, it became harder and harder for me to think of anything else. *It's when you choose not to look.*

I'd stopped searching for Bella. I'd pulled back. And, a voice deep inside me whispered, I'd never looked for answers about my own past—the nightmares, the woods, how I'd survived, why there had been no family to claim me. . . .

The front door creaked open, snapping me out of it. The world came instantly into focus. There was a mug of hot chocolate sitting on the floor beside me, ringed in a confetti heart—clearly, a present from Jude. He wasn't the one who'd opened the front door, though.

Cady was.

"You got somewhere to stay?" I heard her ask gruffly.

"I imagine I can rustle something up."

I couldn't see Mac, but I recognized his voice. For a moment, I was back in the cave, lying flat on my stomach opposite Saskia, trusting him to do no harm—to her, to me.

"You are *not* sleeping in your car." There was no give whatsoever in Cady's voice. "Or the barn." She stalked into the house, banged open a linen closet, and unceremoniously shoved a bundle of blankets in Mac's general direction. He stepped into the house, and a moment later, his gaze fell on me.

I'd been sitting with my feet flat on the ground and my knees in the air, my weight braced against my palms in what Cady referred to as my "ready position."

Ready to jump to my feet.

Ready to skitter backward.

Ready to fight.

"Waiting up to see if I made it home by curfew?" Cady asked me.

I shrugged. "Something like that."

She squatted down opposite me and nodded toward the mug of hot chocolate. "I'm guessing the confetti wasn't your idea."

I snorted and shifted my weight, lowering my knees. She

held out a hand, and when I took it, she stood and pulled me to my feet. The motion was utterly familiar.

It wasn't as comforting as usual.

It's not the things you can't find that haunt you. It's when you choose not to look. I hadn't chosen to step back from this search.

Cady bent to pick up the hot chocolate Jude had left me. "It's cold," she commented.

"It's late," I shot back. "Bella?"

I'd stopped looking because Cady had *made* me stop looking. The least she could do was give me an update.

"We'll regroup once the storm passes." Cady paused, but she seemed to sense that stopping there wasn't an option. "We traced Bella's scent out of the cave system and into the valley before we lost the trail again. Whoever took her knows the mountain better than I do."

The implication of that was clear. "The person who took Bella is local," I said.

Mac saved Cady from having to reply. "The rangers are coordinating with the FBI and talking to the family to figure out who might have had access and motive."

Bella's kidnapper knows the mountain. The storm is washing away trace evidence as we speak.

"Saskia and I could go back out tomorrow." I took a step toward Cady. "We're fresh, and you need the numbers. When the storm passes—"

"When the storm passes, I'll be rested." Cady didn't let

me finish. "So will Mac. So will our K9s. I know you want to help, Kira, but the answer is no."

It's not the things you can't find that haunt you. I didn't want to feel like I'd been backed into a corner, but what Cady was asking of me wasn't fair. Leaving me here, tying my hands, treating me like a *child*—

"It was my life and my choice," I said softly. "That's what you told Bales." I should have stopped there. "You told him that Ash was worth it to you. *This* is my life, and my choice, Cady, and Bella—"

"Kira," Mac cut in. "You do not want to go there."

Cady whirled on him. *"Don't tell my daughter what to do."*

I heard the pain in her voice—worse than a yelp or a whine or a mewl. I knew that Mac wasn't the one who'd hurt her. He wasn't the one who'd lashed out.

"Cady," I started to say, my mouth dry.

"Upstairs." Cady stared at and into me. "We'll finish this discussion upstairs."

I waited for Cady in her room. When she came in, she was still holding the mug of hot chocolate. After a moment, she sat down on the end of the bed and held the mug out to me. "I heated it up."

She wasn't angry. I wasn't sure why I'd expected her to be. Even when I was young, even when I'd lashed out physically, even when I'd drawn blood—all she'd ever done was *be there*.

I'd hurt her. She wouldn't hurt me.

"Cady, I shouldn't have—"

"You hate inaction." Cady reached out and ran her free hand over my hair, no muss, no fuss, no frills in her tone. "You look at Bella, and you see yourself. You want to help. Taking a step back is killing you. I get that, Kira. But the answer is still no."

She held out the hot chocolate again, and I took it. I wasn't in the mood for something sweet, but I needed the warmth. I needed to take what she was giving me.

"I shouldn't have brought up . . ." I stared down into the dark liquid, unable to say the name *Ash*. "I'm supposed to be on your side. I'm supposed to *protect* you."

"No," Cady countered. "I'm supposed to protect *you*. You're supposed to rebel and think I'm a totally lame adult who just doesn't understand and might also be the densest person on the planet."

I snorted into my hot chocolate.

Cady measured her next words. "Coming back here hasn't been easy for me." She paused. "You and Jude haven't asked about why I left. About why I don't speak to my father."

I'd brought up Ash. I'd made her think she had to do this. "We don't have to talk about—" I started to say, but Cady spoke over me.

"His name was John Ashby." She managed a slight smile. "Though I suspect the three of you have probably sorted that out."

Cady didn't owe me this. If anyone had a right to ask her about Ash, it was Jude.

"We grew up together. Like you and Jude and Free. We were a team."

Given what I already knew, I suspected that *team* wasn't just another word for family.

"Military search and rescue?" I asked.

My knowledge took Cady momentarily off guard. "Small town," she muttered. Then she corrected me, "Not military. More like military-adjacent." She pressed her lips together for several seconds. They were chapped, pale. The search had taken a physical toll.

I was the reason she wasn't resting.

"You don't have to tell me anything you don't want to tell me, Cady. I don't need to know what happened."

"You wouldn't have brought it up if you didn't." She rubbed the thumb on her left hand over the fingers on her right. "The team was called down to South America." The story came in pieces and spurts. "The job was in cartel territory. Four of us went into the jungle. Only three of us came out."

It was difficult to picture Cady—*my* Cady—trekking through the jungle, facing off against a drug cartel. "You must have gone down there to find something," I said, my mind reeling. "Or someone."

"The details of the job don't matter," Cady said, which was another way of saying that the details of the job were none of my business. "What matters is that things went south, and if we hadn't pulled out when we did, we'd all be dead."

"And Ash?" My grip tightened around the mug in my hands.

"He wasn't dead when we left." Cady let out a long, uneven breath. "That's all I know. Mac and I went back for him as soon as we could, but he was . . . gone." Cady's voice was hoarse. "I would have moved hell and high water to bring Ash home, even if there was nothing to find."

I tried to imagine what it would have been like if the search for Bella had been a search for Free or Jude. I wouldn't have stopped.

I *couldn't* have stopped.

"My father gave up." Cady shook, physically *shook* as she spoke. "Mac gave up."

"You didn't," I said, because I *knew* Cady.

"I had to." I could see the muscles in Cady's throat tensing. She braced her palms against the bed. *Ready position.* "I was pregnant, Kira."

I heard my own sharp intake of breath.

"My father didn't know," Cady murmured, the words catching. "Neither did Mac. But every time they hammered me for taking risks with my own life, I knew that I was taking risks with his." She closed her eyes, just for a moment. "So I stopped."

Cady had given up looking for Ash—for *Jude*. This was what I'd thrown in her face downstairs.

"I'm sorry," I said. My voice cracked, and I stalked toward the window. My back to Cady, I stared out into the darkness.

"I know that you're just watching out for me. I know that this situation with Bella—it's not the same."

Cady joined me at the window, staring out into the night. We couldn't see the mountain through the darkness, but I could feel it.

"One to ten?" Cady asked me.

"Eight." I wouldn't lie to her, not after the truths she'd just given me. "Girl is back. The flashbacks—I'm handling them."

"I don't have to go back out there," Cady told me. "The search can carry on without me. I can take you home."

"No," I said, stepping back from Cady and from the window. My hands shook, and I used the mug to steady them.

Cady had given up the search for Ash for Jude's sake. I wouldn't let her give up this one for mine.

CHAPTER 27

I crept into the room I was sharing with Free at a quarter to two, but didn't fall asleep until the sun began to peek over the horizon the next morning. I dreamed of darkness—not the forest, but the kind of darkness that comes with walls on four sides, closing in.

Bad things happen to bad little girls.

I knew it was a dream, but it didn't matter. I could still feel myself clawing at the tiny crack beneath a shadow-cast door, a whimper rising in the back of my throat. I was still whimpering when I woke up—and I wasn't the only one.

Silver stood over me, nudging me awake. *Pup. Wake up, pup.* Her high-pitched whine broke off as the world came into focus for me and her tongue lapped at my face.

Kira, I thought. *I'm Kira. That's Silver. Kira and Silver. We're fine.*

In the early years, I'd woken up like this more mornings than I could count.

"Good morning, Sleeping Beauty." Free tossed something at me. It wasn't until it landed on my stomach that I realized it was a Pop-Tart. I sat up before Silver could get ideas about snatching it.

"Breakfast?" I asked Free.

"Breakfast, part two. Part one was rough. Ness is down with the flu, and let's just say that Bales Bennett's culinary skills leave something to be desired."

Given the size of Free's appetite, I deeply suspected she'd eaten whatever it was that Bales had attempted to cook anyway. As I eyed the Pop-Tart, she tossed something else at me—a file folder.

"What's this?" I asked, shoving Silver over after a quick scratch behind her ears. I flipped open the folder just as Free answered my question.

"An overview of Miss Penelope Ferris's research into our missing persons."

"The librarian?" My mind went immediately to the conversation I'd overhead between Gabriel and Bales the day before.

"One and the same," Free replied. "Jude has developed an ill-fated crush on her—he digs the glasses." Free hopped up on the dresser, her heels bouncing lightly against the drawers. "Boy is still hanging out at the library in what he insists is 'completely necessary recon' and not at all an effort to prove himself helpful to his new lady love by stacking shelves."

"Did he tell you he's a lover, not a fighter?" I asked.

"I believe the direct quote was 'Make love, not war or questionable breakfast choices.'"

As the last remnants of the dream slid off me, I wondered whether or not I should break it to Jude that the current object of his affection had almost married someone else. Deciding it wouldn't make much difference either way, I bit into the Pop-Tart and began thumbing through the files Free had given me. *So many people, gone without a trace.* I read over their names one by one. When I got to the last one, my gaze darted up to Free's.

She would have married my brother, Gabriel had said, *if things had turned out differently.*

"I see you've come to the first case our librarian friend documented." Free turned toward the window. "One Andrés Cortez."

One hour, multiple readings of the files, two Pop-Tarts, and three split-second, gut-clawing flashbacks later, this is what I knew: Andrés Cortez had gone missing four years earlier, at the age of nineteen. He'd dropped out of high school the day after his sixteenth birthday to help support his family and had been working as an unofficial guide on the mountain since he was twelve. For eighteen months prior to his disappearance, he'd also held down a day job as a mechanic two towns over.

He'd been reported missing by his fourteen-year-old

brother. *Gabriel.* I felt like I should have known, like I should have been able to scent the tragedy on him.

According to the official records, the investigation had found no evidence of foul play. The working theory seemed to have been that Andrés had kicked the small-town dust off his feet and left his life and responsibilities behind, the way his own father had years before. In the weeks leading up to his disappearance, he'd spent several hundred dollars on wilderness supplies.

People around here go missing all the time. I could hear shades of meaning in Gabriel's words now that I hadn't before.

"Makes you wonder, doesn't it?" Free asked.

With effort, I pulled my attention from the file and looked up at her. "Wonder what?"

Free leaned back against the wall. "Nine people in the last four years, starting with Andrés Cortez. I'm asking myself what a 'normal' number of disappearances around here might be."

Over half a million people are reported missing each year. I didn't recognize the statistic, not at first. Unlike my time in the forest, this was a memory I had to search for. When I found it, I felt like I was watching it unfold from under water.

"Over half a million people are reported missing each year." The doctor pauses.

"How does that make you feel?" She leans back in her chair. "Kira?"

"Hungry."

"It makes you feel hungry?"

I shrug.

"Let's try something different. Let's talk about the dog."

I cock my head to the side. "Silver?"

"The new dog. Saskia." Another pause—longer, leaner somehow. "Someone hurt her."

There was a roar in my ears, a whisper, and then *nothing*.

"The cases might not be connected," Free was saying. "These missing persons might have nothing to do with Bella."

And how, I thought, *does that make you feel?* I had to stifle the urge to physically shake off the question. Feeling was dangerous. Thinking was better.

As long as I was thinking, I was *me*.

"Say the cases were connected." I turned to Free, my focus intense. "Andrés Cortez is the earliest case we have a file for. Do you think he was the first?"

Free balanced precariously on the windowsill, one knee pulled to her chest and the other dangling toward the ground. "The first what?"

I thought of the doctor, asking me about Saskia. *Someone hurt her.* There was still a part of me that believed that was what humans did. They hurt things—not because they had to, not in self-defense, not to sate their hunger.

Because they *could*.

"The first victim." Free answered her own question—or maybe the expression on my face answered it for her. "You think all these people were kidnapped, like Bella?"

I didn't know what to think.

CHAPTER 28

It was Free's suggestion that we talk to Gabriel. It was my idea to go alone. Every instinct I had said that Gabriel wouldn't do well with being outnumbered. I was the one who'd spent the most time with him. I was the logical choice. Free wasn't happy about that, but she agreed: I would talk to Gabriel.

I would ask him about his brother.

For the first time since Cady had sent me off the mountain, my body and the restless energy inside it felt aligned. I made it to the shack I'd seen Gabriel disappear into the night before and paused. Up close, the term *shack* seemed insufficient. It wasn't big—maybe twenty feet by twenty—but it was solid. It had been made with wood but made well. The color had faded with time, enough so that I doubted Gabriel was the one who'd taken hammer to nail. But someone had built this place, board by board.

I understood, objectively, that knocking was something

people did. But announcing my presence—giving away my position and waiting, open and exposed—wasn't something I'd ever been able to bring myself to do. Jude had joked for years that my version of *knocking* was to stand silently outside a door, glaring intensely.

I might have given up on this particular door—I wasn't even sure why I'd come—but I heard something. The sound was muted, but I had a way of listening, focusing on one thing and blocking out everything else.

And there it was again—a low-pitched murmur. *A moan.*

A breath caught in my throat, I pressed the door inward, slowly at first. The hinge creaked, the old wooden boards protesting beneath my feet as I shifted my weight. Allowing the house to announce my entry sent my shoulders hunching upward, but after freezing on the makeshift porch for a moment or two, I made my way inside.

The first thing I noticed was that the cabin consisted of a single room, plumbing on one side, a shelf with non-perishables on the other, and a bed in between.

The second thing I noticed was the body on the floor.

Body. For an instant, I was somewhere else, looking at *someone* else. I could see long, dark hair. I could see blood pooling on white tile.

I stumbled backward, my hand grappling for the wall and hitting paper. I didn't turn to see what I was touching. I couldn't tear my eyes from the floor. Sunlight streamed in from the door and a nearby window, illuminating the shape of the form sprawled there.

Not a woman. Not bleeding.
Gabriel.

I was used to the forest haunting my dreams, used to shades of memory bleeding over into the light of day. But this was different.

This wasn't the forest.

This wasn't Girl.

My breath was coming quickly, my heart hammering in my chest as I knelt next to Gabriel's body. He lay facedown, his head turned to one side. My hand crept toward his face. It was only after I'd felt his breath, warm against my palm, that I realized why I'd reached out.

To make sure he was breathing.

To make sure he was alive.

I could see now, the way his chest rose and fell. He let out another low-pitched moan, and I understood what I should have assumed from the onset—he was sleeping.

How many nights had I spent on the floor instead of pinned down under covers in a bed? How many times had I woken, a strangled cry dying in my throat?

And yet, when I'd seen him lying there, I hadn't thought that he was sleeping.

I shouldn't be here.

In the months after Cady had found me, that feeling had been with me constantly. Even once I'd accepted that I was Kira, that I was human, that I was *wanted*, the white-hot realization that I wouldn't ever fully belong in this world could hit me in an instant.

Get it together, Kira. Bales had said the day before that Gabriel wouldn't thank me for having overheard their conversation. I doubted he'd be any more charitable finding me crouched over his sleeping body.

I stood and backed away in a single, liquid motion. I turned toward the door, intending to flee, but as I did, I caught sight of the wall I'd reached for when I'd stumbled backward. My hand had hit paper, and now I could see why.

The surface was covered, ceiling to floor, with notes and maps, photographs and pins. I recognized bits and pieces from the missing persons reports I'd read over, but that was nothing compared to the whole.

An eight-foot-by-ten-foot map of Hunter's Point and the adjacent mountain hung in the center, marked up so thoroughly with black marker and flags that I could barely make out the words underneath. Smaller maps broke the rest of the Sierra Glades into quadrants.

Seven hundred and fifty thousand acres, I thought, reaching up to press my fingertips gently against the map in the center. In a lifetime, Gabriel couldn't cover that much ground.

But he could try.

CHAPTER 29

ales had claimed that Gabriel knew the mountain better than anyone. Now I understood why. I thought back to the way that Gabriel had helped me find Saskia when she'd gone missing.

Caves, I could hear him telling me. *My brother used to insist that they were out here, but I spent an entire summer looking and never found one.*

Based on what I'd seen on Gabriel's wall, I was willing to bet he'd spent longer than one summer looking. In fact, I would have bet the clothes off my back that he'd spent *years*.

"A quiet Kira bodes well, I always say!" Jude plopped down beside me. I was sitting with my back up against the tree I'd slept under our first night in Hunter's Point.

"Is this an 'obsessing over the fact that I'm stuck here instead of out searching' quiet or a 'meditating on what was in those files' quiet?" Free asked, jumping to catch hold of the tree's lowest branch and pulling herself effortlessly up.

"Or an 'I should have taken Free with me to talk to Gabriel' one?"

Jude stretched out his mile-long legs and laid the folder of information we'd obtained from the librarian delicately on his lap. "I have always felt, deep down," he said once it became clear that I wasn't going to answer Free's question, "like I might be the second coming of Sherlock Holmes."

Jude had also, at various points in time, claimed to be the second coming of Ann Landers, William Shakespeare, and Princess Di. I said as much out loud, and my foster brother adopted a serene expression.

"I have layers."

Above us, Free positioned herself on the branch, allowing her legs to dangle down. "And what, oh second coming of Sherlock, are your finely honed instincts telling you about our missing persons?"

Jude pressed two fingers on his right hand to his temple, like a medium communing with the spirits. A look of intense concentration settled over his face.

"Now would be a good time for you to say something," he told me in a stage whisper. "Propose a theory, and I will do my Sherlockian duty and tell you why you're wrong."

A theory? I was about as much use at putting together theories as Saskia was at putting people at ease.

"I believe in you," Jude told me. "I really do."

"And I believe you're keeping something from us," Free added. "I really do."

One for all, and all for trouble.

"I don't think Gabriel believes his brother just walked away from their family." I should have told them more than that. I should have told them exactly what I'd seen at Gabriel's place—and exactly what the sheriff had told me. But Gabriel had helped me find Saskia the day before.

Gabriel and I were both the kind of people who slept on the floor.

"Do you think good old Gabe believes that his brother's case might be connected to Bella's?" Jude asked.

Yes. The force of my instinctual response was savage in my mind, but I was saved from responding by the sound of the world's most mournful baying. NATO had found us, Duchess on his heels. As Free tore a stick off the tree and tossed it for Her Ladyship, NATO hunkered down between Jude and me and continued the hound dog version of a tragic ballad.

Jude tousled his K9's head back and forth, scratching at just the right spot behind his ears. "The world isn't as bad as all that, old man."

I felt, rather than saw, Saskia edging toward us. She'd spent the past twenty-four hours giving everyone myself included—a wide berth. Meeting her liquid gaze, I had the oddest sense that she was on the verge of adding her howls to NATO's.

I didn't *know* the reason for their canine melancholy, but I had my suspicions. "We train them to find what they're looking for." I turned from Saskia to study NATO's deep brown eyes. "And in training, that's something they can do."

But out in the real world, that wasn't how search and rescue worked.

"First the river," I said, reaching up to stroke a hand along NATO's velvety-soft ears. "Then the mountain . . ."

In both cases, the hounds had caught Bella's trail. And both times, that trail had gone cold. Whoever had taken Bella knew how to cover their own tracks—and hers. *A local. Someone who knows that mountain.*

Duchess dumped the stick she'd fetched for Free ceremoniously at my feet. I picked it up and threw it again for her. This time, Her Ladyship did not deign to fetch. She sat down next to NATO and bit his tail—gently enough to tell me that she wasn't really looking for a fight. In response, NATO licked her face and cuddled up. Saskia took up position three or four feet from the pair of them.

"It can't be easy," Free said overhead. "Looking and looking for something you know you'll never find."

Something about her tone made me wonder if there was more to that statement than I could hear. I glanced toward Jude and he elaborated.

"Things you know you'll never find," he translated, "like the identity of one's father, a way to be normal, or a family who cares when you hang-glide off the neighbor's roof."

Free held a hand to her heart. "Ouch. In case you didn't pick up on it, K, the bit about being normal was for you."

Jude was right. We were all looking for something. I'd been too focused on myself—and on the files and on Gabriel—to have thought about sharing what I'd learned about Ash. Now that I *was* thinking about it, I wasn't sure if it was my place to tell him that Cady had been pregnant when Ash had disappeared.

Jude leapt abruptly to a standing position and bounded back and forth on the balls of his feet until he'd captured NATO's full and undivided attention.

Play.

"We should give you something that you actually *can* find, boy." Jude turned back to Free and me, like he'd never uttered the word *father* at all. "What say you, ladies? Up for a little Extreme Hide-and-Seek?"

CHAPTER 30

Free hid first. We ordered Duchess and Saskia to stay by the tree and let NATO loose. Sass and Her Ladyship were not always the best of friends, but I was fairly certain they wouldn't get into it with each other today.

"Find her," Jude told NATO.

Our boy practically shook with glee. This time, when he followed the trail, he'd find something. We'd make sure of it. As the K9 worked, nose to the ground, Jude and I fell into silence.

"So," Jude said finally, drumming his fingertips absent-mindedly against the side of his leg. "Gabriel Cortez. Intriguing fellow." When I didn't reply, he elaborated. "Might I be sensing some sexual tension?"

I narrowed my eyes at him.

"Just tension, then," Jude said quickly. "Right-o."

NATO took a sharp right and began picking up speed. Jude and I hung back but picked up our pace as well.

"You have to be wondering," I said, turning the tables on Jude and stealing a look at him out of the corner of my eye. "About Cady's past. About what it means for you."

Jude gave me a long, considering look. "I asked Mom about my father once." He paused. "*Just* once. It was right before you came to live with us. I had formed theories, you see, mostly involving astronauts, but also the occasional space alien taking on humanoid form."

I could see a teeny tiny Jude saying exactly that.

"She told me that she'd loved my father, and that he'd loved her, and that she knew for a fact that he would have loved me. And that was it. She neither confirmed nor denied his astronaut status, but that night, when I went to get a glass of water from the kitchen, I saw her. She was crying—not sobbing, exactly. It was more like her eyes were malfunctioning—leaking. I remember thinking that the leak might never stop."

Even as a child, Jude would have eaten his own hand to keep from seeing Cady like that again. He never asked for more than you could give.

"I've been keeping secrets from you." The admission slipped across my lips.

"I know," Jude replied airily.

That was all it took for the secrets to come pouring out. I told him about Gabriel's maps and notes, about *kidnapping* and *assault*. I almost told him about the conversation I'd had with Cady the night before, but I hesitated. *That might not be my secret to tell.*

171

"I think Cady would answer your question now," I said instead. "If you asked her who your father was."

"And that," Jude said, "is *exactly* why I won't ask. She'd answer, but it would cost her. And for what?" He tweaked the end of my ponytail. "I have all the family I need."

Up ahead, NATO dropped to his belly, pushing his head under an old log and letting out a joyful bark.

"Methinks he doth found something," Jude said, wiggling his eyebrows. "Or rather, some*one*."

"Get off of me," Free said, shoving NATO gently as she pulled herself out from her hiding place. "You big, slobbery mess," she crooned, pouncing on him as she made it to her feet. "You clever, clever boy."

Unlike Saskia, NATO wasn't trained to loop back. He worked primarily on a lead, and Jude was never far behind, so he just kept barking until Jude and I caught up.

"Well done, my good man!" Jude said, adopting a very poor British accent. NATO leapt up to press his front paws to Jude's thighs, to which Jude replied, almost immediately, "Shall we waltz?"

The sight of Jude taking NATO's paws in hand and beginning the world's most awkward ballroom dance jarred a laugh out of me. Eventually, Jude let go of NATO's paws and whirled gracefully back to Free and me. "Who's next?"

"For dancing?" I asked, wrinkling my nose. "Or Extreme Hide-and-Seek?"

Jude kept right on waltzing. "Dealer's choice!"

"I'll double back for Duchess." Free brushed the dirt off

her jeans, very deliberately not mentioning *dancing* at all. "She could use some cheering up, too. You up for hiding this round, K?"

We'd played this game a million times before. At one point, Cady had banned it, because Extreme Hide-and-Seek had gotten a little *too* extreme. Duct tape, rappelling equipment, and paintball guns were now permanently outlawed from game play.

"Cut Saskia loose if she's getting antsy," I told the others. "And let Duchess know she can bring it on." I hesitated, then nudged Jude in the side. "You can tell Free what I told you," I said softly. "About Gabriel."

He nudged me back, and a split second later, I took off running. The three of us needed this as much as the dogs did. The longer and faster I ran, the easier it was to push the events of the past couple of days out of my mind. I didn't have to think about what I'd seen in Gabriel's cabin. I didn't have to think about missing persons reports, or hold the image of that flyer with Bella Anthony's picture in my mind.

I didn't have to think about the blanket.

I didn't have to think about Girl.

I just ran. I dodged through the trees. I pulled myself up into one, allowing the branches to hide my body from the naked eye. I sat there, and I waited, freer than I'd felt in days.

And then I caught sight of another figure moving through the forest—lean and lithe.

So much for not thinking about Gabriel Cortez.

I willed myself to stay where I was. Gabriel passed under my tree, and I realized that he was wearing a pack and carrying a flashlight.

It's still light outside. Without even thinking about it, I dropped down from the tree, landing silently in a crouch. I watched Gabriel hop the fence at the back of the property. I watched him hang a right.

Toward the mountain.

———

CHAPTER 31

I followed Gabriel, hanging back far enough that he couldn't sense my presence. I should have been thinking about Jude and Free and the game I'd left behind. But *promises* and *worry* and *logic*—those were just words. They were abstract. Tracking, trailing, stalking, waiting—those were now. I might have started off curious about where Gabriel was going and why, but the act of following him pushed all conscious thought to the back of my head. There was nothing but the hum of anticipation and my own silent, liquid movement through the brush—until we hit the base of the mountain.

I stopped. Gabriel started to climb.

I watched, camouflaged. We were on the near side of Bear Mountain, opposite the place where the copter had dropped us the day before. Soon, Gabriel stopped climbing. He contorted his body, and in the space between one blink and the next, he'd disappeared from sight.

The tracker in me said that no one ever really disappeared, and as I climbed, following the path he'd laid, I
knew exactly what I was looking for.

An opening.

A cave.

Cady had said there was a whole system of underground
caverns. Multiple entrances—or depending on your inten-
tion, multiple *exits*. My foster mother had estimated that
it could take the rangers weeks to map them all. My first
thought, when I started *thinking* again, was that it could
take one person—one single-minded, driven person—years.

I almost missed the gap between one rock and the next,
where Gabriel had vanished. The opening was small—
smaller than the one I'd entered the day before.

Fortunately, this time, there wasn't a drop.

I squeezed through. What little light followed me told me
that it was going to get very dark very quickly, and unlike
Gabriel, I hadn't brought a flashlight. I was far enough
behind that I couldn't even tell, for certain, which way he'd
gone.

What are you doing, Gabriel? The question kept me from
turning back. *Just how well do you know these caves?*

I braced my right hand against the wall, steadying myself
as I crossed slowly into darkness.

This was probably a bad idea. I was following someone
who'd been accused of kidnapping and assault, someone
who'd lied to me the day before and was behaving suspiciously now. I was perfectly aware of those facts, but I also

knew that Gabriel had been at the Bennett house when we'd arrived. I knew that he'd made another appearance there that night, that he'd been on the property when I'd woken up the next morning, that he'd spent hours that day searching alongside me.

If he'd been the one to stash Bella in the cave, he wouldn't have had time to move her.

Would he? That thought batted at me as my surroundings went from dark to pitch-black to eerie, velvety nothingness. Up ahead, I heard something. As I inched along the wall and slowly made my way around the bend, the uncompromising darkness began to recede.

Within minutes, I saw it. *Light.*

I'd found Gabriel. He'd left his flashlight on the cave floor, pointed upward, illuminating his climb. By the time I spotted the outline of his form, he was already ten or fifteen feet overhead.

I had no idea how Gabriel was creeping his way up the cave wall—or why—but as I watched, he reached some kind of landing and pulled himself onto it, stomach first. He inched forward, then disappeared.

Again.

This time, I didn't follow. Despite what Cady thought, I did know my own limitations. Specifically, I knew that I couldn't make that climb. I hadn't grown up on a mountain.

I hadn't had to fight for survival *here*.

Listening for any indication that Gabriel was on the verge of returning, I heard nothing but a hollow echo and the distant sound of running water. I cocked my head to the side, closing my eyes and absorbing the sound.

When I opened my eyes again, they landed on the flashlight. The human part of my brain said that taking it would be wrong. Girl—buried deep in the recesses of my mind—said that Gabriel had left it.

You had to protect what was yours.

Kneeling down, I closed my fingers around the flashlight. I hesitated only a moment before I stood and did a 360, taking in my surroundings. I could feel the otherness of this place. Even with the light from the flashlight illuminating the space around me, my senses stayed on high alert. Unsure what I was doing—or why—I found myself moving toward the sound of the running water.

Drink. Girl thirsty—

I shook off the memory. I wasn't dying of thirst. I just needed to know where I was, *what* this place was. The farther I went toward the sound of the water, the colder it got. I rounded another bend, the din of rushing water building. I'd expected a stream or possibly a continuation of the river we'd seen before. What I found wasn't just water.

It was a waterfall.

The river rushed over the edge into a straight drop, crashing into razor-sharp rocks twenty feet below. I lost track of how long I stood there, watching the water descend into darkness, listening to its deafening roar.

Rumbling. Shaking. At first, I thought the jolt to my bones was nothing more than the power of the falls taking hold, but as my balance gave way, I realized that something was wrong.

The mountain was moving.

The tremor only lasted for a moment, but this close to the waterfall's edge, I had to scramble for purchase. I backed away from the roar of the water, from the drop. A hand closed over my bicep.

Gabriel. I sensed him—smelled him—before I turned to face him head-on. His hold steadied me. A fraction of a second later, he dropped my arm, pulling his hand back like the act of touching me had burned him.

I wondered if he was thinking about the way I'd reacted the last time he'd grabbed me.

"Earthquake," Gabriel commented casually. "You know, that thing where the ground shakes for a brief period of time, during which it is typically considered *not good* to be inside a mountain."

I tried to get a read on his posture, his expression. My fight-or-flight instincts hadn't kicked in when he'd touched me. Because he'd reached out to steady me?

"Far be it from me to state the obvious, but you took my flashlight." Gabriel gave me an indecipherable look.

"I did."

Gabriel arched an eyebrow. "Is this the part where I ask why you followed me here and committed petty larceny against my person?"

I got the distinct feeling that he wasn't amused, even though he smiled like he was. I should have been on guard.

When he asked me why I'd followed him, I shouldn't have wanted to reply.

"Your brother disappeared four years ago," I said. Facts were easier than answers. "You've been mapping out this mountain ever since. Yesterday, you told me that you'd spent a summer looking for these caves. You said you'd never found them." My heart gave no signs of thundering in my chest. My breath didn't come quickly. "You lied. Why?"

I braced myself for him to lash out, to go on the defensive, to demand to know how I knew about his brother.

Instead, he reached forward—and plucked the flashlight from my fingertips.

"I told you I wasn't the trustworthy type." He stared at me for a moment longer, then turned. "Come on."

CHAPTER 32

As we approached the entrance, I became acutely aware of the fact that the only light in the cave came from the flashlight in Gabriel's hand. It wasn't until we came face-to-face with a wall of rock that I processed the implication of that darkness.

"Rockslide." I beat Gabriel to the observation. He placed his hand flat on the rocks blocking our exit, testing their stability. I assumed he was trying to calculate the odds that we could dig our way out.

"You know those movies where two people get caught in an elevator together at the worst possible time?" he asked.

It took me a moment to understand what he was saying: We were trapped. The earthquake must have triggered the slide. The opening hadn't been that big to begin with.

I could feel an old, familiar sense of dread rising up inside me, like a whisper of smoke slithering its way up my spine. *Trapped. Dark. Let me out. I'll be good—*

"If it's any consolation, I have it on good authority that being trapped in a confined space with me is a fate at least marginally better than death."

"I don't need you to distract me," I gritted out. I'd seen Jude and Free doing it often enough to recognize the technique.

"Of course you don't. But for the record, if you find yourself needing to hit something, hit me." He smiled. Or smirked. Or both. "After all, I lied to you, and if it weren't for my sheer animal magnetism, you probably wouldn't have followed me into the depths."

"Shut up," I said, but now I wanted to throw something at him, which was significantly more comfortable than allowing in the lurking memories.

"Shut up," Gabriel countered, "or get you out of here?"

I didn't waste any time with my reply. "Both."

I couldn't stop expecting my eyes to adjust to the darkness, but even with the flashlight, we couldn't see more than three or four feet ahead. The air down here was damp, and my heart beat a little harder and a little faster with every turn. The longer the two of us trekked toward what Gabriel insisted was an alternate way out of the mountain, the harder it was to stop from going over everything I knew— about Bella's disappearance, about Gabriel's brother and the other missing persons reports, about the research I'd seen on Gabriel's wall.

"I know what you're thinking," Gabriel said, pausing to

remove a canteen from his pack. "This would be an excellent place to ax-murder someone." He took a swig of water before passing the canteen to me. "It occurs to me," he continued, "that it's also a *horrible* place to talk about ax-murdering."

Given the circumstances, I suspected Gabriel was employing what Jude would have referred to as *dark humor*. I took a drink of the water. "Why would you need an ax?"

There was a long pause. "What I love about you is your ability to make a rhetorical question sound disturbingly not rhetorical at all."

He handed me the flashlight. I took it, unsure why he was giving it to me.

"You're not going to like this part."

I processed that statement a moment before I steadied the flashlight and saw the opening. It was two feet in diameter, if that.

"This is the only other way out of the mountain," Gabriel told me. "Or at least, the only one I've found."

This. As in a tunnel so small that the only way through was on your stomach. The muscles in my throat clenched a moment before the wave of nausea hit me.

Trapped. Dark.

"You take the flashlight and go in first. I'll follow."

Bad things happen to bad little girls.

"Kira?"

The wisp of control I'd been holding on to snapped. "If I go first," I said, the words forming in the back of my throat, "you'll be *behind me*."

183

"In retrospect, maybe I shouldn't have made inappropriate jokes about murder," Gabriel replied. "Hindsight is twenty-twenty." Whatever he could see of my face must have made an impact, because he stopped cracking jokes. "If I go first, and you freeze, I won't be able to help you. But if you go first, and something happens, I can get you out."

"I don't . . ." My muscles were already going rigid. There was a roaring in my ears, an indescribable *whisper*—

"You don't need protection—check. We've been through this. Are you, by any chance, capable of humoring me?"

I was vaguely aware that his tone was low and soothing, like the one Mac had used with Saskia the day before.

"Okay, so no humoring. What about a bribe?" He paused and waited for my eyes to find his. Eventually, they did. "You asked me why I lied to you about the caves. In response, I deflected, rather skillfully, if I do say so myself." He waited until he had my full attention. "You want to know what I'm doing out here, if it has something to do with my brother. Under normal circumstances, I'd deflect those questions, too. But if you do *this* for me"—he jerked his head toward the tunnel—"I'll tell you whatever you want to know."

CHAPTER 33

Gravel and stone bit into the flesh of my forearms as I pulled myself forward. I could feel my heart beating in my abdomen. I concentrated on the visceral sensation of my flesh scraping against the tunnel floor. Pain would keep me in the here and now—pain and my awareness of another living being, right behind me.

"Why did you lie to me?" It probably said something about me that this was my first question. "Yesterday, when you pretended that you didn't know the cave was there—"

"I wasn't pretending." Gabriel made good on his promise: no flippant comments about how untrustworthy he was this time. "Like you said earlier, I've been mapping out the caves for years. I thought they might go all the way through Bear Mountain. I *looked* for an entrance on the northern slope. But yesterday was the first time I'd found any evidence to back that up."

I kept a hold on the flashlight as I dragged myself forward on my stomach. The beam of light was lost in the black hole ahead of us, the end of the tunnel nowhere in sight. I focused on forming my next question. If I could think—if I could *talk*—then I could believe that the flashlight wouldn't go out, that the mountain wouldn't shake again.

That I wouldn't die in the dark.

"Do you think your brother's disappearance is related to Bella's?" I focused on forming the question, and then I focused on waiting for his answer.

"Anything is possible, right?"

I was breathing evenly, but each time air exited my lungs, they seemed to shrink, and the next breath was harder won. I thought of the maps on Gabriel's wall. *Questions,* I thought. *Ask them.*

"Are you looking for your brother," I asked through clenched teeth, "or for his body?"

Gabriel stopped moving behind me, but just for an instant. "I could have left you down here."

"You could have tried," I returned. "Now, answer. You promised."

I heard a faint scratching sound—not Gabriel and not me.

Bad things happen in the dark. Bad things happen to bad little girls.

Maybe I hesitated, or maybe Gabriel just sensed that he was on the verge of losing me. He started talking again and didn't stop. "I never believed that Andrés just took off. I can buy that he might have wanted a weekend to himself, but if he didn't come back, it was because he *couldn't*. I used to think that something had happened to him—an accident. Maybe he was climbing and he fell. Or maybe he had one of those heart murmurs you read about, and he just dropped dead one day while he was out here exploring. Maybe he ran into the wrong predator." There was a pause, a slight one. "It didn't occur to me until much later that the predator could be human."

Like the person who took Bella. The world around me was getting smaller. My fingernails bit into the palms of my hands as I pulled myself forward. My next question unwound inside me slowly, like a snake rising from coiled position. "Why were you arrested for kidnapping and assault?"

The question had teeth. To Gabriel, it probably seemed like it came out of nowhere, but in my mind, it was all tangled together: Gabriel and his brother, the missing persons reports, Bella, the sheriff.

"Been talking to the law?" Gabriel asked me, his voice echoing in close space.

"Is that your way of deflecting the question?"

He'd promised me not to deflect—and he knew it. As long as I kept going, he'd keep talking. He'd promised.

"When Andrés disappeared, I could have gone off the rails. Instead, I got my act together. I spent every spare second I could out on the mountain, looking for my brother, but I also made varsity soccer, joined the debate team, started pulling straight As. My mother had just remarried. I thought her husband was a good guy. I thought that if I was that kind of guy, people would believe me when I told them that Andrés hadn't just left."

The muscles in my arms were starting to ache.

"The joke was on me, though. My good-guy stepfather was the one who convinced my mother to stop looking for Andrés. He almost convinced me."

"Almost?"

"My mom and my stepdad had a baby. The novelty of a newborn wore off for that *good guy* pretty fast. Five weeks in, my mom was barely sleeping, and my stepfather would look at the dishes in the sink or bang around making himself dinner and say that if she would just be a little *smarter* about how she handled things, she wouldn't be falling down on the job. My sister had colic. He thought that was my mom's fault, too."

I could hear Gabriel grinding his teeth. As the first shard of light became visible at the end of the tunnel, I ground mine as well.

"I got used to him making my mother cry. Every time that it happened, he'd tell her—and me—that she had postpartum depression. She didn't, but he didn't want to admit that it was something he'd said or something he'd done that had upset her. He'd start talking about how she was emotionally unstable, about how maybe she couldn't be trusted with my baby sister because she was so illogical and irresponsible and erratic. He said it often enough that she started to believe it, and when he told her she was failing as a wife, she believed that, too."

Gabriel was breathing more heavily now. Every once in a while, his arm would brush my leg.

"He never hit her," Gabriel said.

The end of the tunnel was close—five feet away, or six.

"He never hit me, but he did like slamming things around. Punching walls, right next to her face. If they were fighting and the baby started crying, he wouldn't let my mother leave the room. He'd stand in the doorway and block her when she tried to go, telling her that if she wasn't such a horrible excuse for a mother, maybe my sister would be sleeping through the night."

We were almost out now.

"One day, she said something he didn't like, and he threw a glass into the wall. It shattered. A shard hit my mother's arm. Another came *this* close to my infant sister's face." Gabriel paused, ever so slightly. "I snapped."

I didn't need to ask what that meant. It meant the same thing it would have if someone had threatened Cady and Jude in front of me. *Attack.*

Assault.

The muscles in my neck and stomach tensing, I rolled over to my back and pulled my upper body out of the tunnel. I placed my palms beside my legs, braced, and lowered them to the ground. I was out. I was through.

Fresh air had never tasted so good. The muscles in my chest loosened, and I breathed in hungrily—again and again, like a drowning man who'd made it up for air.

"So that's the assault charge." Gabriel made it out and rose to his full height beside me. He examined a cut on the heel of his hand. "I clocked the guy, knocked him out. I was in a bad situation, and I made a bad choice. Pretty sure I'd make it again. Just between you and me? Part of me even enjoyed it." He paused. "Would you like to hear about the kidnapping charge next?"

"Your sister?" I guessed. He'd said that she was a baby, that she was there, that she was almost hurt. I wondered if he'd meant to take her for good, or if he'd just wanted to get her out of the house.

"She's almost four now," Gabriel said quietly. "I'm supposed to stay away from her—and my mother. That was part of the deal I struck with the DA. I pleaded guilty to assault, they dropped the kidnapping charge, and my mother didn't have to testify."

"But if your mother had testified—"

He cut me off, his brown eyes capturing mine. "She wasn't going to testify on *my* behalf."

I blinked back against the sun and managed one last question, though now that we were out, he was under no obligation to answer.

"The sheriff, he was the one who arrested you?"

No answer.

"You told him the truth, and he didn't believe you?" I guessed.

Gabriel's dark hair caught the sun. "Oh, he believed me. He was my soccer coach. I thought he was such a good guy." The gleam in Gabriel's eyes nearly took on a life of its own. "The sheriff knew exactly what happened, because my mom is *his* wife."

CHAPTER 34

The hike down from the mountain didn't take us to Hunter's Point. We ended up two towns over instead.

"Wait here," Gabriel said, like he hadn't bared his soul to me, like I hadn't been searching for the right words to say in return the whole way down. "I know the guys who work here." He nodded to the local auto shop. "I'll see if someone can give us a ride."

I would have snapped, too. He was hurting the people you love. I'm sorry. All the things I hadn't said cycled through my head as Gabriel disappeared into the garage. I'd known him just long enough to suspect he wouldn't want *sorry*.

"Still too good for the job I offered you?"

The question made its way to my ears over the din coming out of the garage. If I'd been one of the dogs, my ears would have perked up. The missing persons report had said that Andrés Cortez had worked in an auto shop. I slipped inside, ignoring Gabriel's command to wait.

"I have a job," Gabriel was telling a man whose upper half was hidden beneath a car.

"Old man Bennett will get tired of you someday," came the reply. "If I were you, I'd clear out before he gets sick of playing Daddy Warbucks."

"That old man," Gabriel said, each word pleasant and precise, "could take on everyone in here—and then some."

I wasn't an expert at the art of persuasion, but that didn't seem like the most effective way to ask for a ride.

"Can I help you, sweetheart?"

I turned toward the mechanic who'd asked that question. I couldn't offer Gabriel anything in exchange for what he'd given me up on the mountain, but I could save him from having to ask someone who was giving him a hard time for a ride. "I need to borrow a phone."

I dialed Jude's number from memory. He answered on the first ring.

"Kira?" The hope—and tension—in Jude's voice reminded me that I'd taken off without a word. Jude and Free would have set Duchess on my trail.

She didn't find me. Knowing Jude and Free, they'd probably tried Saskia next. *And she couldn't find me, either.*

"I'm fine," I said quickly. "I'm with Gabriel."

Jude let out a long breath. "I was in no way concerned that you might have been snatched by the person who took Bella or buried in post-tremor rubble. The phrase *lying in a ditch somewhere* never even crossed my mind."

There was no guilt trip like a Jude guilt trip.

"It's a long story," I told him, "but I promise that I'm fine. I just need you to come pick me and Gabriel up."

There was a brief pause on the other end of the line. "Dare I hope this long story will be accompanied by an elaborate reenactment? Preferably with musical numbers?"

I told him where I was.

"On my way," Jude told me cheerfully. "But fair warning: Free might have been slightly less optimistic than I was when your trail disappeared in the mountains. She called Mom."

Jude came to get us in Gabriel's truck. Free was with him.

"You abscond with our Kira," Jude informed Gabriel cheerfully, "we abscond with your truck!" He paused. "I've never driven a stick shift before."

Gabriel audibly groaned. "Move," he told Jude. Free was sitting in the back of the truck. NATO, Duchess, and Silver were with her. Saskia was there, too, but the other three were giving her a wide berth. I took that to mean that she'd been a bit testy. I climbed in, positioning myself next to Sass.

If Jude had been worried, there was a very good chance that Free was *pissed*.

"Hey, Free," I said, well aware that I might be poking a bear. Free stared at me. NATO snuffed in my general direction, and Duchess farted—loudly.

"Serves you right," Free told me. She tossed my cell phone in my general direction. "How many times do I have to tell you that if you're going to do something completely stupid and utterly inadvisable, *I want in.*"

"I saw Gabriel leaving the property. I followed him. And once I was following . . ."

"I've seen you in stalk mode," Free said. "I know what it's like, but I also know that at some point, you had a choice, just like you had a choice about keeping secrets."

Right before I'd left, I'd told Jude what the sheriff had said about Gabriel. I could see how dumping the words *kidnapping* and *assault* on a person and then pulling a disappearing act might have been cause for some concern.

"The sheriff is Gabriel's stepfather," I told Free. It was easier to share a secret than to promise to stop keeping them.

Free processed the barbed edge in my voice. "On a scale of one to ten, how much do we hate the sheriff?"

In answer, I let my upper lip pull back from my teeth. Then I snapped them together. Saskia was on all four feet in an instant.

"That much." Free let out a low whistle. NATO ambled into her lap, and she gave him a good scratch before pushing him off. Duchess farted again.

"You'll have to excuse Her Ladyship," Free said. "Being left high and dry at Extreme Hide-and-Seek gives her indigestion."

Free wouldn't hold a grudge, not if she so much as suspected I might need her. But she *hated* being left behind. She probably wouldn't say another word about it, but if a dog wanted to continually fart in my general direction, she was all for it.

I was still weathering Duchess's onslaught when Free's phone rang. Free glanced down at the caller ID, then tossed it to me.

Cady.

This was not going to be pretty.

"Hello." I answered calmly and heard Cady let out a breath the moment she recognized my voice.

"You want to explain to me why I have a message on my phone from Free, claiming you'd gone missing?"

Cady didn't *sound* angry, but that dry, no-nonsense tone never boded well.

"Not particularly."

I expected Cady to rephrase the question as an order, but instead, she hesitated. "Are the flashbacks getting worse?"

That question was a visceral reminder that there had been a time in my life when taking off—*running, hiding, holing up*—had been my MO.

"I just got caught up in doing something," I said. *Something* seemed so much less likely to set Cady off than the words *earthquake* and *rockslide* and *juvenile delinquent*.

"Do me a favor," Cady ordered. "Don't get caught up again."

I had control. She expected me to use it.

"Cell reception here is coming in and out." Cady's words proved almost prophetic. Whatever she said next, I didn't hear it.

"Go," I said. "Find Bella."

"Kira." There was another long pause on the other end of the line. "I'm not sure there will be anything left to find."

"You think she's dead?" I felt like I had a piece of bone caught in my throat. This was what I got for letting myself be taken off the case, for taking a step back and even entertaining the notion that reading missing persons reports and asking questions qualified as *doing something*. "You think she's been murdered?"

Silver rolled over, pressing her body against mine and stretching out along the length of my legs. To my surprise, Saskia didn't just tolerate it, she lay down on my other side.

"We're not giving up." Cady hesitated, just for a moment. "In the meantime, if you see Gabriel, give him a wide berth."

If I'd been walking, that instruction would have stopped me dead in my tracks. "What?" I said. "Why?"

Had the sheriff said something to her? Why would Cady—who had better sense than anyone I knew—listen?

"Gabriel's volatile, Kira. If the circumstances were different, I would be fighting for him every bit as much as my father is, but he's not my kid. You are, and you have a lot going on right now. Whatever Gabriel's been through, whatever anger he's carrying—it's not good for you."

Hearing her say those words should have made me angry. Instead, it hurt.

"I'm not fragile," I said. "I'm not going to break."

Cady's reply was lost under a web of static, and then the line went dead. Free arched an eyebrow at me in question.

"She wants me to stay away from Gabriel," I said flatly.

I could see the wheels in Free's head turning. If she told me that Cady was right, if *she* acted like I was broken—I wouldn't be able to take it.

Instead, Free twisted and pounded a fist on the window separating us from the truck's cab. Jude opened it.

"What can I do for you?" he asked pleasantly. "Gabriel and I are *bonding*."

Free just smiled beatifically. "How would you gentlemen feel about a little road trip?"

CHAPTER 35

Gabriel didn't particularly feel like taking us anywhere, but Free could be very convincing. She requested a place with a view. That was how the four of us came to be standing on a stone ledge in the shape of an arrowhead, facing away from the national park. At first, all I could see as I looked out was green—a thousand and one shades of it. The landscape stretching toward the horizon looked like it had been painted with a knife: thick and textured and *alive*. I could see civilization if I looked for it. But why would I? Why would anyone?

Free walked right up to the edge and looked down. "How far is the drop?"

"Maybe a hundred feet?" Gabriel guessed.

Jude looked at me. He looked at Free. And then he peeked over the edge of the ledge, threw his head back, and howled. Free joined in: half yodel, half victory scream.

"Don't you ever just want to yell?" Jude asked a visibly

startled Gabriel. "To take everything inside of you—every worry, every *what if*, every question that haunts you—and just . . . let go?"

"Not particularly."

Free flipped her ponytail back over her shoulder. "Are you a liar or a stick-in-the-mud?" she asked Gabriel.

He probably had a smart-mouthed response to that question, but he didn't get a chance to use it, because I *did* know what it was like to swallow screams and howls. My dark place was a living, breathing thing. I'd barely held it at bay in the caves. It rose up like a wave inside me with each setback in the search for Bella, and in between, it churned. *Watching, waiting, feeling, scratching against the door to be let out—*

I raised my face to the sky and let loose a howl of my own. Jude whooped, and Free joined in, and soon, the dogs had added their voices, all except for Saskia, who was pacing the fringes, her blue eyes focused on Gabriel. The edges of his lips had just started to curve upward when, suddenly, he paused, cocked his head to one side, and then started jogging back toward his truck.

I followed him, and Saskia followed me. I made it back to Gabriel's truck just in time to see him reach through the open window and fiddle with the dial on what looked to be a radio. It took me a few seconds to register the fact that the radio was on when the truck was not, and another after that to process the muffled words coming out of the speaker.

This wasn't a radio.

This was a police scanner.

Gabriel must have realized I was standing there, because he turned toward me. "Kira."

I bristled. He hadn't mentioned owning a police scanner. He hadn't even hinted that he was keeping tabs on the sheriff's department.

"Kira," Gabriel said again, his voice softer this time and oddly devoid of emotion.

"What are you doing?" I asked him. "What is this?"

Very slowly, he straightened his body. He dropped his arms to his side. "Behind you."

As I turned, I became acutely aware of the world around us. *The smell of dirt. The sound of Free and Jude and the dogs on the ledge.*

The feeling of being watched.

I scanned our surroundings, pushed back against the sound of my own heartbeat, my breath, and *listened.* I heard nothing, but my head swiveled to the left of its own accord. There, in a tree less than ten feet away, I made out two eyes glowing an unearthly yellow.

Reflecting the sun, I thought, but the words were distant, like someone else had thought them and I'd only overheard. My own thoughts—the ones I lived and breathed and *felt* rushing like blood through my veins—were entirely focused on the shape of the animal watching us from that tree.

Bigger than Girl. Faster.

"Mountain lion," Gabriel said. "They rarely attack humans."

That was what he thought.

That was what the statistics said.

That wasn't the message I received from the liquid grace with which the predator leapt down from the tree.

Food. Hungry. I remembered being hungry. I remembered hunting.

I remembered being prey.

The mountain lion stood between us and the others. Saskia was the first one to notice. I knew her. I knew what she looked like when she was on the verge of a lunge.

"Stay." The word burst out of me. Saskia growled, and the mountain lion's head swiveled from me to her.

No.

I took a step forward. Gabriel caught my arm, but I shook him off. Another step, and the animal's gaze was right back on me. I knew better than to corner a predator. I also knew that Saskia's control was even more tenuous than mine.

"Don't turn around," I told Gabriel, fighting the instinct to lower my voice. "Raise your hands. Make noise."

The way to fight a predator was to convince it you were the bigger threat.

"Don't look away," I continued, my eyes on the cat's as I felt a scream bubbling up in my own throat. *Not terror. Not fear. Rage* was a human word. The yell I let out when the cat took a languid step toward us was anything but.

Beside me Gabriel added his own voice to the chaos, stomping, taking up space, staring the mountain lion straight in the eye. The animal eyed us for a moment, then made a chuffing sound, deep in its throat.

But it didn't come any closer.

As quickly as it had begun, it was over, the mountain lion melting back into the wilderness—all 130 pounds of it.

Sharp teeth. Strong jaw. Claws. Lethal. The drumbeat of warnings thrumming in my brain persisted long after the threat was gone.

"You okay?" Gabriel asked me.

"I'm fine."

What I didn't say was that there was a part of me—hidden and wild and *free*—that was better than fine. There was a part of me that had *enjoyed* it.

Saskia let out a sound—half growl, half whine—and I realized I hadn't dropped the order to stay yet. When I did so, she bolted for me. The second she reached us, she turned around, snarling.

Another predator would approach *her* human over her dead and rotting corpse.

"Now was that so hard?" Jude called out to Gabriel. "See what I mean about letting go?"

"You get all the fun," Free told me.

"I understand now," Gabriel said thoughtfully. "The three of you share a single iota of common sense. I'm just a little unclear on which one of you has custody of it now."

"I'm not positive," Jude told Free. "But I *think* that's a compliment."

"No," Gabriel replied. "No, it is not."

A sound from the truck reminded me of why I'd followed Gabriel off the ledge in the first place. "Gabriel was just about to get over himself and tell us why he has a police scanner."

"Gabriel," Jude declared, "is my *favorite*."

CHAPTER 36

According to what Gabriel had told us, he'd acquired the police scanner for the same reason Jude, Free, and I had wanted to get our hands on the missing persons reports. He wanted to know when someone in Hunter's Point went missing,

He was looking for a pattern.

"Anything else you feel like sharing?" Free asked him, her tone casual, but her eyes intensely focused on his face. In her free time at school, Free played poker. That never turned out well for her opponents. She was an expert at finding tells.

"The police found something in Alden." Gabriel addressed the answer to me, not Free. "Town about an hour from here. Witness thinks she saw the missing girl. Sounds like the FBI is canvassing the streets." He gave us exactly two seconds to process that. "I'm going."

This wasn't just about Bella, not for him. The maps on

his walls, every piece of research he'd done—none of that was for *Bella*.

Not knowing. There should have been a word to describe the emotion that went along with that. It wasn't a longing or a need or a fear, not exactly.

"I can drop you off back at the house, or you can walk." Gabriel didn't wait for a response before he climbed into the truck and jammed the key into the ignition.

I knew, beyond any shadow of a doubt, that Cady wouldn't want me sticking my nose into this, but when she'd kicked me off the search, I'd let her. I'd sat back, and I'd done nothing, and look where that had gotten us.

Nowhere.

I turned toward Jude and Free. The moment our eyes met, a silent, split-second conversation followed. Jude held out his hand, palm down. Free and I mimicked the motion, and then, in unison, we voted.

My fingers curled into a fist. *Yes.*

Jude—*yes.*

Free was the last one to vote, but we all knew that her fingers were going to fist, too. *One for all, and all for trouble.*

"You're not dropping us off anywhere." Free climbed into the truck next to Gabriel. "We're coming with."

By the time we arrived in Alden, I wasn't sure who was more ready for our road trip to be over: Saskia, Gabriel, or me. All three of us were out of the truck before Free had even unbuckled her seat belt.

Alden wasn't much bigger than Hunter's Point, just a dot on the map that people passed through without giving the town or its inhabitants a second thought.

"We're dealing with a kidnapper who knows how to survive in the wilderness. Someone who knows Sierra Glades National Park." Gabriel shut his car door, harder than necessary. "The person who took Bella knows how to cover their tracks."

I thought of the number of times the trail had gone cold and Bella—and the person who took her—had seemingly just vanished. "This person doesn't just know how to cover their tracks," I said. "They know how to disappear."

A muscle in Gabriel's jaw ticced. I wasn't sure what to make of that. Free gave him a once-over, then threw out a question. "So why would a wilderness expert give up that advantage and bring Bella back to civilization?"

Jude was the first one to come up with a response. "If they're local, they might have been afraid that if they stayed gone too long, someone would notice their absence."

"Or maybe the kidnapper wants to take Bella somewhere." Free squatted next to Duchess, scratching behind her ear. "Or the witness was mistaken. Or this sicko is just playing with us."

"This isn't a game." Gabriel's voice was so low that I had to strain to hear it. I tracked his gaze to a man and a woman in dark colored suits across the street. "Feds," Gabriel continued, muted. "Kidnapping is a federal offense."

As if she'd heard Gabriel, the female in the pair glanced

our way. I wondered what she saw. Four teens and four dogs? Could she tell that we weren't supposed to be here?

"Should we mosey?" Jude asked brightly. "I suggest we mosey."

We *moseyed* away from the street and down to a creek to regroup. The trees were thicker here than in Hunter's Point, the divide between civilization and the Glades less sharp. I wondered how many people in Alden had land that backed right up to the national park.

If Bella's kidnapper had that kind of access . . . I couldn't keep my mind from sorting through the possibilities. Beside me, Saskia lowered her head to the creek, her front paws braced against the rocks. She drank for a moment, then went stiff and still, her blue eyes focused on something in the distance.

"We should go back," Gabriel was saying. "Ask the people in town some questions. If the feds realize we're asking around about Bella, so be it."

I barely heard him. My muscles had gone as taut as Saskia's. She sensed something—heard it, smelled it, *felt* it, I wasn't sure—but I knew in my bones that my K9 knew something in hers.

"Kira?" Jude got out my name an instant before Saskia bolted across the creek and into the densest part of the woods. The other dogs took off after her, like this was a game, just another round of Extreme Hide-and-Seek.

Except that we hadn't given them a scent to find.

I sprinted after them, barely aware of the creek water

seeping through my jeans. Free called for Duchess to heel. NATO managed to wait for Jude. But Saskia didn't stop, and neither did I, not even when it became clear that Silver couldn't keep up.

I could hear the others on my heels, but I didn't turn to look at them, my attention focused on tracing the path my K9 was blazing. I didn't stand a prayer of a chance of keeping pace, but as my leg muscles began to scream in protest, as stones and limbs bit haphazardly at my flesh, Saskia slowed.

She stood, regal and still, just long enough for me to catch sight of her again, and then she took off once more.

It continued that way for a small eternity, Saskia leading us farther and farther into the wilderness, over the border into the park. I wished that I'd memorized the maps on Gabriel's wall, wished that I had more of an idea of where we were than "in the shadow of the mountain" and "deeper into the park than we meant to go."

This section of Sierra Glades had no rangers' stations, no trails. There was nothing special about it, nothing majestic. Just trees and dirt and rocks—and us, chasing after my possibly unhinged, possibly on the trail of who knows what, dog.

Finally, Saskia stopped. Finally, I caught up with her—and finally, the others caught up with me.

"Bella?" Jude was the one who managed the question.

I knelt next to Saskia. "I don't know." I sank my fingers into my girl's fur, scratching softly behind her ears. She turned her head toward me and whined.

None of this made sense. This wasn't how Saskia had been trained. This wasn't what we did. *What is going on?*

Saskia butted my hand with her head, and my breath stilled in my throat. *I trust you, girl.* I felt those words, more than thought them. Whatever instinct had possessed Saskia, whatever had led her here—whatever she'd smelled, whatever she'd followed—I trusted that, too.

Standing up, I did a 360, taking in our surroundings. What if the person who'd taken Bella *hadn't* left the park permanently? What if this latest lead was just another misdirection? Another game?

What if Saskia had recognized the kidnapper's scent?

What if she'd recognized Bella's?

Slowly, I began to make my way from tree to tree, toward a clearing maybe fifty yards away. Two-thirds of the way there, my toe caught on a stone, and I stumbled.

Free caught me. For a moment, her eyes held mine, and I saw in them the same sense of eerie foreboding I felt.

This is it. This is something.

I caught sight of the stone that had tripped me. And the stone next to that—and the one next to that . . . Each of the rocks was about the size of a bag of flour. They lay in a perfect circle, each one half-buried in the ground.

"That's not a natural formation." Gabriel knelt next to me, examining the ground.

"Forest art?" Jude suggested, but even he couldn't manage a hopeful tone.

Someone had dug into the dirt, buried the rocks, arranged them just so. It felt intentional. It felt *ritualistic*.

I sank to the ground to get a better look. Saskia came up behind me, pushing herself between my arm and my body. I followed her gaze—uncanny and intense—to a tree positioned at the base of the circle.

A breath caught in my throat. Hash marks—thousands of ragged hash marks—had been carved into the trunk of the tree.

Why? I ran my fingertips over the marks. *What do they stand for?*

"I choose to believe that those are hash marks of the non-nefarious variety," Jude said, but the sound of a twig snapping—of footsteps—in the distance had him taking three steps back.

These marks weren't made all at once, I thought, my heart beating viciously in my throat. *Someone has been coming back to this tree—someone has been marking* something—*for years.*

Gabriel stood and positioned himself in front of the rest of us. Saskia whined again, then bolted forward. I grabbed for her but missed.

No. Sass— The words died in my throat, and I was on my feet in seconds.

"Saskia?" A familiar voice broke the tension building in the pit of my stomach a moment before an even more familiar figure came into view.

Cady?

Of all the things—and people—I'd thought Saskia might have scented, this option hadn't occurred to me. Saskia took up position at Cady's side, then turned back to me, her tail wagging.

"Mom," Jude said awkwardly, keeping one hand on NATO to keep him from bolting to bestow doggie kisses upon her. "Fancy meeting you here!"

Cady spent exactly two seconds narrowing her eyes first at Jude and then at Free before turning 100 percent of her attention to me.

Walking toward her, I was fairly certain that this was about to get ugly, but before she could say anything, before *I* could say anything—about the rocks, the hash marks, the tree—a loud, sharp bark broke through the summer air.

At first, I thought it was Pad, thought that she'd found something, but then I realized that the golden retriever was standing just behind Cady. *NATO, Duchess, Saskia, Silver* . . . they were all *here*.

The barking came from farther down.

I pushed past Cady, pushed toward the clearing. I told myself that the rangers might have brought in another team, that the feds might have had an SAR expert of their own, but the deep tenor of the bark suggested that the K9 in question was large.

As large for its species as Mackinnon Wade was for his.

I broke through the tree line, and the world fell into slow motion. Mac's dog was barking, nose to the ground.

"Cadaver dog." I heard myself say the words. "Mac's dog is trained to find bodies."

Human remains.

I thought of Bella, of rocks laid in a perfect circle and hash marks scratched into the bark of a tree. Someone had come back to this place, again and again. It held meaning— for someone.

"Kira." Cady came up behind me, wrapping an arm around me and coaxing my head onto her shoulder. "It's okay. I promise you—you're going to be okay."

I wanted to really hear those words. I wanted to believe them. But I couldn't, because as Mac bent down to mark the spot his dog had indicated, the animal lumbered through the clearing, nose in air, then started pawing at another spot, a few feet away.

The cadaver dog barked. *More remains.* When Mac came to mark that spot, the K9 repeated the process.

Again.

And again.

CHAPTER 37

'd thought that the worst-case scenario was that the search for Bella ended with a body. Instead, it ended with five. Five unmarked graves, one visibly more recent than the others.

I tried not to think about Bella's blanket, about her mother.

Soon, the place was crawling with feds. The sheriff's men ushered us to the side. At some point, someone draped a rough brown blanket over my shoulders. Like I was capable of feeling the chill that came with nightfall.

Or like I was in shock.

The sheriff arrived not long after they removed the first body. When I looked for Gabriel, I realized, through a thick fog in my brain, that he was gone.

"Come on." Cady squatted beside me. "You don't need to see this."

See this.

See this.

There were so many people on the scene that I could make out very little. So why could I almost *see* a woman, lying prone on the floor? Why could I *smell* blood? My mind was a mess of *traps* and *guns* and *teeth*. *It hurts—*

"Hey. Look at me." That wasn't Cady's voice. It was deep and gentle. Somehow, I focused on Mac's eyes, focused on the fact that he was kneeling in front of me, steady and real.

He glanced at Cady. "You round up the other kids," he told her. "Kira and I will be just fine."

After a long moment, Cady went to find Free and Jude. Mac and I sat side by side on the ground in silence.

"When you do what I do, you see things." Mackinnon Wade was nothing if not soft-spoken. "Natural disasters. Mass graves. The worst tragedies humanity has to offer." He stretched his right hand out, looking at the back of his knuckles, like the story of those atrocities was inked into his very skin. "And then you come back to civilization, and you bring it with you. Sometimes, you keep those memories under lock and key. And sometimes, they get out. Sometimes, they drag you under, and you're there, *right there*, all over again."

I closed my eyes. *Girl.*

Running—

Hurts—

The fragments of memory stabbed at me like shards of glass. I breathed in, and I breathed out, and I breathed through them. Mac's massive hand covered mine. I forced my eyes open. I didn't like being touched. I didn't like to show weakness. I didn't know this man.

But somehow, I didn't want him to let go.

"It's nothing to be ashamed of," Mac said. "Having ghosts. It took me a long time to learn that, a long time to feel like I was fit for human company, and even longer to believe: The things that haunt us, they *make* us human."

He laid my hand gently in my lap and reached up to unclasp a pendant he wore around his neck. "When I met Cady, I was sixteen. She was fourteen, nosy, and somehow figured out that I was living in my car."

I thought that maybe he'd changed the subject for my benefit, to make it clear that he wasn't talking to get a reply.

That let me form one. "I bet Cady didn't like that."

"Me living in my car? She hated it. Somehow—and to this day, I don't know how—I ended up living on the Bennett property." He looked down at his massive hands. "I built the place myself."

I thought of the makeshift cabin where Gabriel was living. Suddenly and without warning, the dam inside me broke.

"How do you do it?" I asked Mac, rushing the question, the words piling on top of each other like trucks on the freeway. "How do you go out there, again and again, knowing what you're going to find?"

"I tell myself that I don't find bodies," Mac replied evenly. "I find answers. I find lost ones, and I bring them home."

He held out the pendant he'd removed from around his

neck. I realized, belatedly, that he wanted me to take it. As my fingers latched around the gift, my chest loosened enough to stop fighting every breath.

I turned the medallion over to get a better look at it.

"My personal patron saint," Mac offered. "The Wades—lovely bunch that we are—happen to be the world's worst Catholics. You're looking at the patron saint of lost causes."

My fingers tightened around the medallion. *Saint Jude.* A breath caught in my throat, and slowly, I began to understand why Cady hadn't been glad to see Mac, why I was okay sitting next to a complete stranger, why Saskia had let him pet her. Mackinnon Wade was calm and collected and centered—and *familiar.*

Ash isn't Jude's father. Before I could say anything out loud, Cady came back to retrieve me and took us home.

CHAPTER 38

When I was younger, I had trouble closing my eyes. I needed to be able to see things coming. Changes to routine, sudden movements, unfamiliar environments, unfamiliar people—those sent me straight to high alert.

Surprises were indistinguishable from attacks.

Jude had made it his mission in life to run interference on my behalf. *Not this time.* I felt motion sick, though I knew the gut-rending nausea had nothing to do with the way Cady was driving. *Jude can't run interference, because he doesn't know. He doesn't know that Mac is his father. He doesn't know, and I do.*

As a child, I'd been taught by specialist after specialist to recognize, regulate, and appropriately express my emotions. *How do you feel?* The question was a thorn, wedged into my flesh. *How do I feel?* I thought angrily.

I *felt* like I'd seen a mass grave. I *felt* complicit in the way that Bella Anthony's story had ended. I *felt* like I had no right to have been the one that Mac told about Saint Jude.

"Out." Cady didn't bother to issue separate orders to the dogs and the three of us when we arrived back at the house. She didn't say a word to Free, Jude, and me about the way we'd moseyed right into a crime scene. Part of me wanted her to read us the riot act. At least that would have been predictable.

"Go on," Cady said once we were inside. "Pack your bags. We leave in the morning."

Jude and Free bolted for the stairs like prisoners who'd received a last minute stay of execution, but my feet felt like they'd been welded to the entryway floor, my chest muscles tightening like a vise around my lungs.

"We can't leave," I burst out.

"We're search and rescue, Kira. If you choose this life, you won't always like what you find." Cady could have stopped there, but she didn't. "Do you think I wouldn't give my right arm to bring that little girl home? Do you think I wanted it to end like this?"

No. That was what I meant to say. What came out was "It's not over. It can't be."

I'd stepped back from this search, and where had that gotten us? A barking cadaver dog and unmarked graves. I could picture Bella's blanket in my mind. I could feel it in my hands.

"Someone has to tell Bella's mother," I said hoarsely. "The police will identify the bodies, and then someone has to tell Bella's mother. It's not over."

It wouldn't be over until Bella—like Mac's *lost ones*—got to go home.

"There's nothing more I can do, Kira," Cady told me, her voice tight. "And what I've already done—it's cost you and Jude enough."

"Jude and I are fine," I insisted.

Cady gave me a look. "Jude is the world's leading expert at pretending to be fine, at *willing* himself to be fine, but even he has his limits. And don't tell me that this search hasn't taken a toll on you. I saw you back at the clearing. I *felt* you remembering things that no child should ever have to experience." Cady's voice was shot through with emotion. "I won't stand by and watch you go through it all a second time."

"What if I want to remember?" I'd spent a lifetime walking in minefields. If *I* was the one who blew them up, at least I'd have a choice about it.

At least I'd see it coming.

Cady pressed her eyes closed—just for a second—before she responded. "If that's what you want, then I can set up an appointment with Dr. Wilder. But not yet—not until you're sure, not here, not because I dragged you into this mess."

This mess. As in the search she'd kicked me off of? The child we couldn't save? Or the entire life she'd hidden from us, like we didn't—like *Jude* didn't—have a right to know?

"Mac is Jude's father." I tried out the words. It felt like ripping off a bandage, though whether the wound in question was mine or Jude's or Cady's, I wasn't sure.

Opposite me, Cady fell silent.

"Does Mac know?" I asked, taking a step forward. "Does Jude?"

"I can't do this with you, Kira."

"We could stay," I told Cady, reaching out to lay a hand on her arm. "Just for a few days. Just until they catch the person who took Bella."

"They might *never* catch the person who took Bella." Cady took a step back, away from my touch. "Get packed. I want to be on the road at first light."

Cady knew that I didn't do physical contact easily. I couldn't ever remember her shrugging me off. It made me want to fold in on myself, retreat.

"So that's the plan, is it? You're just going to run away again?"

I turned to see Ness standing in the doorway between the entry and the kitchen. The older woman coughed, and I remembered Free mentioning that she was down with the flu. Dark smudges circled her eyes, but her posture more closely resembled a general on the verge of leading his troops into battle.

"I'm not running away," Cady said carefully.

Ness gave Cady a look that reminded me of every warning look Cady had ever given Free, Jude, and me. "Little girl, you've been running for years." The old woman let those words sink in, then turned on her heel. I could hear her slamming her way through the kitchen, banging open a cabinet.

"Ness." Cady followed her. I followed Cady, then pulled back when Ness turned from filling a teapot with water to whomping it down onto the stove.

"You need to forgive your father, Cadence." Ness didn't pull her punches.

"That's between him and me."

Ness turned on the stove, then pivoted to face Cady. "I love you. I raised you as much as Bales did, and Ash was *my* son. I'd say that gives me a stake in this."

"My kids come first," Cady said, her voice steely. "And I—"

Ness didn't let her finish. "Your father's dying."

Cady stepped back, her right hand gripping the kitchen sink so hard that even from my spot in the doorway, I could see her knuckles turning white. Silence reigned between the two of them until the teapot began to whistle. Ness grabbed a faded kitchen towel, moved the pot off the stove, then grabbed a mug from the still-open cabinet overhead.

"The stubborn old coot won't tell you that he's sick. He's too proud to ask you to stay." Ness poured hot water into a mug. Her hands shook slightly as she fetched a tea bag. "So I will."

"That's why Bales asked Cady to come back for *this* search." I wasn't usually a person who thought out loud, but Cady was still standing there, white-knuckled and frozen, and all I could think about was what Bales had said about regret. "He wanted another chance."

"Smart girl," Ness commented. She nodded toward the open cabinet. "If you're the type for tea, help yourself."

Cady let go of the sink and walked over to Ness. "He could have just *told* me."

Ness fixed Cady with a look over her mug. "Your daddy's been trying to get in touch with you for years, Cady. Letters. Calls. Emails. You never even responded."

"You know what he did." Cady didn't just sound angry. She sounded *gutted*. "You were there, Ness. When I came to my father on bended knee, when I groveled, when I *begged*—"

"There was nothing he could do." Ness slammed her tea down onto the counter.

"He had contacts," Cady insisted quietly. "In South America. But calling them in was too dangerous. He wouldn't—"

"He *couldn't*," Ness insisted. She shook her head and quietly got two more mugs down from the cabinet. "Not with the risks you'd already taken. Not when it was clear as day you'd take more."

"That was my choice."

"It was a suicide mission," Ness countered, her mouth set into a grim line. "Do you think, even for a second, that's what Ash would have wanted? My son loved you, Cady. He was in love with you. And you were *pregnant*."

I saw Cady swallow. "Ash and I weren't . . ." she started to say. "Jude isn't . . . Ash isn't his . . ."

Ness poured two more mugs of tea—one for Cady and one for me. "Whatever you were or weren't," Ness said, brushing off Cady's words like they were nothing, "we're family, Cadence Bennett, and if you're half the woman I raised you to be, you'll think long and hard about what that means."

CHAPTER 39

By daybreak, our car was packed. Four humans, five large dogs, and a metric ton of family secrets took the atmosphere right from *claustrophobic* to *suffocating*.

I felt like I'd left a part of myself—maybe the most important part—back in the park.

When Cady pulled off at a gas station on the way out of town, a niggling panic built inside me. She hadn't given me a choice about being kicked off the search. She wasn't giving me a choice about leaving now. She hadn't told Jude the truth about Mac *or* the truth about Bales.

"I will admit that this is an unfortunate turn of events." Jude turned in the front seat to look at me the moment Cady got out to pump the gas. "I had hoped for at least one family bonding moment before we left." He swallowed. "And Bella . . ."

Hearing Jude's voice break broke me.

"We did what we could." Free set her jaw, but even I could see that she didn't believe what she'd just said.

We should have done more.

"Darn our human limitations," Jude said out loud.

Bales is dying, I thought in reply. *Mac is your father, and Cady's just running away.*

"Don't look now," Free murmured, "but we've got company."

I turned to look just in time to see Mackinnon Wade climb out of his car and stride toward Cady. The pendant he had given me was in my pocket. My fingers closed around it as Cady turned toward him. I searched Mac's face for some resemblance to Jude's.

"What do you think they're saying?" my foster brother asked. "Do you think it's dramatic? I bet it's dramatic."

"Whatever the Gentle Giant is saying," Free interjected, "Cady does *not* look happy about it."

I could make out tension in Cady's lips, an odd glint in her eyes.

"That's not anger," Jude said quietly. "It's not sadness. It's *hope.*"

Hope? Hope for what? I didn't risk asking that question aloud, in case he was wrong.

Cady opened the driver's side door. "Something's come up. Pad"—the dog's ears twitched forward—"you're with me." Cady snapped her fingers, and the golden leapt from the car to stand beside her. "As for the rest of you . . ." Cady tossed her car keys to Jude. "Head back to the house. Tell Ness and Bales that preliminary analysis suggests that all five bodies we recovered yesterday were adults."

Adults. My heart slammed against my rib cage. *As in, not Bella.*

She's alive.

"Mac and I are headed back to the site," Cady continued, "and so help me, if you three even *think* about following, I will devote the time between now and your eighteenth birthdays to constructing new and inventive ways to make you rue your collective existence on this planet. Is that clear?"

"Crystal!" Jude chirped.

"Message received," Free confirmed.

Cady turned to me. I said nothing, but I did reach forward to grip her hand. I thought she might push me away again. Instead, she squeezed back.

"No giving up this time," she told me. "No running away."

A ball of emotion rose in my throat, and a moment later, Cady was gone.

"Bella might still be out there," I said. If I could say it, maybe I could believe it. "She might still be alive."

I hadn't promised Cady that I would stay out of this, because I wasn't sure that I could—or should. We needed to do everything we could for a child people had given up on. For Bella.

For Girl.

I blinked, and suddenly, Jude was pulling the car onto the gravel drive leading up to the Bennett property. I'd lost time. Seconds? Minutes? I wasn't sure. I focused on the here and now—and the fact that we weren't alone.

"That's the sheriff's car," Jude commented, pulling up beside it. "And that's the sheriff. And that's—"

"Gabriel." I finished Jude's sentence, my jaw clamping down as I registered the way the sheriff shoved Gabriel as he marched him toward the car.

As I registered the handcuffs on Gabriel's wrists.

Trapped. I felt like I was looking at the wolf from my memory, his leg caught between vicious metal jaws. But Gabriel didn't thrash or fight, didn't so much as resist as the sheriff put a hand on the back of his neck and roughly pushed him into the backseat of the police cruiser.

"Don't. Touch. Him." I was out of the car and inches from the sheriff in a heartbeat. I was vaguely aware that Saskia had followed me, that Silver—as old as she was—stood at my other side, her teeth bared.

"Don't," Gabriel said sharply. I wasn't sure if he was talking to me or the dogs. He didn't have a chance to say anything else before the sheriff shut the car door.

"I would advise you to take a step back," the sheriff told me before shifting his gaze to my canine companions, like *they* were the real threat.

"Stepping back now!" Jude put himself between me and the sheriff. "And since we're stepping back," he said cheerfully, as he began herding me away from the sheriff, inch by inch, "I'm sure you wouldn't mind telling us exactly what you've arrested our good friend Gabriel for."

"He's not under arrest." The sheriff didn't sound particularly happy about that. "He's just coming down to the station to answer some questions."

"Without a lawyer?" Free inquired politely, squatting down next to the dogs, calming them the way Jude had calmed me. "And under duress?"

"Do you want to mention the handcuffs?" Jude asked me. "Or should I?"

I wanted to show *my* teeth. I wanted the sheriff to look at me and know that I knew exactly what kind of coward he was.

"We have reason to believe that Gabriel might know something about Bella's kidnapper," the sheriff told us before offering me a very small close-lipped smile. "But if *you* would like to explain how it is that you and Gabriel found the cave where Bella was being kept, why Gabriel decided to take a road trip to Alden, and how the whole lot of you just happened to stumble across a mass burial site exactly as it was being uncovered, I'd be glad to take your statement as well, Kira."

What could Gabriel possibly know about Bella's kidnapper? I thought about the maps on his walls, the police scanner. I thought about the way he'd left the crime scene yesterday before the sheriff had arrived.

"What do you say?" the sheriff asked me flatly. "Would you care to join us down at the station?"

That was a threat, an attempt to control me. I could feel Girl inside me, the pressure in my head building as I kept a rein on the desire to let her out.

Jude shot me a look that I clearly interpreted to mean *For the love of all things good and holy, do not go down to the station.*

I tamped down my instincts and shot Jude a look that I hoped communicated something along the lines of *Find Ness or Bales.* I wanted to be out there, searching for Bella, but I also knew, deep in the pit of my stomach, that I couldn't leave Gabriel with Sheriff Rawlins.

Gabriel's stepfather didn't get to control me. He didn't get to haul Gabriel off alone. Pushing down the roar of the forest, I responded the way I thought Cady would have, if someone had tried to strong-arm her.

I held out my wrists and met the sheriff's gaze head-on. "Do you want to cuff me, too?"

CHAPTER 40

When we arrived at the station, they separated us. I'd expected that. I hadn't expected the room they put me in to be so small. The longer I sat there, waiting for the sheriff, the closer the walls on all sides seemed.

I can do this. I'd come with Gabriel because there was strength in numbers. *Confined space. Stale air.* Awareness of the lack of windows pulsated through me. I set my jaw and stared straight ahead. Free and Jude wouldn't leave me— or Gabriel—here for long.

The door to the interrogation room opened. I tracked the sound of footsteps coming toward the table. The sheriff sat down across from me.

Confined space. Stale air. Predator. I thought of my encounter with the mountain lion the day before. If I could handle that, I could handle this.

"I'll be straight with you, Kira." The sheriff paused, waiting for a response—not a verbal one, but a shift in my position, a blink of my eyes. "We know that the person who took Bella has a high degree of familiarity with Sierra Glades National Park, particularly, though not exclusively, the mountains. Your foster mother and Mackinnon Wade were tracking Bella and her kidnapper when the trail brought them to that clearing—and those bodies. At a minimum, Bella and her kidnapper stopped there. The FBI's profilers believe it's more than that—they believe the person who took Bella is also the person responsible for the grave site. That person is almost certainly local, and yesterday's discovery suggests that he or she may have been using the park as their own personal hunting grounds for four to five years." The sheriff tilted his head to the right, his eyes sharp. "What has Gabriel told you about his brother?"

I hadn't seen that question coming. I tried not to let that matter. "I know that Gabriel's brother went missing four years ago."

The sheriff laid his hands flat on the table between us. It was a casual gesture that didn't feel *casual* at all. "We're still waiting on forensic analysis and full autopsies," he said, his knuckles rising slightly off the table, "but I suspect they'll date the oldest body to the summer of Andrés Cortez's disappearance."

My brain latched onto certain words. *Body* first, then *Andrés*.

"Now, maybe one of those bodies belongs to Andrés Cortez," the sheriff allowed, "but between you and me, I doubt it. More important, *Gabriel* doubts it."

I found the will and ability to reply. "What are you talking about?"

"Andrés Cortez was an incredible tracker." The sheriff shifted his weight back in his chair, but somehow, the space between us seemed to shrink. "Gabriel's brother was downright gifted at wilderness survival, and he worked as a guide on that mountain from the time he was a boy. Do you understand what I'm telling you?" He rapped the table, then spread his fingers flat again. "Somebody took Bella. Somebody killed the people we found yesterday, and I think that person has been living off the grid in the Sierra Glades for *years.*"

The sheriff shifted his weight again—forward, this time. "When you first joined the search, did Gabriel ask you about your progress? Did he pump you for information? Do you have any reason to believe that he knew of the cave's existence? Does *he* think Andrés is alive?"

Each question made it a little harder for me to breathe. The table separating my body from the sheriff's wasn't big enough. The room was getting smaller.

"Before Andrés disappeared, he purchased a great deal of wilderness equipment." The intensity in the sheriff's voice didn't match the odd almost-smile on his face. "Enough to spend at least a year out there, trekking the glades."

A year. I knew that at a certain point, a person stopped needing store-bought supplies to survive. If what Sheriff Rawlins was saying was true, Gabriel's brother could still be out there, and if he had spent that long in the wilderness, alone, by choice—he might not be in his right mind.

"You're probably wondering why I'm telling you this, Kira. You're just a kid. You're not even a local, but for some reason, you seem to want to protect Gabriel. That's interesting to me. Gabriel doesn't have many friends. He's too volatile. You might even say he's aggressive."

The sheriff was a hypocrite. He wanted me to believe that Gabriel was the one who was out of control.

"Loyalty can be a wonderful trait, until it's misplaced." The sheriff stared at me. "Misplaced loyalty can be very dangerous."

The emphasis he placed on the word *dangerous* triggered something inside me. My adrenaline surged. I tried to tell myself that there was no real threat. *Confined space. Stale air. Man wants to hurt Girl.* I cut that thought off at the knees. It was all I could do not to lunge at him.

"All I need you to do is tell me what Gabriel has been up to for the past twenty-four hours." The sheriff smiled, like he'd already won.

Breathe in. Breathe out. Gabriel hadn't said anything about suspecting his brother. He'd gone back out to the caves, but he'd just been looking for the pathway through the mountain.

Hadn't he?

Even if he *had* been looking for his brother, that was because he'd spent years looking for Andrés. Not because he believed Andrés was the one who had taken Bella.

Right? I kept breathing. *In* and *out.*

The sheriff lifted his hand. I almost flinched, almost lunged, but he wasn't reaching for me. He pulled a photograph out of a thick manila envelope.

The stone formation, half-buried in front of the hash-marked tree.

"Why are you showing me this?" I asked.

The sheriff's teeth flashed—almost, but not quite a smile. "I'm showing you what I need to show you to remind you that I am not the enemy here, Kira." He paused. "Do you recognize this?" The sheriff tapped the photograph. He waited until he saw a spark of recognition in my eyes before continuing. "Gabriel did." He pulled out a second picture—smaller stones, buried in a similar formation near some kind of fort. "The Circle for the Lost."

The sheriff's voice was soft now. *He wants me to lean forward to hear him,* I thought. *He wants me to let my guard down.* Maybe that was paranoia, and maybe I was right. Either way, I didn't move.

"The Circle is an old Hunter's Point tradition, dating back to the town's founding when winters were long and some of the people who went off to explore the surrounding terrain were never seen or heard from again." The sheriff let his index finger trail the two nearly identical stone circles. "Think of it as halfway between a grave marker and a prayer."

Think. As long as I was thinking, I was in control. *Gabriel knelt next to the stone circle,* I thought. He'd said it wasn't a natural formation, but that was all.

"Gabriel and Andrés built this Circle," the sheriff said, tapping two fingers against the picture with the fort. "Their mother was a Turner before she married Daniel Cortez, and the Turners are one of five founding families, the very people most likely to remember—and keep—a tradition as archaic as this one."

Founding families. I thought about the book the librarian had given me. I tried to keep thinking, but an unsettled feeling slithered through my gut. *Why didn't Gabriel say something? Why pretend he had no idea what the Circle was?*

The sheriff slammed the folder shut, hard enough to shake the table. I flinched. Was he trying to scare me? Maybe he'd expected me to say something. Maybe I'd waited too long to reply.

This room was too small.

The door was shut.

I felt a change in his demeanor, like the rattle on a snake, sending warning vibrations in the air. An instant later, all trace of tension on the sheriff's face was gone, like I'd imagined it, like he'd never lost his temper.

"What were you doing in Alden yesterday?" The question was reasonable, and so, his manner implied, was the man.

Answer. Answer, and he won't hurt you. Answer, and he'll leave you alone.

"We heard there was a development in the search for Bella."

"Who heard?" the sheriff prodded. "You?"

No. Gabriel was the one with the police scanner. He was the one who'd decided to go—the rest of us had tagged along for the ride.

"I am not your enemy here," the sheriff told me.

The muscles in the back of my neck tightened, one by one. He'd scared me. He'd *tried* to scare me. "You're not my friend."

The sheriff flipped open a second folder. There was a photograph on top: a filthy child crouched in the corner of a hospital room, her hair in knots, her skin caked with mud and blood.

If I'd been capable of moving, I would have squeezed my eyes shut.

"You've had a difficult life." The sheriff turned the picture around so that I was staring straight into the eyes of my younger self. "I understand that, Kira. I understand how you could look at someone like Gabriel and feel like you were looking at some dark, twisted version of yourself."

I couldn't look away from the photo. If the sheriff had thought this would jar me into talking, he'd miscalculated.

He'd shown me Girl.

"How strong you must have been," the sheriff murmured, "to survive."

Jaw hurts. I was grinding my teeth. Inside I was shaking. Outside, I was frozen. *Everything hurts.*

"How naïve of Cady," the sheriff continued gently, "to think that you could ever be anything but an animal."

No.

"A dirty little animal. That's what you are, isn't it? If you weren't, you'd *want* to help Bella. You'd want to help me." He was standing. He was walking around to my side of the table. "I'm sure Gabriel has been filling your head with lies. He likes to talk, and he's perceptive enough to use your . . . *history* to try for common ground."

"I'm not an animal." My chair clattered to the floor. If I'd been in my right mind, I would have stood my ground. Instead, I skittered backward.

"I'm not going to hurt you." The sheriff took one step toward me, then another. "I've given you no reason to be afraid of me."

Control. I had to stay in control. *Breathe in. Breathe out.* "I want to leave now. You can't keep me here."

"I can if I'm concerned that you're a threat to yourself or others." He was within a few feet of me now. "It would be a shame to have to tell Cady that, despite all her work, you're still what your mother made you."

"Cady. Is. My. Mother." If I could form words, I could think them, think: *He can't hurt me. It's just talk. He can't do anything but talk.*

My back was up against the wall. The tangled mess of

thoughts and images in my brain flashed in pace with my heart, racing, pounding.

The sheriff turned and reached for the folder on the table—my file. The space that put between us let me breathe. A single breath—just one, then he pulled out a photograph of a woman with dark hair and blue eyes and features that looked altogether too much like my own.

"Your *real* mother," the sheriff clarified needlessly. He studied me. "You don't recognize her. You don't remember."

He was moving toward me again. There was nowhere left for me to go.

"Haven't you ever wondered? Why you survived? How a child could live like an animal, lost in the wild for weeks?" He lowered his voice to a bone-shuddering hum. "Your biological mother was some kind of conspiracy nut. She lived off the grid. No one even knew she had a child, and that meant that she could do whatever she wanted to you." He was too close to me—and coming closer.

Can't think. Can't breathe. There was a roar in my ears, and a rush of emotion—not mine.

Girl's.

"The police described the abuse as intermittent but severe. They think you used to take refuge in the forest to escape."

No. He wouldn't stop advancing. My body was a live wire, every nerve ending screaming. *Man wants to hurt Girl.*

"With trauma like that in your background, you must see the world as such a hostile place."

Man is right on top of Girl. Man reaches—

The motion flipped a switch inside of me. Like a rubber band stretched past its limit, something inside me snapped. I stopped fighting. I stopped trying.

I lunged.

No control, no thoughts, no words.

CHAPTER 41

My hands swiped air. Strong arms clamped around me. My eyes darted to the door—it was open. I was so far gone that I almost didn't recognize Bales as he pulled me away from the sheriff. I fought the old man, bucking against his hold, arching my back, twisting my neck, my teeth going for his—

"You'll be wanting to take a step back, Sheriff."

Even with my mind a twisted mess of *images* and *feelings* and *hurt*, I could hear the lethal note in Bales Bennett's tone.

The sheriff's voice broke through the red haze next. "I was just talking to her, and she went feral. I should arrest her for assaulting an officer."

He was lying. He was a *threat*, and he was *lying*, and I would . . .

Bales tightened his hold, forcing me to still. "Kira didn't assault anyone." He kept his tone low. "She's going to breathe and calm down, and the two of us are going to walk out of here."

Breathe. Calm down. Breathe.

Bales whispered into the back of my head, "Jude said that I should offer you confetti. He also said that if the confetti didn't work, I should up my game and bribe you with glitter."

Jude. I recognized the name and clung on for dear life. *Jude. Free. Cady. Me.*

Kira. I'm Kira.

"Your granddaughter is a very disturbed child." The sheriff shook his head sadly. "What Cady's tried to do for her is admirable, really, but—"

One second, Bales was restraining me, and the next, he'd let loose of me and had the sheriff by the throat. Bales slammed him against the wall, like the sheriff weighed no more than a rag doll.

"I'll have *you* arrested," the sheriff wheezed.

"I'm dying." Bales offered the sheriff a glittering smile, his knuckles whitening as his hand tightened around his target's neck. "I've got weeks, maybe months to live."

On one level, I was surprised Bales had volunteered that information in my presence. But on another, more immediate level, I was entranced by the superhuman control with which Bales held his prey in place. Long seconds ticked by as the sheriff's fingers scraped futilely against the vise on his neck. With no warning, Bales dropped his hold. The sheriff wheezed, and Bales took a single step backward.

"Funny thing about dying," Bales said, his voice contemplative. "You don't have much to lose." He let his hands fall to his sides, his palms facing outward. "Go ahead and arrest me. I'd love to hear you telling a judge that you were brutalized by a frail, dying old man."

I thought of the sheriff, puffing himself up to seem bigger—and then I realized that I could think again. Bales had attacked, so I didn't have to. But thinking was a double-edged sword.

My eyes went to the folder still lying open on the table. My picture was still visible. So was *hers*. Long dark hair. Eyes like mine.

"Gabriel's outside," Bales told me. "It was everything I could do to keep *him* from coming after you. I'd take it as a kindness if you could go tell him you're in one piece."

A kindness? I thought incredulously. If Bales hadn't come into this room, there was no telling what I would have done. I'd lost control, and I knew from experience that for weeks—maybe even months—I'd be standing right on the verge of losing it again.

An animal. A dirty little animal. I swallowed. I reached and closed my hand around the file folder. I picked it up, and step-by-step, I made my way toward the door.

"The next time you come after my family?" I heard Bales tell the sheriff behind me, his voice low. "I'll take advantage of the fact that I'm dying and make it a point to take you with me when I go."

CHAPTER 42

Bales led the way out of the sheriff's office. Gabriel was standing on the street outside. He wasn't alone.

The librarian who'd caught Jude's fancy was standing beside him. When she saw Bales and me, she laid a hand lightly on Gabriel's shoulder, then took her leave.

"Checking up on you?" Bales asked.

Gabriel shrugged. "Apparently, I need checking up on." As if to prove the point, he brandished his wrists in my direction. "Look," he said. "No cuffs."

Was he really joking around right now?

"I'll get the truck." Bales raised an eyebrow at the two of us. "Try not to kill each other before I get back."

Moments later, Gabriel and I were alone. His smirk wavered ever so slightly. "I didn't ask you to come with me."

"So?" I didn't have energy or words to waste on why I'd come. I was literally holding my past in my hand, and I had just as literally gone for the sheriff's jugular. If Bales had arrived a minute later, there might have been no coming back.

"I could have told you they would separate us, Kira." Gabriel kept his tone light, but the glint in his eyes was anything but. "Do you think I was in a *better* position knowing that if I didn't give him what he wanted, he'd be more than happy to go play games with you in the other room?"

What he wanted, I thought. *And what exactly did he want, Gabriel?*

"Seriously, princess, do you really think having you here helped?"

The fact that he could stand there and call me *princess,* like I was some pampered, spoiled little girl, like *he* had to protect *me,* pushed me over the edge.

"Do you really think," I echoed his own phrasing back to him, "that your brother is dead?" That was what he'd led me to believe back in the caves—he'd talked about accidents, about dropping dead, about predators.

Gabriel's face went blank.

"Or do you think," I continued, "that he has Bella?"

Gabriel didn't give me an answer. He split the second we got back to the house.

"I'll send Jude and Free out," Bales told me. Cady's father seemed to know that he couldn't fix this—or me.

"Don't," I said abruptly. "I want to be alone."

"I find myself doubting that, Kira," Bales said gently.

"Please." That was all I could manage—and all it took for him to leave me to my own devices. The file I'd taken from

the sheriff's office was heavy in my hands. It had my picture in it. It had my mother's. But a file that thick? There had to be more.

Police described the abuse as intermittent but severe. They think you used to take refuge in the forest to escape.

Something wet and cold brushed the back of my hand—NATO. When I looked down at him, his tail started to wag.

"Go away, NATO."

If Jude's hound had been capable of smiling, he would have beamed at me—right until Saskia appeared between us and bit his nose. NATO yelped and backed up. After a moment's contemplation, he darted forward again to lick Saskia's face, then took off running before she could respond.

"That wasn't very nice," I told Saskia. I wondered if she could tell from my tone that I wasn't feeling very nice, either. Looking at her, I saw her the way she'd looked when we'd found her, bone-thin and bleeding. Someone had dumped her in Cady's yard because they knew that Cady wouldn't turn away a stray.

My fingers tightened around the police file in my hand. *My* file. Something unnameable inside me cracked slowly open, something dark and cavernous and ugly.

I read the file.

The writing was detailed. The pictures were worse. My initial medical exam had been intensive. The doctors had documented my injuries, old and new. I'd always thought that the scars that marked my body were from the forest. According to what I read, some were.

Some weren't.

That truth was like a shard of glass ground into my stomach. Everything inside me threatened to come up. I'd known—of course I'd known—that whatever family I'd had before was probably either dead or didn't care much if I was. I had to have ended up in the forest somehow. But part of me—the stupid part, the hopeful part, the part that hadn't looked for answers—had wanted to believe that I was normal once.

That before I'd been Girl, I'd just been a girl. *Not a dirty little animal who deserved what happened to her.*

"Kira!" Jude appeared beside me and hooked his arm through mine. "I have gathered that Gabriel Cortez is a withholding withholder who withholds."

Jude thought I was out here because of Gabriel—because Gabriel had lied to me. Misled me.

Same difference.

"In his defense, he just met us." Listening to Jude's voice was like looking unblinkingly into a too-bright light. "We can hardly blame him for not realizing how awesomely trustworthy and mind-blowingly nonjudgmental we are."

Go away, Jude. I wanted to send him running, the way Saskia had done to NATO. But I couldn't, and Saskia took one look at the two of us and left me to fend for myself.

"I am sure all our questions will be answered in time," Jude declared. He was always sure. He never doubted.

Jude had never had the underside of his arm pressed into a hot stove.

"Kira?" Jude's gaze fell on the police file in my hand.

I jerked my arm away from his and stepped back. I didn't want him to see the pictures.

Stomach hurts. The memory pulled me under. *It's dark outside. I'm hungry. So hungry. Maybe she's asleep. I can be quiet. I can be small. I can be quick.*

I almost make it to the kitchen. Then I see her. She's face-down on the tile floor.

Not moving.

Blood. The memories started piling on, fast and frantic, spinning. I could only see bits and pieces, but I could feel—*running. Don't stop. Don't look back. You'll be safe in the forest.*

Hide.

"Hey." Jude bent down until his face was even with mine. "It's okay, Kira. Whatever you're remembering—it's not real. You're safe now. You're here."

"It *is* real." I expected that statement to come out garbled, but it didn't. My eyes were dry, but I couldn't stand to blink. The thick folder in my hands blurred in front of me. "The sheriff had my file. I have it now."

Jude sucked in a breath. "You don't have to read it."

"I already have." It was right there on the tip of my tongue to tell him everything, to purge the poison, to bleed it onto him. *My biological mother hurt me. Whenever she was drinking—I learned to stay away. The police thought I used to take refuge in the forest when it was bad.*

When it was bad . . .

"Whatever the file says . . ." Jude's voice somehow broke through the cacophony in my head. "It doesn't matter, Kira mine. It doesn't change anything."

"You don't know." The words flew out of me, living, breathing, *angry.*

An expression flickered over Jude's achingly familiar features. Not quite sorrow.

Guilt?

"Jude?" I managed.

He didn't reply. The last thing I'd said hung between us. *You don't know.*

"Mom had a talk with me when you came to live with us," he said softly.

I realized then what should have been obvious: Cady knew. Of course she knew. She'd adopted me. She'd been a part of the search. She'd probably seen this file.

Cady knew. Jude knew.

"Mom said not to ask you about it—not unless you brought it up first. She said . . ." Jude swallowed, his Adam's apple tensing against his skin. "She said that if the worst thing you could remember was the forest, then maybe that was a blessing. She said that it was our job to protect you."

At some point in Jude's confession, my grip on the file must have loosened, because I dropped it. A gust of wind blew the folder open. My past—the statements, the pictures—scattered.

Anyone could see them.

I lunged, stumbling to my knees to get them back. Jude

knelt beside me, his fingers capturing a wayward page. I ripped it away from him.

"Go," I said.

"You don't mean that."

"You lied to me," I said, my voice eerily calm, even to my own ears. "My whole life—you *knew*, and you kept this from me." I'd told Bales not to send Jude out here. And now I was naked and raw and bleeding, and Jude wouldn't leave.

"I've been keeping things from you, too," I heard myself say. "Bales is dying." I wanted to stop, but I couldn't. Sometimes, a wounded animal nipped as a warning.

And sometimes it bit to draw blood.

"Cady knows," I continued, "but she won't forgive him. She won't stay."

Hurting Jude didn't make me hurt any less.

"Ash isn't your father. He had a thing for Cady, but she had one for Mac." I pulled the Saint Jude pendant from the pocket of my jeans and held it out to the boy who'd been my anchor, my friend, my *everything* before I'd known how to be anything back. "Mac gave me this." I nodded to the medallion as Jude took the necklace from my hand. "That's his patron saint."

"Saint Jude." Jude's voice was as quiet as mine now.

He left.

CHAPTER 43

I chased down most of the pages, but a few got away from me. Within an hour, I was tired of looking and done running after ghosts. Most of all, I was sick of replaying my conversation with Jude. I'd hurt him. I'd known I was doing it, and I'd done it anyway, and why?

Because he knew what I was, what I'd survived. He'd always known—and maybe he thought he'd been protecting me. Maybe he and Cady had done what needed to be done, but I didn't want to be that girl.

I didn't *want* to know, and I didn't want them to know, either.

For once, the open sky overhead did nothing to calm the twisting, aching *awful* inside me. The trees and grass and dirt weren't comforting or familiar. They just reminded me what I'd known as a child: No matter how far you ran, you couldn't stay out of arm's reach forever.

Sooner or later, you had to go home.

I made it into the house and up to the bedroom Free and I had been sharing without running into Jude or Bales, for which I was grateful. But my luck ran out when I opened the bedroom door.

"You look about as good as Jude does." Free was standing near the window. I wondered where she'd been, wondered if she'd talked to Jude, wondered if *she* knew.

"I need to lie down," I said.

I need you to not be here.

"Jude is a happy guy," Free commented, ignoring my silent message. "Pathologically, unerringly, purposefully happy at almost all times." She paused. "If I were a betting woman, I'd wager that if the two of you had a fight, Jude's not the one who picked it."

"It wasn't a fight." I didn't elaborate. What did you call using the truth as a weapon? What was the word for looking at someone you loved and feeling like your guts had been hollowed out?

"You hurt him." Free was never one to sugarcoat things. "Whether you meant to or not—"

"I meant to," I said quietly.

Free gave me a long, assessing look. "Then you and I have a fundamental disagreement about how you treat family."

She was right. I knew she was right. But all I could do was repeat myself as I turned my back on her. "I need to lie down."

I need you to go away.

"Not until you tell me what happened." Free's hand closed around my arm. She forced me to face her, and for a moment—just a moment—I wanted to hurt her. Not the way I'd hurt Jude. I wanted to hurt her the way I'd hurt Gabriel when he'd grabbed me. I wanted to let everything inside me—the anger and the sorrow and the fear—out.

No.

"Seriously, K, Miscreant to Miscreant—"

"Go away, Free." I felt desperate, but I sounded angry.

Free dropped my arm. For a split second, I saw something raw and vulnerable cross her features, and then all hint of emotion disappeared from her face. "Fine."

When I heard the bedroom door shut behind her, I shuddered. Once I started shaking, I couldn't stop. I curled into a ball on the bed, and a desperate, keening sound made its way out of my throat.

I was supposed to be stronger than this.

I was supposed to be better than this.

I was supposed to *protect* the people I loved.

I noticed my bag sitting beside the bed. Free must have brought it up, just like she'd packed it for me. A horrible, twisting tension spread from my stomach outward. Sadness was a visceral emotion for me, as white-hot and sharp-edged as rage. One second I was lying there, and the next, my hands were tearing through my bag. I hurled the things Free had packed for me to the ground, one by one. I ripped a shirt, the cotton giving way beneath my need to do something, to *hurt* something. I heard the shirt tearing, and I felt it, and it wasn't enough. I couldn't stop, not until my fingernails scraped the bottom of the bag and hit fabric. *Threadbare. Soft.*

Free had packed my blanket.

I stopped breathing and sank to the floor, pressing it to my face, a sob caught in my throat. I heard someone padding toward me—Silver. I hadn't even realized she was in the room. This had been her blanket once.

She'd seen me at my worst. *Then. Now.*

My constant guardian pressed her nose to my neck. I didn't push her away. I hadn't, even when I was wild and hurting and small.

"It shouldn't matter," I said through the blanket, squeezing my eyes shut and breathing in Silver's smell. "What happened to me before the forest shouldn't matter. Whether or not Jude knew—it shouldn't matter."

I fisted my hands in her fur—gently, but I couldn't let go. "I know that I'm your pup, and I'm Cady's kid and Jude's sister and Free's friend, but when you all treat me like I'm fragile, like I'm some bomb on the verge of going off . . ."

I don't feel human. I don't feel like a person at all.

Silver lay down next to me, her body pressed up against mine. *Silver is here. Kira is here. Silver is here with Kira.* I buried my face in her fur. I listened for her heartbeat instead of my own.

I broke.

I didn't understand why I'd let a man like the sheriff do

this to me. I choked on my own sobs, unable to understand what was wrong with me.

And Silver nudged my neck with her wet nose, saying—for the hundredth time or the thousandth or the millionth— that there was nothing wrong with me at all.

CHAPTER 44

Girl's mouth is dry. Her lips are cracked. There's dried blood beneath her nails.

She tries to sit up but can't. Can't move—

"There you are." The woman's voice is sweet. She kneels next to Girl, and Girl flinches, but the hand that touches her face is gentle.

Soft.

In the light of the moon, the woman begins digging. She half buries first one rock, then another. Girl's fingernails claw at the grass beneath her. Her body writhes, but she still can't sit up. She can't run.

No. This can't be happening.

This never happened.

The world shudders with that realization, and suddenly, I'm standing beside my younger self and watching—watching the dark-haired woman and the writhing child, and I know that this isn't a memory. It's a dream—just a dream—but still,

I can't turn away. I can't stop watching the dark-haired woman as she completes the Circle and stands to examine her work.

Her eyes meet mine.

"Someone's coming," she whispers. "Hide."

I bolted up in bed. A glance at the clock told me that I hadn't been asleep for more than an hour. The sun was still shining outside. Jude and Free were nowhere in sight.

Except for Silver, I was alone.

My canine guardian was asleep beside me, lying on her side. I laid a hand on her head, stroked it down the length of her body, the dream lingering in my mind. I forced myself to sort through the tangle of *now* and *then, imaginary* and *real*, and at some point, I realized that Silver wasn't moving.

She wasn't responding to my touch.

Her chest wasn't rising or falling.

She's not breathing. That thought stilled the breath in my own lungs. "Silver." I said her name quietly at first, then louder. I cupped her head in my hands. I petted her, and I told her that she was a good girl, and I waited for her to wake up.

Wake up, Silver. Please—

I'd known objectively that she was old for a German shepherd. I'd known that she wouldn't be with me forever. But not now, not like this—

"She's gone." I wanted to take back the whispered words. Saying it made it real, and I needed it not to be real. I needed her to wake up. I needed to save her, the way that she had saved me.

That day in the ravine. The weeks and months that followed. Every nightmare, every morning when I woke up—

I didn't cry. I couldn't, because Silver wasn't there to put me back together, to lick my face and nudge my neck and let me *break*.

She was gone.

I curled my body around hers. I held her, the way a man dangling off a cliff holds on to the side. But I couldn't hold on forever. Slowly, I wrapped my oldest friend in a sheet from the bed. I carried her down the stairs, struggling under the weight, but unwilling to let myself even think about dropping her. If it killed me, I'd get her out of this house.

I'd get her outside.

I laid her out beneath the tree where I'd slept my first night. I knelt down next to her. I told her, again and again, that she was brave, that she was good, that she was perfect.

You were mine.

I wanted Jude and Free, but most of all, I wanted Cady. I wanted someone who'd loved Silver as much as I had, who'd loved me as fiercely and as steadfastly as the faithful dog had—day after day, year after year, even when there was nothing in me to love.

"How old was she?" Gabriel knelt beside me, his eyes on Silver's body, his voice gentler than I'd ever heard it.

"Twelve. Almost thirteen."

Gabriel was quiet for almost a minute. "Doesn't make it any easier," he said.

I shook my head. Someday, it would be Saskia—and

NATO and Duchess and every dog I loved, unless something killed me first.

"Do you want to bury her?" Gabriel asked me.

No. I didn't want to put Silver in the ground. I didn't want to pile dirt on top of her. I didn't want to say good-bye.

I forced myself to nod. When Gabriel fetched a shovel, I took it from his hands, and I wouldn't give it back—not even when my fingers began to blister from digging and my palms began to bleed.

Silver had spent most of her life taking care of me. I could do this—*this one thing*—for her.

As Gabriel and I lowered Silver's body into the grave, Saskia found us. She stood silently beside me, and when I began shoveling dirt onto Silver, the husky threw back her head and howled.

CHAPTER 45

"The Andrés I knew wouldn't have hurt anyone. He wouldn't have taken that girl." Gabriel gave me the answer I'd asked for earlier. I barely even heard it now. "But when we found Bella's jacket in the cave . . . when we knew she wasn't alone . . ."

"Do you know where he'd take her?" I asked dully. "If he was the one, do you—"

"I'd tell the FBI myself if I did." Gabriel left it at that. He held my gaze for just a moment. I had the sense that if I'd been a normal person—if he had—he might have made physical contact. Instead, he inclined his head slightly.

And then he was gone.

Maybe he thought I wanted to be alone. Maybe this was what being given space felt like—space to mourn, to grieve.

I couldn't stay here. Silver was in the ground. I'd pushed Jude and Free away. I needed out.

As I stared at the fresh dirt of Silver's grave, I thought

of the Circle for the Lost—*halfway,* the sheriff had said, *between a grave marker and a prayer.*

I could go back to Alden, back to the clearing where we'd found the bodies, and try to pick up the search for Bella. But what good could I possibly do there? The place was still crawling with law enforcement. It was their job to identify the victims, to follow up on any physical evidence. Whatever scent path Bella and her kidnapper had laid, the police had almost certainly disturbed it.

There's nothing I can do.

Cady had made a difference for me. *Silver* had made a difference for me. I'd spent years throwing everything I had into learning search and rescue, because if I could someday do the same for someone else, then maybe I could prove, even just to myself, that I was worth it.

That I'd deserved to be saved.

That I was *good.*

My eyes stung as I turned and walked back toward the house, forcing myself to focus on the search, on Bella, on anything but Silver lying in a hole she'd never climb out of.

This is what I knew: Bella's kidnapper had taken her to a mass grave site. Was Bella meant to join those bodies? Had something gone wrong with the kidnapper's plan? Or was the person who'd taken Bella just leading us all on a merry chase? If the sheriff had been telling the truth, the FBI believed that the kidnapper and the person who'd put those five bodies in the ground were one and the same. That meant that he or she had also probably erected the stone circle we'd found near the clearing. I had no idea what the hash marks on the tree stood for, what any of it meant to the kidnapper, but the sheriff had said that the Circle for the Lost was a Hunter's Point tradition, dating back to the town's founding.

As it so happened, I had a copy of the town history.

I flipped through page after page of *A History of Hunter's Point*, looking for any trace of the Circle for the Lost. I found it in a set of pictures from 1922. Winter had come early that year. A group of a dozen young people—including a Ferris, a Turner, and a Rawlins—had left on what was supposed to be a months-long journey into the wilderness. It was doubtful they'd made it beyond Sorrow's Pass.

I hadn't thought before about the pass's name—or where it had come from—but as the pictures told the story of the explorers' disappearance, the word *sorrow* stuck with me, right up until I saw a photograph of the adjacent valley.

There, butting up against the riverbed, was a stone circle. *Halfway between a grave marker and a prayer.*

"Sorrow's Pass." I looked from one picture to the next. "The valley. The river."

Maybe it was a coincidence. Maybe it meant nothing that I could see parallels—no matter how thin—between these pictures and the path our kidnapper had taken. There was nothing in the *History* about the caves, nothing about Alden or the clearing.

But we'd lost—and found—Bella's trail multiple times in

the first forty-eight hours. At the river. At Sorrow's Pass. In the valley.

Tracking Bella and her abductor from one location to the next had proven futile, again and again. Whoever had taken her was too savvy, knew the park too well. The only thing I could think to do—*had* to do—was to stop following, stop tracking, and start figuring out where that person might be headed next.

Andrés? I wondered. *Someone else?* Whoever it was, the person who'd taken Bella had a reason. The Circle, the hash marks on the tree, the disappearing and reappearing trail . . .

I stood. Cady and the other searchers would have attempted to pick up Bella's scent where they'd had it last. They'd be searching downriver. That made sense. It was the right call.

But I wasn't in a place to make the *right* call.

I left a note for Jude and Free. I wasn't sure where either one of them had gone, only that I'd chased them away. A note wasn't much, but it was something.

I wanted to leave them *something*.

I borrowed the keys to the truck. And Saskia and I set off for the park—for the campsite where Bella's family had been staying.

Back to the start.

CHAPTER 46

Sass and I retraced our steps: along the river, through the woods, up into the base of the mountain. I didn't know what I was looking for. Maybe, like some of the hikers who'd passed through Hunter's Point over the years, I was looking to get lost.

I hadn't had a fresh scent to give Saskia, but my K9 pushed forward with uncompromising determination, as if knowing that *I* was looking for something was, in and of itself, enough.

Instead of attempting to make our way up to the pass, sans helicopter, I doubled back to the river, the photograph from the *History* still fresh in my mind. Running water was useful if you were looking to evade trackers. It wasn't foolproof, but if I had to venture a guess about how Bella's abductor had managed zigzagging back and forth across the park, it was a good bet the river had played some role.

Sorrow's Pass is downriver from the campsite. Alden is downriver from Sorrow's Pass.

As Saskia and I made our way along the riverbank, the terrain grew rougher and the water picked up steam. If we wanted to cross to the other side, we'd need to do it soon.

Why? a voice inside me insisted. *What are you looking for, Kira? What could you possibly hope to find?*

I thought back to my dream, to the claustrophobic panic of being pinned to the ground and watching the dark-haired woman bury rock after rock, feeling like she was burying me.

I don't know.

The only thing that I knew was that I couldn't turn back. I'd brought a map with me, but even when I twisted away from the rushing river, unfolding the map and shielding it from the wind, it couldn't tell me what I wanted to know.

What happened to those people in 1922? Where did they disappear to? Where did they go?

Maybe Gabriel—or Bales or the librarian who'd given me the book in the first place—could have told me if local legend held the answer. Maybe it didn't matter—maybe *none* of this mattered. But there was nothing left to do but push on.

Saskia darted in and out of the forest. The longer we forged on—the farther from civilization we went—the faster my K9 ran, her movements liquid-smooth and wild, like the day's events had unleashed in her the opposite of what they'd loosed in me.

No doubt. No hesitation. No pain.

As if summoned by my thoughts, Sass barreled back out of the forest. I willed her to bark. I willed her to signal that she'd found *something*.

But there was nothing to find.

I'm not going to find Bella or her kidnapper. I was never going to find them. I tried to fight that admission, but lost. I'd wanted so badly to do something, to believe that I *could* do something, to make it so that doing something would somehow fix everything I'd broken.

I was so caught up in wanting that—mourning even the possibility of it—that I almost missed the small stone circle. The landscape of the riverbank had changed since 1922. Time and nature had worn away at the rocks. Only the very edges stuck out of the dirt. I stepped into the Circle and turned, 360 degrees. Nearly a century before, someone in Hunter's Point had erected this memorial.

I'd expected that to mean something.

I'd expected that to *matter*.

But the Circle I'd found was barely a Circle at all.

A wave of emotion rising up inside me, I squatted down, my fingernails digging at the dirt around the nearest stone. *It's not fair,* I thought. Pain shot up through my hands as I dug faster and harder, one nail snapping and then another.

Saskia barked. She didn't like seeing me like this.

I couldn't stop.

When the rock came free, I lifted it with two hands and

stared at it, then hurled it into the river with everything I had.

Saskia barked again, and I turned to her, as shredded inside as the skin on my battered hands. And then I took in her posture and she let out a third bark, sharp and crisp. *Unmistakable.*

I whirled, scanning our surroundings, trying to figure out what she'd found. My gaze stopped on a tree, older and thicker around the base than any of the others. Etched into the trunk of that tree was a series of hash marks.

Hundreds of them.

Thousands.

I made my way toward the tree, let my bleeding fingers trail over the hash marks before I could bring myself to believe that this was real. Bella's kidnapper had been here.

Sound. To my left. I turned on my heels. Willing my heart to hush in my chest, I prepared to bolt, but when the sound made its way to my ears a second time, I recognized it as human, young.

Alive.

Saskia lay down on her stomach and poked her nose under the brush. I knelt, blood rushing in my ears, and a pair of muddy brown eyes stared back at me.

There, beneath a makeshift canopy made of dirt and wood, lying on her stomach, was the missing girl.

CHAPTER 47

"Bella?" I kept my voice soft and made no move to touch her.

The little girl stared at me, her face smudged with dirt, her expression eerie and calm. "The angel said someone would come for me."

Her voice was high-pitched but coarse. Moving slowly and keeping my hands where she could see them, I withdrew a bottle of water from my pack. I opened it and set it on the ground in front of her.

Seconds passed before she sat up, still hunched beneath the canopy's branches. First one hand closed around the bottle, then the other. Her eyes never left mine as she lifted it to her mouth.

"Slowly," I told her, unsure how dehydrated she was.

After a moment, she lowered the bottle, her hands still wrapped tightly around it.

"Are you hurt?" I asked. So far, Bella had been calmer

than I would have expected. I didn't want to spook her, but I needed to know what I was dealing with.

Her expression impossible to read, the child answered my question by sticking out her right leg. She pulled up the mud-caked pajama bottoms she was wearing and showed me a long scratch that ran the length of her shin. The wound looked clean, all things considered.

It had already started to heal.

"Anyplace else?" I asked her.

Bella shook her head.

I heard movement to my right a second before Saskia took up position in front of Bella. The combination of movement and sound reminded me that we had no way of knowing if Bella was alone out here.

No way of knowing when the person who'd taken her would be back.

"Bella," I said carefully, when she didn't shrink back from Saskia's presence, "the person who took you—"

"Took me?" Bella held the water bottle closer. "No one took me." For the first time since we'd found her, she smiled. "My angel *saved* me."

"Saved you," I repeated. Someone had hauled Bella all over this mountain. Someone had built the rudimentary shelter she was sitting under now.

"Mommy and Daddy said I wasn't supposed to wander off." Bella looked down, pulling her legs tight to her chest. "I wasn't supposed to, but I did."

She shivered. I knew the chilling shadow of memory

when I saw it. Without much thought, I pulled closer to her.

"I wanted to see the river." Bella squeezed her eyes shut. "The side was slick. It didn't *look* slick. . . ."

"You're okay," I murmured. "You got out." I found myself thinking back to her earlier claim. "The person who took you—"

"My angel."

"Your angel . . . saved you." I brought my hand very close to Bella's but left it to her to close the distance. "You fell in the river, and this . . . angel . . . pulled you out."

"I was so cold." Bella opened her eyes, but I knew instinctively that she couldn't see me. She was seeing something else. "The angel wrapped me in a blanket. The angel built a fire."

I had no doubts that Bella's "angel" was a person—just like I had no doubts that the person in question had been dodging the authorities for days.

"This angel," I said, trying to keep my voice neutral. "Why didn't they bring you back to camp?"

"Mommy and Daddy left." Bella's voice was matter-of-fact. "I was bad, and they left, and the angel promised to take care of me until they got back."

Whoever had pulled Bella from the river had told her that her parents were gone. They'd let her believe it was *her* fault. A spark of rage caught fire inside me, but I smothered it, lest Bella see even a hint of anger on my face.

"The angel promised to take care of me," Bella repeated softly. "And *I* promised to help the angel."

Those words sent a chill down my spine. "Help?" I repeated. "Help with what?"

Bella didn't answer.

"Your angel," I said, suddenly on high alert. "Are they close by? Are they coming back?"

Still no answer from Bella.

"Can you tell me what the angel looks like?" I knew, even before I asked the question, that Bella wouldn't answer this, either. The tiny hand that had been creeping toward mine pulled back, her fingers curling inward.

Don't push. Don't scare her. Don't force her to talk.

I shifted backward, giving her space, even as my mind began to race. I had to get her out of here. I had to get her home.

I wished—desperately—that Cady were here in my place. I had enough trouble dealing with my own emotions. Dealing with a child's felt like juggling glass. "Guess what?" I said, hoping that I hadn't spooked her past the point of reply.

After a long moment, Bella whispered, "What?"

I let out a breath. "Mommy and Daddy are back now," I said softly. "They're waiting for you, and, Bella?" My voice caught in my throat. "They're going to be so happy to see you."

Bella had a family. She had people who loved her. She had something to go home to. Concentrating on that—and ignoring the lump in my throat—I took my cell phone out of my pack. *No service.* I hadn't really expected that there would be. I went for the radio next and dialed it in to the station the rangers used.

"Can anyone hear me?" I put the words out into the ether but got nothing but static in response. "Come in." I heard the faintest hint of something on the other end of the line. "Come in. This is Kira Bennett. I found Bella. I repeat, I found Bella. Our coordinates are . . ." As I gave them our coordinates, I stood, appraising our surroundings, all too aware of the fact that Bella's kidnapper could—and probably *would*—return.

"Did you get those coordinates?" I waited for a response and got none. "Do you read me? Come in." I repeated myself several times, then took my fingers off the call button but didn't stop speaking. "Please . . ." I found myself saying, "Cady . . . come in."

Find me. Bring me home.

I ground my teeth together and swallowed. I hadn't cried when I'd buried Silver. I couldn't afford to lose it now. If I couldn't be certain that help was coming, I'd have to break protocol and bring Bella in myself. I was fairly certain that she wasn't injured—at least not the type of injury that would prevent me from moving her—and the longer we stayed here, the greater the chances that Bella's *angel* would be back.

"Is Cady coming?"

I looked down to see Bella at my side, Saskia standing guard between us.

Smiling, Bella reached a hand out to mine. I took it, marveling at the change in her demeanor.

"The angel said that Cady saves people," Bella whispered. "And the angel doesn't lie."

CHAPTER 48

The trip back was slower with a child in tow, but Bella didn't show any signs of hunger or dehydration—or fear. If anything, from the moment she'd heard me say Cady's name, she'd been ready and willing to follow wherever Saskia and I led.

As much easier as that made things for me, I couldn't keep from turning the last thing Bella had said over and over in my mind. Bella's kidnapper had told her about Cady. That was disconcerting enough, but the way Bella had phrased it—*the angel said that Cady saves people*—made me think that the kidnapper hadn't just expected the girl to be found.

He wanted Cady to find her.

Somehow, I doubted the *he* in question was Andrés Cortez. Andrés had never met Cady. He'd have no way of knowing what she did for a living. The person who'd taken Bella had led us on an elaborate chase. Every time we'd lost the trail, we'd found it again, farther on. *The strip of cloth telling us that Bella made it out of the river. The smear of blood at Sorrow's Point. The windbreaker the kidnapper left in the cave. The spotting in Alden.*

And now I'd found Bella, less than two miles from where she'd been taken.

Why?

The hairs on the back of my neck stood up a second before I heard a twig break in the distance. The sound of footsteps followed, and I immediately put my body in front of Bella's. My senses alive, every muscle on high alert, I tracked the footfalls coming closer.

Why leave Bella so close to where she was taken? The question morphed in my mind. *Why set her out like bait in a trap?*

I bent and picked up a rock. As weapons went, it was unimpressive, but if I'd been caught in a hunter's snare, I wasn't going down without a fight.

A flash of motion was the only warning I got before an animal barreled out of the forest. *Canine. Dog.* My brain cycled through a start-stop chain of recognition before focusing on the animal's familiar lines. *Pad.*

Cady followed a moment later, and on her heels, there were others—Mac and his dog, a handful of rangers.

I forced my fingers to loose the rock in my hand. As it thudded to the ground, I met Cady's eyes. "You got my message?"

"Message?" Cady stared at me for a moment before shifting her gaze to Bella. *"Oh."* That sound was gut-wrenching, like Cady hadn't let herself believe that this story could have a happy ending—like she'd needed one, even more than I had. She dropped to her knees in front of Bella. "Are you okay?" she asked. "Are you hurt?"

Bella didn't answer the questions. Instead, she stared intently at my foster mother. "Are you Cady?"

With a glance at me, Cady nodded. I expected Bella to leave me and go to my foster mother, but she didn't. Instead, the little girl pushed close to my side.

Too many people, I thought, staring up at the rangers. *Too much noise.*

Somehow, my arm found its way around Bella, like human contact was my native language instead of one I'd struggled with for years. "She's fine," I said. "A scratch on her leg, but no other noticeable injuries. I found her farther upriver—a mile or two. I think she was waiting."

For you. I couldn't say those words to Cady—not in front of an audience.

"Any sign of her kidnapper?" Mac drew my attention from Cady.

I shook my head. "I tried to radio for help. I thought it went through, but I couldn't get a clear response, so I decided to bring Bella in myself."

One of the rangers took out a first aid kit. Another had a blanket to wrap around Bella's shoulders, but when they stepped forward, the little girl stepped back.

"She just wants to go home," I said, wishing I couldn't

hear an echo of that desire, an ache in my own tone. "She wants her family."

Cady stood, bringing her face from Bella's eye level to mine. "Are *you* okay?"

Finding Bella was supposed to fix whatever had broken inside me. It was supposed to give me the magical ability to step back and see that Cady and Jude had only ever tried to protect me. It was supposed to tell me how to fix things with Free.

It was supposed to make me *worthy* and *good* and *whole*.

"I'm fine," I said, but what I was thinking was, *You lied to me my whole life*. Worse than that, I was thinking that the reason Cady had lied was that she thought I couldn't handle the truth—and she was right.

Cady knew I wasn't strong enough. She knew the only way I could ever be normal was to pretend.

Cady tucked a strand of stray hair gently behind my right ear, and then she looked down at Bella. "Let's get you girls home."

CHAPTER 49

Bella sat next to me on the ride to the sheriff's office. She didn't say a word. Even once we'd arrived, and a pair of FBI agents came in with a child advocate, she refused to answer their questions—about where she'd been, about the person who'd taken her.

They thought she was traumatized. They let me stay because Bella had attached herself firmly to my side, and they let Cady stay because she was my guardian. What no one but me realized was that Bella wasn't keeping quiet because of *trauma*. I'd tried to tell the FBI what Bella had told me, I'd tried to make them listen, but each time someone spoke over me, the words got a little harder to find.

"You're not asking the right questions." I hadn't meant to raise my voice, but at least this time, they heard me. Every adult in the room turned my way. "You keep asking about the person who took Bella. You should be asking about her angel." I met Bella's eyes and softened my tone. "Bella's angel pulled her from the river, wrapped her in a blanket—*saved her.*" I swallowed. "Bella's parents were gone, so the angel promised to take care of Bella until they got back. And in return . . ." I glanced down at the little girl. "Bella promised to help."

"Help with what?" The sheriff inserted himself into the conversation. Even the sound of his voice put me on edge, but I refused to give him the satisfaction of showing it.

"I don't know," I said, turning to the little girl sitting beside me. "Bella? Why did the angel need your help?"

Bella caught her lip between her teeth. Seconds ticked by in silence, but eventually, she answered, "The angel needed to save someone else."

"This angel . . ." The sheriff took a step toward Bella, but a glare from the child advocate cut him off midsentence and froze him in his tracks.

"Who did the angel need to save?" the woman asked quietly.

Before Bella could answer, the door opened, and the little girl's entire face lit up. "Mommy!" She was on her feet in an instant. "Daddy!" She started forward, then paused, and I remembered that Bella's angel had told her they'd left because they were mad.

"Baby." Bella's mom fell to her knees, her arms opening. The expression on her face was halfway between torture and exaltation. I thought of the way she'd refused to go back to the hotel, the way she'd fought for Bella, the only way she could. "You're okay. You're okay, Belly. Baby, you're okay."

Bella's father showed no visible emotion until Bella launched herself into her mother's grasp, and then without warning, he let out a sob and collapsed, his arms encircling them both.

It felt wrong to watch—*too intimate, too private*—but I couldn't drag my eyes away. I heard every catch of Bella's mother's breath, saw every frantic kiss they pressed to her head.

I promised I'd find her, I thought. My eyes stung. *I promised I'd bring her home.*

I fought the tsunami of emotion welling up inside me. I turned my back on the reunion. A pair of familiar arms wrapped around me. I didn't fight Cady's embrace, but I couldn't make my own arms move. I couldn't hug her back.

"Perhaps Kira could enlighten us on how she found Bella?" The sheriff managed to make the question sound reasonable, almost comforting, as if he was asking to give me something to focus on, rather than launching a veiled attack.

Something snapped inside me. Finding Bella hadn't changed anything. It hadn't changed *me*, but I didn't have to pretend that this was okay, that *I* was okay.

"You need to leave," I said, my voice low, my body remembering what it had felt like to lunge for his throat. I forced my gaze to Cady's. "He called me an animal." The words cost me. They *hurt* me. "A dirty little animal."

"What are you talking about?" Cady rounded on the sheriff. "What is she talking about?"

"He had my file," I said quietly. "I have it now."

The FBI chose—wisely—to escort the sheriff elsewhere and give Cady a moment alone with me.

"Kira." My name caught in Cady's throat. "Baby, I am so sorry."

"Sorry that he told me?" I asked, the question physically painful. "Or sorry that you didn't?"

I never got an answer to that question.

"Excuse me?" Bella's mother interrupted the two of us. "You're the one who found her?" she asked me.

I nodded, and a moment later, the woman's arms were wrapped around me. I breathed through the bone-crushing hug. She touched me, and I let her.

After a small eternity, Mrs. Anthony gathered herself together and pulled back. She pressed something into my hand. "Bella asked me to give this to you. I have no idea where she got it, but . . ." The woman bowed her head, tears streaming down her cheeks. "If you ever need *anything* . . ."

I didn't reply. One hundred percent of my attention was focused on the item that Bella's mother had placed in my hand. It was a medallion, silver and tarnished, with two figures engraved on its surface. There was writing etched around the edge, but I couldn't read it.

It's a saint, I thought, a chill crawling down my spine. *A pendant, like the one Mac gave me.* I knew, in the pit of my stomach, where Bella had gotten it. Her angel had given it to her.

The same angel that had erected the Circle for the Lost. The one who'd told Bella that Cady would come.

There are five founding families, I thought, my racing mind going back to the town history. *Turner. Ferris. Ashby. Rawlins. Wade.*

"What do you have there?" Mac's voice was as low and soothing as ever when he leaned over to see the medallion I held in my hand. My fingers closed over it. I surged forward, catching Bella and her family as the FBI was guiding them toward a private room.

"Bella," I called.

The little girl turned to look at me. I knelt down to her level and held out the medallion. "Who did the angel need to save?" I repeated the question that the child advocate had asked Bella.

Bella crooked a finger at me, indicating that I should bend down. And then she finally gave me an answer. "Someone she loves."

CHAPTER 50

The word *she* fell over the room with the force of military-grade explosives. Bella's angel was a woman.

A woman. From one of the founding families. Wants to save someone—someone she loves. My mind racing, I looked down at my hand, my fingers unfurling to reveal the pendant.

"May I?" Mac asked me. This time, I allowed him to take it from my grasp.

"Mac?" Cady fit a thousand questions into a single word.

Mac swallowed. "Saint Anne," he said finally, his blue eyes intent on Cady's. "She's the patron saint of mothers and grandmothers."

Images flashed through my head. *Hash marks on trees. The Circle for the Lost. Five founding families.*

In 1922, three children of founding families had gone off into the wilderness and never returned. More than three-quarters of a century later, Cady, Mac, and John Ashby had taken a job in South America—and only two of them had come back.

Ash was my son. The words Ness had said to Cady the day before echoed in my mind. *I'd say that gives me a stake in this.*

"No," Cady said. "I know what you're thinking, Mac— but no."

"She taught us every bit as much about survival as your father did," Mac countered. "And she's been down with the flu for days."

Ness had been at the house when we'd arrived, but by that point, Bella had already been missing for more than a day. *Enough time for Ness to get her settled in the cave. Enough time for her to come home and convince Bales to bring Cady in on the search.*

"Bales is dying." I knew, somehow, that Cady couldn't ignore the words if I was the one who said them. "Ness said that he'd been trying to get in touch with you, but you wouldn't reply."

Cady weathered that statement like a blow. "My father wouldn't have asked me to come back for himself. I wouldn't have come back *for him.*"

Mac wove a hand through Cady's, as if he could some-how channel strength from his body into hers. "Ness knows you. She knows Bales. She knows me. It makes sense, Cady. If she wanted to bring us back here . . ."

"It doesn't make sense." Cady took a step away from him,

releasing his hand. "There were five bodies in that clearing, Mac. *Five.*"

Some things cut all the way to the bone.

"The autopsies came back." The male FBI agent took that moment to remind us of his presence. "We're still waiting on DNA and some other higher-level tests, but the ME has tentative rulings on cause of death." He paused. "At least two died of exposure, one appears to have been attacked by some kind of animal, a fourth has the kind of blunt-force trauma we would associate with a fall."

"And the fifth?" Cady asked, her voice hoarse.

"Drowned," the female agent replied. "Most likely in the river." She stopped dancing around the point and laid it out for us. "We've found no evidence of foul play. In at least two cases, we believe the bodies were buried a month or more *after* the victims died."

It was hard for me to imagine Ness killing someone, but it was strikingly easy to imagine her laying a stranger to rest.

The day before, Mac had told me that he didn't find bodies. *I find lost ones,* he'd said, *and I bring them home.*

CHAPTER 51

Ness Ashby was nowhere to be found. The FBI searched the Bennett property. They went through her cabin with a fine-tooth comb, and they didn't find a trace of the old woman.

Not so old that she can't still take to the mountain, I thought. *Not too old to pull Bella out of the river or take advantage of the kind of search that people will mount for a missing little girl.*

"I'm mad at you." Free came to stand right beside me. "But for the next ten seconds, I'm going to pretend that I'm not."

I felt like I'd swallowed a tennis ball, but I managed to respond. "You want me to tell you what's going on?"

"Eight seconds."

Luckily, I was an expert at keeping things short. "I found Bella. The person who took her wanted us to find her."

"Three seconds," Free said lazily.

"The person who took her was Ness."

"Ness?" Free repeated, forgetting all about her countdown. "Older woman about yea tall? Tough as nails and makes corn bread even better than Cady's?"

When I'd gone out to search, I should have taken her with me. Free *and* Jude should have been there when we'd found out the truth. Gabriel, too.

"Ness did it for Cady," I told Free. "And for Bales."

Free was quiet for long enough that I wondered if she was trying to make sense of what I'd said or if my temporary pardon had run out.

"Finding Bella was supposed to fix me." I didn't know what else to say or how to explain what I was talking about or why it mattered.

Fortunately, Free didn't believe in segues between one subject and the next. "We're unconventional," she told me. "Not broken."

We. I took a hesitant step toward her. "New part of the Creed?"

Free folded her arms over her chest. "Maybe." She paused. "I care about you, Kira," she told me, in a tone that would have been more appropriate for cursing. "And Jude cares, and you don't *get* to hold that against us. You don't get to lick your wounds in a corner and snarl when one of us gets too close, and you don't ever get to stand there bleeding and tell me that it's none of my business if you bleed out."

I meant to say okay, but what came out was "You packed my blanket."

"Of course I did!" Free exploded. "I thought you might need it."

"Not to interrupt what appears to be an extremely emotionally laden conversation about blankets . . ." Gabriel announced his presence and waited for the two of us to turn toward him before continuing, "but your dog is giving every appearance of having lost her freaking mind."

I started scanning the area for Saskia, but Gabriel stopped me. "Not your dog," he told me. "Hers." He nodded his head toward Free. "The female bloodhound is attacking the barn door like her family honor depends on it."

"Her Ladyship does have very strong feelings about doors," Free allowed. "You could say she doesn't like being shut out."

I had a feeling that pointed comment was aimed at me, but something about what Gabriel had said crept under my skin and lingered. "Was NATO with her?" I asked.

Gabriel turned to look at me.

"The male bloodhound," I clarified. "Jude's dog. Was he with Duchess?"

"No." Gabriel stared at me. "Why?"

"Speaking of Jude," Free put in, "given recent revelations, we could all use some unrelenting, reality-defying optimism right about now. Where is he?"

It took me a moment to realize that she was asking me. "I haven't seen Jude since the two of us fought," I said, suddenly able to feel my heartbeat in my stomach.

"He didn't go with you?" Free asked.

I scanned the property, half expecting Jude to pop out

of nowhere. Cady and Mac were moving from Ness's cabin toward the main house. A pair of FBI agents had cornered Bales, who looked like he'd aged a decade in a day.

No Jude.

That was when I heard the howling. I broke into a run without any conscious awareness of where I was going or why, but the moment the barn came into view, I realized that Duchess wasn't the only one pawing madly at the door. Saskia was right beside her, howling the way she had at Silver's graveside.

Wrong. Something is wrong. I made it to the barn door first. Gabriel and Free were right behind me. Free ducked down to the dogs' level, but all I could think about was the way that Silver's body had looked, wrapped in a blanket.

I pried the door open. Somehow, Gabriel made it inside first. I *felt* Duchess flying by us, but visually, the only thing I could see was the outline of NATO's form on the ground.

"No," I said. "Not after Silver. *I can't—*"

"Kira." I heard Free, but it took me a moment to realize that she'd somehow made her way past me and was kneeling next to NATO. "He's got a pulse."

Alive. I made my way toward them. *He's alive.* I went to the ground and laid a hand on NATO's neck. Beside me, Duchess whined. Saskia was still howling. My hands searched NATO for an injury but found nothing. He stirred beneath my touch. He tried to climb to his feet but stumbled.

"Ketamine." Gabriel's voice was tight. "The vet uses it to knock animals out. He'll be groggy. . . ."

Whatever else Gabriel was saying, I didn't hear it. The world slowed down around me, because Saskia was still howling, and NATO was trying to drag himself toward the back of the barn, and all I could think was that no one had seen Jude.

Ness had disappeared, and no one had seen Jude.

I took off in the direction that NATO was trying to go. There, at the back of the barn, a dozen rocks lay in a neat circle. In the middle of the circle, there was a large envelope. Behind it, a single white candle burned, the flame flickering before my eyes.

Unable to hear anything but the sound of my own ragged breathing, I bent to pick up the envelope. Before I could think better of it, I slid my finger beneath the flap, tearing it open. The sting of a paper cut barely registered as I removed the contents.

Three items.

The first was a map. A quick glance told me that someone had marked a spot, deep in the depths of the park, with a thick red X. The next two items were photographs. The first was one I'd never seen: Cady and Mac and Ash, older than they'd been in the last picture I'd seen—early twenties. Mac's expression was still serious. Ash's devil-may-care grin had taken on an edge. And Cady looked . . .

Happy.

I turned the picture over, half expecting a caption, but the back was blank. Ignoring the tightness in my chest, I turned my attention to the second photograph. It was facedown, and for several long seconds, I couldn't bring myself to turn it over.

Free reached over and did it for me. Her sharp intake of breath was the only warning I got before the face in that photo cut me, straight to the core.

"Jude." I bit down, like I could somehow unsay it. Like I could make the familiar, loopy grin in that photograph any less Jude's. The picture was old a year or two at least—but Jude still looked like himself. He'd been unmistakably *Jude* since he was a kid.

"Silver died." I wasn't sure why I was telling Free this now. "Silver is dead, and Ness drugged NATO, and Jude . . ."

I couldn't keep talking, but I refused to give in to the haze of shock that threatened to fog my mind. I didn't have the luxury of losing it right now. There was one thing that mattered and *only* one thing.

There was a white cloth, nailed to the wall, directly over the circle. I grabbed it and pulled it down, the sound of the ripping fabric jarring the rest of my senses back into play. I lifted the cloth to my nose. A faintly sweet, faintly chemical smell had me jerking it away from my face.

I didn't recognize the scent. I didn't have to in order to picture weatherworn hands pressing this cloth over Jude's face. The fingers on my left hand held tight to the pair of photographs from the envelope, to the map, and I thought back to the moment when I'd found Bella, lying beneath that canopy. I thought about how the child had said that her angel needed her help.

I remembered wondering if Bella had been bait, if I'd fallen into a trap.

Not a trap, I thought, bending at the waist with the force of the realization, the chloroformed rag in my hand. *A distraction.*

CHAPTER 52

The FBI confiscated the map, the pictures, and the cloth. The rangers began coordinating transportation to the far end of the park, an expansive ancient forest as different from the mountains as night from day.

We were told, by people who knew what they were doing, that Jude would be returned to us unharmed. That meant nothing to NATO. Jude's dog was groggy—and inconsolable.

I wasn't much better.

Inside the main house, Bales immediately started packing. He had an emergency pack half-ready to go, and the crisp, dispassionate way he moved reminded me that he'd been military—either intelligence or special forces. Without a word to the rest of us, he took out his phone, sent a text, and reached into his bag.

Cady caught his arm halfway there. "You're going after her."

"The FBI thinks the place Ness marked on that map is an end point," Bales said gruffly. "I happen to know the woman well enough to know that she wouldn't give away the game."

"You think the map is a starting point." Mac's eyes were sharp.

"I should have seen it." Bales never stopped moving, never sped up or slowed down or showed any hint of the toll this had to be taking. "The way the trail kept disappearing and reappearing. The way she was keeping to herself."

"You couldn't have known." Cady wasn't being generous. If she hadn't believed that, she wouldn't have said it.

Every muscle in Bales Bennett's body went taut. "She did this for me."

Ness had taken Bella to bring Cady home, to bring Mac home, to give Cady's father one last chance to make things right. I could see that but couldn't bring myself to care, because Ness Ashby had victimized an innocent child. She'd taken Jude. Whatever *game* she was playing, whatever her goal was now, she was using the person I loved most in this world to do it.

The person I'd hurt. The person I'd *meant* to hurt. The person who'd never done anything but try to take care of me.

"She did this," Bales said a second time, his voice sharp, "*for me.*"

"And what about the bodies she buried?" Gabriel had hung back, silent in the shadows, from the moment the FBI had taken the evidence we'd found. Now he didn't seem to be able to stop himself from speaking. "If one of them is Andrés—did she do that for *me*?"

I hadn't stopped once to think about what Ness being the kidnapper might mean for Gabriel. He'd known her. He'd trusted her.

"Whatever she's done or hasn't done," Bales said, meeting Gabriel's gaze and holding it, "I cannot believe the woman I know would have kept *any* information about your brother's disappearance from you."

"The woman you know took Jude." Free was on the warpath. "She knocked him out and *took* him and left some sick treasure map behind. I don't think we can assume there's much she wouldn't do."

"Free's right." Cady's voice resonated with the ache I could feel building deep in the pit of my stomach, deep in my bones. "The Ness I thought I knew wouldn't have taken my son. She couldn't have."

"You didn't see her," Bales said, his head bowed, his fingers holding tight to his pack. "When Ash went missing, you were too caught up in your own grief to see hers. But I saw it, day in and day out." He forced his eyes back up to Cady's, his head still bowed. "I made the call to my contacts in South America."

Cady took a literal step back from that admission.

"I told you that I wouldn't," Bales continued. "I told you that some things weren't worth the cost, but I loved Ash, too, and eventually, I broke. I called in favors that I never should have called in. I paid a price I never should have paid, and I went down there."

"You should have told me." Cady shuddered. "If I'd known . . ."

"You would have insisted on coming with me," Bales said. "I couldn't let that happen. So I went alone. And when I came back, when I told Ness that there was no trace of her boy—not a body, not rumors, *nothing*—she accepted it. She let go. She moved on." Bales swallowed. "And she started spending more and more time in the park."

Ash had been gone for eighteen years. I thought of the hash marks on the tree. *Days since he went missing?* I wondered. *Weeks?*

I tried to make this—any of it—make sense. "She didn't start burying people who died in the park until recently," I said. "Four years ago—or five."

"What changed?" Free asked.

"Five years ago," Bales Bennett said finally, "I broke down and hired a private detective to find my daughter."

"Five years ago"—Mac laid a hand on Cady's shoulder—"she realized that you had a son. She would have thought Jude was Ash's. She always thought that someday, for you, it was going to be Ash."

I couldn't tell how Mac felt about that—*any* of it.

"I told her the truth yesterday," Cady uttered desperately. "I told her that Ash and I weren't . . . that Jude wasn't . . ." She shuddered. "What if she takes that out on him?"

"Jude is yours, Cady." Mac drew in closer to her. "And

he's mine." That acknowledgment sucked the air from the room. "Whatever she's gone through—whatever she's going through—Ness wouldn't hurt him."

"She won't hurt the boy." Bales sounded infinitely surer of that than I felt. "But if we don't find her before the authorities do, she might hurt herself."

The deafening sound of a chopper drowned out Cady's reply. Bales strode toward the door.

"Let me guess," Mac called as we followed Bales out and saw a massive military-grade helicopter landing on the lawn. "You called in another favor."

Saskia pressed to my side the moment my foot hit dirt. Up ahead of us, Cady didn't tell her father that she was coming with him. She just climbed onto the chopper, calling Pad to her as she did. Mac followed but ordered his K9 to stay.

"Come on," Free told me, grabbing hold of my arm and pulling me toward the chopper. I signaled for Saskia. Duchess hesitated, reluctant to leave NATO to come to Free.

"You two stay here," Cady yelled over the sound of the blades.

"It's Jude," I said. When my words were lost to the din, I repeated them, yelled them. *"It's Jude."*

"I'll stay." Free pulled back. Nothing she could have said or done would have surprised me more. "I'll take care of NATO." She had to shout to be heard, but the look on her face was far fiercer than her tone. "Duchess and I will stay here, but Kira goes. Gabriel, too."

Free hated being left behind. She hated being left out. She was fearless—but she would stay if it meant that I didn't have to. She would take care of Jude's dog the same casual and no-nonsense way she took care of Jude and me.

One for all, and all for trouble.

Cady shook her head. "Kira, I can't let you—"

Free folded her arms over her chest and offered Cady a dangerous, glittering smile. "If you think I'm not resourceful enough to somehow rustle up an airlift of my own for Kira and Gabriel," she commented pointedly, "you'd be wrong."

CHAPTER 53

Stepping foot into a grove of giant sequoias was like walking back into the Jurassic age. All around me, trees that had stood for thousands of years stretched skyward, as tall as twenty-story buildings and thicker through the base than some apartments. In my entire life, I'd never seen something so majestic, so primal.

"There are dozens of groves in the Sierra Glades," Bales said, his voice echoing through the silent forest. "Ness marked one of the smaller ones on her map." He paused. "This one's the largest."

"And you think we're in the right place why?" Gabriel asked.

"I don't think," Bales replied evenly. "I know, because I know her." He lingered on that statement for a fraction of a second before returning to military strategist mode. "We've got a thousand acres to cover and depending on how competent the official search teams are, we could have less than an hour's head start."

None of us asked what Bales thought might happen if the FBI got to Ness and Jude first.

"There's upward of twenty thousand trees in this grove," Bales continued, his enunciation crisp. "Ness and Jude could be anywhere. The rest of you will take the dogs and search in pairs. Stay aware. With the drought, we've had more than our fair share of dying branches, and from that height . . ." He angled his head toward the breathtaking treetops. "Any falling item could be lethal."

"What about you?" Cady asked, staring at her father with an expression on her face that I couldn't quite parse.

"I'll head west," Bales replied. "I know a thing or two about hiding, and I might not need a K9 to pick up her trail."

That was the only good-bye the four of us got. Within seconds, Bales had disappeared into the forest. I turned toward Gabriel, but Cady stepped between us. "You'll go with Saskia and Kira?" she asked Mac. He nodded, and Cady spared a single glance at Gabriel. "You're with me."

Before I could formulate a reply, Cady drew a plastic bag out of the pocket of her cargo pants. Inside was a plain white T-shirt.

Jude's.

I stared at it, unable to draw my eyes away as Cady let Pad get the familiar scent. Moving robotically, I took it and offered it to Saskia next. And just like that, we were off.

Mac was a silent companion. He kept pace with me as my K9 blew past us both.

"You didn't bring your dog," I said as minutes ticked by and the silence of the forest overwhelmed me.

Mac said exactly what I needed to hear. "We're not looking for a body."

My eyes threatened to leak. *"Thank you."* I heard a tremor in my voice, but I didn't have the time for or the luxury of breaking down. Mac believed Jude was alive, believed that Ness wouldn't hurt him.

I could believe that, too.

Focus. Listen. Feel. Mountains and underground caverns weren't my territory. Waterfalls and rivers weren't home. But this was a forest—the *ultimate* forest—and I would be whatever I had to be, open the door on any memory and every instinct, to bring Jude home.

As I pushed onward in the direction Saskia had gone, I found myself wanting to say something. "I told Jude about you." I wasn't sure if that was a confession or a statement. "I told him that you were his father."

"If I'd known . . ." Mac replied, his voice lost to the massiveness of the wilderness around us. "If I could have been there, I would have."

I hadn't been sure until that moment that I would ever be able to look at Cady and not think about the way she'd kept my past a secret. But now? Now I knew that when I looked at her, I'd think about what—and who—she'd kept from Jude.

"He's loyal." Suddenly, I needed Mac to know that. "Funny. Stupid when it comes to girls. A total geek." I managed a smile that almost broke me. "He loves too easily and gives too much, and he's never even heard of a glass that's only partway full."

There was a sound like a *crack*. Mac lunged at me, grabbed me, twisting our bodies to the side. A massive branch crashed to the ground, an inch away from my face.

An instant later—if Mac had moved an instant slower—I would have been dead.

"Kira." Mac's tone was urgent. It was another second or two before I realized why. A dog was barking in the distance.

Not Saskia, I realized. *Pad.* Darting from Mac's grasp, I bolted toward the sound. The forest, the mammoth trees overhead, the burning in my muscles as I pushed myself to the brink and past it—none of that mattered.

Find. Recall. Re-find.

Pad was the best we'd ever trained. Cady was with her. They'd found something.

When Saskia fell in beside me, I followed her lead. Mac yelled my name, but I didn't care what he was saying.

The only thing that I cared about was Jude.

Saskia made it to Cady before I did and added her voice to Pad's. The woman who'd raised me stood with her hand on the trunk of one of the giants, its gnarled bark twisting like something out of a fairy tale.

Like something out of a nightmare.

It was only when Cady stepped forward that I realized

that the dogs weren't barking at the tree. They were barking at what was inside.

I hadn't seen it at first, but as Cady disappeared, I made out an opening in the tree's base, a doorway. I was halfway to following when Mac locked a hand around my shoulder. An instant later, Gabriel appeared, winded, and skittered to a stop beside us.

It's hollow, I thought. *The tree is hollow, and my family's inside.*

Before I could shrug off Mac's grip, a familiar form appeared where Cady had stood a moment before.

Ness held a hand up to the dogs. "Stay."

There was enough casual oomph to that command that Pad looked to me. It took every ounce of control I could muster not to tear into Ness myself, but we still hadn't seen Jude.

"Stay." I repeated Ness's command. Pad sat, her ears flicking forward, but Saskia took a threatening step toward the old woman.

"I guess Saskia won't be staying out here," Ness commented wryly, "though I'm afraid I can't vouch for her safety inside."

Jude was inside. Cady was inside.

"Well," Ness said, turning her attention to Gabriel and Mac. "Don't just stand there, boys. Come in."

CHAPTER 54

The sequoia wasn't completely hollow, but someone had carved out enough space for a small room. Jude lay prone on the floor. Cady knelt beside him, trembling. I started for them, but Ness stopped me, something metal digging into my side.

Gun. My brain processed the situation on a delay. *Rifle.* Saskia had bolted ahead. She nosed at Jude's still body.

"Get away from my daughter."

I could barely hear Cady's words over the ringing in my ears. Jude wasn't moving. Guns were *blood.* Guns were *vicious.* Guns were *cheating.*

"Whatever this is, Ness, it's between you and me. Leave my kids out of it."

I forced myself to focus on Cady's voice. On the other end of the gun, Ness looked at me, the oddest expression in her eyes. "It's amazing, isn't it?" she asked Cady softly. "How much you can love a child?"

Ash. I struggled to form the name in my mind. *She's talking about Ash. Not me. Not Jude. We don't have anything to do with this.*

But there was a gun pointed at me, and Jude was . . .

"Unconscious," Cady told me. She latched a hand around Saskia's collar. If Saskia attacked, Ness might shoot me.

And if I attack . . . That was the reason Cady had told me that Jude was unconscious. He wasn't dead, and I was able to keep a whisper's hold on myself.

"You brought me back here." Cady did what she could to draw Ness's attention. "I came." Her voice vibrated with intensity. "I'm here."

"And if I lower this gun," Ness countered, "you'll leave, and whatever you know, whatever secrets you're keeping—they'll walk out of this park with you."

What secrets? I wondered, but deep in my mind, the question was lost under the cacophony of others. I wondered what it would sound like if Ness pulled the trigger. I wondered what it would feel like. I wondered if I would feel anything at all.

"What about *your* secrets, Ness?" Gabriel's voice snapped me into the moment. "What about the things that you've been keeping from me?" Gabriel was smiling, but the curve of his lips was utterly out of place on his face. His eyes glittered dangerously in the scant light. "The bodies," he clarified. "The ones the FBI found. You can't think of any reason I might have a vested interest in how that turns out?"

Ness wavered, just for a moment. The gun never moved,

but her gaze flicked toward Gabriel. Beside me, I saw Mac shift his weight ever so slightly.

"Nature can be merciless," Ness told Gabriel. "I gave them what mercy I could."

Mac eased toward Ness—toward the gun. Her head whipped toward him.

Don't push her, Mac. My pulse jumped in my neck. Saskia strained against Cady's hold, but Mac didn't so much as tense.

When he spoke, it was with the same tone he'd used with me when I was in shock. "You buried the dead. You gave them peace."

For a split second, I was sure that she'd recognize the slight shift of his weight, that she'd react—that I'd pay the price. But instead, Ness pressed her lips together. "I couldn't bring them back, but I could put their bodies to rest. Honor them. Remember them. *Mourn* them."

"And what about Andrés?" Gabriel said. There was nothing light or airy in his voice, no smile on his face as he stepped toward Ness. "Did you mourn my brother? Remember him? Give him peace?"

"Gabriel, no." Ness turned her attention back to him. "I don't know what happened to your brother."

Seconds ticked by, the two of them locked onto each other. Mac lunged forward. Ness turned the gun on him so fast that I wondered if she'd known he'd be the one to make a move the entire time.

"If I knew what happened to Andrés," Ness said, her voice

taking on an uncomfortable edge, her gaze on Mac's now, her finger hovering over the trigger, "I wouldn't have left you to wonder. Not you, Gabriel. You're family." Her chin shook. "*I* wouldn't do that to family."

"We didn't leave you wondering on purpose," Cady said, her throat making an attempt at strangling the words. "If we knew what happened to Ash . . ."

Ness turned the gun on Cady, stepping back from Mac, back from all of us. "You know something," she said, as if willing those words to be true. "When you left, you weren't just running away from your father. You were running away from what happened." Ness's voice went up an octave. "*Something happened.*"

Ness had raised Cady. She loved her. But as I breathed the stale air inside that tree and watched the way Ness looked at *my mother*, at Jude, still unconscious on the floor, I suddenly knew that Bales had been wrong.

Ness might not have come here intending to hurt Cady, but she could do it.

Mac must have sensed the same thing, because he held his hands up, stepping back and away from Ness, and he started to talk. "We went down to South America to retrieve a client's daughter. She'd been taken and was being held at a camp farther into the jungle than anyone else was willing to go."

Cady shifted to put her body more squarely in front of Jude's. She had a two-handed hold on Saskia now. "We found the girl." Cady's voice cracked. I could see her folding in on herself, see the memories taking hold. "We got her out. We made it to the extraction point. But Ash . . ."

Words failed Cady. I'd been there. I wanted, more than anything, to go to her, to block her body with mine the way she was blocking Jude.

"Ash what?" Ness prompted silkily, her voice so soft that the lack of volume almost masked the intensity underneath.

"Ash went back." Mac provided the answer. I could sense him willing Ness to turn the gun his way, but she kept it focused on Cady.

"Why?" Ness demanded. "Why would he go back?"

"I don't know," Cady said.

"Why?" Ness took a step forward, her fingers tightening around the rifle. Saskia strained against Cady's hold, but Cady hauled her back. "Why, Cadence?"

"I don't know." Cady lost it. "The girl we'd saved was in bad shape. Mac had taken enemy fire. We made it back by the skin of our teeth, with minutes to spare, and *Ash went back.*"

I knew, beyond any human knowing, that Cady had relived that moment, again and again. This was her forest. Her Girl.

"You left him," Ness said, her volume rising.

"There was an explosion." Cady shuddered. "Enemy forces were incoming. We were outnumbered and out-gunned, and . . ." Her head bowed with the force of what she was about to say. "We left him."

The silence that followed that statement was deafening. I calculated the space between Cady and me, the space between Cady and Ness, the chances that I could get to the gun, the risk that Saskia would break Cady's hold, the consequences if she did.

"Ash knew." Mac took first one step toward Ness, then another. "When he went back in—whatever he was thinking, whatever he was after—he knew that he wouldn't make it back out." For the first time, I could hear something that wasn't *calm* or *steady* in Mac's tone. "Ash *knew* we'd have to leave him there."

Ness turned her head toward Mac, the gun still aimed at Cady's chest. "Why?"

As hard as it sometimes was for me to read people, I heard echoes of a thousand more questions in that single word. *Why would Ash choose to go back? Why would he take that kind of risk? Why hadn't he thought, in that moment, of her?*

"Ash was always in it for the adrenaline." Mac shook his head. "He liked taking chances. He liked winning. But in the weeks leading up to that mission, he was different. The chances he was taking were less calculated." Mac shook his head, his voice tightening. "I confronted him about it, but he kept pushing, right up to the end."

"He knew," Cady whispered. Then she repeated the words again, louder.

"Knew what?" Mac asked the question before Ness could.

When Cady answered, her answer was only for him. "Ash knew that we were together, Mac." She swallowed, her eyes closing, just for an instant. "He knew that I was pregnant."

Silence fell, for one second, two, three. And then Ness spoke. "Loving you," she told Cady, her voice almost tender, "killed my son."

"You never told me." That was from Mac. "That you were pregnant. You told Ash?"

Cady stared at the barrel of the gun. "He found the test. He asked me. I couldn't lie to him. I was going to tell you, Mac, but then we lost Ash. And I didn't tell you, because I didn't deserve to." She lifted her gaze to Mac's. "I didn't deserve you."

Cady had blamed herself for what had happened with Ash. She'd given up the man she'd loved in penance. It was sick and twisted and wrong, but I'd been to the dark place, too. I knew what it was like to push people away because you couldn't stand to be comforted. I knew what it was like to hurt the people you loved when the person you really wanted to hurt was yourself.

"What else?" Ness said suddenly.

Cady shook her head. "There is nothing else."

"What else don't I know?" Ness asked, like Cady had never spoken. "What else aren't you telling me?"

The answer was *nothing*, and I knew, in the part of my gut that could feel danger like the vibration of a tuning fork struck against metal, that *nothing* was the wrong answer. Ness didn't want to hear it. And if we *made* her hear it . . .

My gaze went to Saskia. She wasn't straining against Cady's hold anymore. She was still, and there was something wild in her eyes.

"Bales couldn't find even a hint of what happened to my son," Ness said, the pace of her words deliberate and slow. "Not even a rumor. People don't just disappear, Cady. Not like that. Not him." Ness let her finger rest on the trigger. "Did he get out?" The question reverberated off the walls. "What happened to him? What did he go back for?"

"I don't know," Cady said softly. Saskia lowered her head slightly.

Ness's finger shook. I stopped breathing, stopped thinking, every muscle in my body preparing to fight. On the ground, Jude stirred, and like a veil had been lifted from her eyes, Ness shifted the gun from Cady to Jude.

I held up my hand. It shook, but I held it up. *Stay, Sass. She'll hurt you. She'll hurt our family.*

Jude groaned and sat up. "I suppose," he said, his voice groggy, "that there are worse places to wake up than inside a tree." Then he registered the rest of his surroundings. "Oh."

Oh as in *Oh, someone is pointing a gun at me.*

Oh as in even Jude couldn't see the bright side of this.

"Tell me my boy got out," Ness said. The words were for Cady's ears, but she was looking at Jude. *Cady's boy.* "Or tell me that my son died there. Tell me something."

She was going to pull the trigger. If Cady couldn't tell her what she wanted to hear, she was going to shoot. And if I tried to stop her . . .

I can hear the gun going off. I can see the blood.

"He got out."

At first, I thought Cady was the one who'd told Ness what she wanted to hear. It wasn't until Gabriel turned toward me that I realized that I was the one who'd spoken.

I couldn't fight a gun—not with claws and teeth, not with every instinct I had. All I could do was *this*. I could keep my hand up. I could keep Saskia from attacking. I could keep Ness's attention on *me*.

"Ash got out." I repeated myself, my voice louder this time, steadier. If Ness Ashby wanted to shoot someone, she could shoot me. She could listen to me telling her what she wanted to hear, realize that I was lying, and shoot *me*.

"Kira." Cady saw what I was doing. More than that, she saw that it might work.

"Everyone wondered how I survived," I said, willing Ness to listen, willing her to aim at me and not Jude. Not at Cady, not at Sass—*at me*. "A little girl, all alone in the woods for weeks." A few days ago, I might not have sounded so close to it—so sure. I waited until I was sure that I had the whole of Ness's attention, and then I lied. "I wasn't alone."

I bent down and pulled up the leg of my jeans, revealing the deep, ridged scars around my ankle. "There was a trap." If I could just keep talking, if I could just keep saying things that *were* true, maybe I could distract her from the one thing that wasn't. "I saw a wolf caught in one, early on. Later, it was me." My mouth tasted metallic. The memory smelled like rust—like blood. "Somebody tipped the police

off about my mother's body. Someone told them about me."
I swallowed. "Someone found me dying in that trap and let
me go."

"You're a bad liar," Ness said, her voice low.

Survival wasn't just about being the fastest or the
strongest or the one who refused to die. When it came to
confrontations, survival was just as much about bluffing,
about pretending strength, when you had none.

"Some people," I said, my voice humming in a way that
didn't sound small or scared or human at all, "don't want to
be found. Ash chose to go back in. Is it so hard to believe
that he might have chosen to disappear? That something
might have pulled him to check in on Cady, year after
year?"

One second I was standing there, and the next, Ness had
me backed up against the wall, the barrel of the gun digging
into my throat.

Good. Let her shoot me. Let her kill *me.* I could hear
Saskia snarling, hear Cady and Jude trying to keep her
under control.

It won't last.

"You expect me to believe," Ness said icily, "that my son
disappeared in the depths of a South American jungle eighteen years ago, but that he just happened to reappear, years
later, in the woods on the outskirts of a nowhere little town,
to save *you*?"

I didn't expect Ness to believe that. I didn't expect anyone to believe it. I couldn't swallow. I couldn't breathe.

But I could keep Ness's attention on me as Gabriel moved in behind her.

"He had a scar." I choked out that sentence. Ness stared at me for a moment, then eased back, just enough to allow me the breath to speak.

"What did you say?" Ness asked, suddenly hoarse.

"The man who saved me," I said quietly. "He had a scar."

Most people did—especially those with devil-may-care grins, who liked winning and taking risks and lived in a dangerous world.

"What scar?"

My heart jarred my rib cage with every beat. Gabriel was nearly behind Ness now. I couldn't let her turn around. I couldn't let her take her eyes off of me. So I thought back— to the picture in Cady's old room, to the one Ness had left in the envelope when she'd taken Jude.

I pictured John Ashby in my mind. I pictured his face.

"Here," I said, raising my hand and sliding it down my jaw and across my chin. "The man I saw in the woods—the man who saved me—he had a scar *here*."

Ness's body seemed to give out beneath her. The gun dipped, and Gabriel lunged, grabbing the barrel with both hands. An instant before Ness collapsed to the ground, Cady lost her hold on Saskia.

I heard my girl go for Ness. I saw it in slow motion—and then I saw Bales. Had he been waiting outside? Had he just found us? He threw himself in front of Ness, and Saskia's teeth sank into *his* arm.

"Bales." Ness choked out his name. Cady called for her father. I threw myself forward, getting a hold on Saskia the way Bales Bennett had held me in the sheriff's office. I whispered to her.

I'm here. I'm okay. Saskia. You're Saskia. I'm Kira. I'm here.

As Saskia turned toward me, her whole body shaking as she attempted to burrow into mine, Bales sank to the ground, where Ness was still saying his name, over and over again.

"FBI is incoming." Bales kept his tone gentle enough that I could barely push air in and out of my chest. "Ness," he said softly. "Nessie."

The glassy look in Ness's eyes disappeared as she turned toward Bales. "I wouldn't have hurt them."

I didn't believe that. Maybe Bales did. Maybe he didn't. Either way, he let his arms curve around her. "I know."

CHAPTER 55

Ness Ashby turned herself in to the FBI. I expected
Cady to have us packed and on the road the moment
we'd finished giving our statements, but this time,
she didn't seem in a hurry to leave. Pandora's box had been
opened inside that ancient sequoia, and not even one of the
most stubborn women I knew could close it.

"Which tie says 'Congratulations, it's a boy, I have completely accepted the fact that my father is not, in fact, an
astronaut'?" Jude held up two nearly identical bow ties for
my inspection. He was preparing to spend the day with
Mac—clearly a bow tie occasion.

"The one on the left," I deadpanned.

Jude smiled beatifically. For someone who'd been kidnapped less than twenty-four hours earlier, he'd bounced
back quickly.

"So," I said. "You and Mac."

"I clearly inherited his manly physique."

"Jude." I gave him a look.

"I don't know what to say, Kira mine. The man is responsible for half my DNA. He seems like a good guy. Broad shoulders, steady in a crisis, likes dogs . . ."

"He would have been there," I said quietly. "If Cady had let him, if she'd told him about you—"

"Mom loves us." Jude stopped messing with the tie. "More than anything, Kira. She would have taken a bullet for me yesterday. Given your newfound proclivity for bluffing gun-toting little old women, I can only conclude that she might still end up taking one for you someday."

Jude wasn't the type to get bogged down in *ifs*. He loved me. He loved Cady. Cady and I loved each other. For Jude, it really was that simple.

I swallowed. "I'm sorry." Those weren't words I'd ever really understood. They weren't words I'd had much—if any practice saying. "About yesterday. The things I said to you. The way I said them."

"You're allowed to have feelings, Kira. In fact"—Jude tweaked the end of my ponytail—"I think it's a good thing. Before you know it, you'll be holding a boom box over *your* head, professing your love for—"

I narrowed my eyes at him.

"Changing the subject now!" Jude declared. "Is it me, or does surviving a kidnapping really bring out my cheekbones?"

I spent the afternoon with Free, out at the tree where I'd buried Silver. She made me tell her about finding Silver, about wrapping her body in the sheet, about digging the grave. We cried, both of us—ugly-cried, with a side of hating the world and loving the ones still with us even harder.

"It means something," I told Free, rubbing NATO's ears as he laid his head down in my lap, "that you stayed so I could go."

"I've never been as good as you are at search and rescue." Free shrugged that statement off like it didn't matter. "But I like to think that when push comes to shove, I'm good at taking care of people."

NATO seemed to appreciate being included in "people."

"Extreme Hide-and-Seek?" Free asked me. She'd mourned. She'd let me thank her. That was about all the sitting around she could take.

"I don't know," I replied slowly. "I was thinking . . . it's an awfully lovely day for mischief. Think we could get a little *creative* in town?"

"Do I even want to know what that means?" Gabriel appeared to have even fewer qualms about eavesdropping than I did. Saskia walked beside him. He gave no signs of treating her like a danger or a liability, and I would have sworn she wasn't so much as even *entertaining* the idea of eating his face.

"I hear you jumped the gun," Free commented, shielding her eyes from the sun and giving Gabriel an assessing look. "Literally. As in, you literally jumped on top of an old lady holding a gun."

"Not actually what the idiom refers to," Gabriel countered. "But who am I to quibble?"

A loud and unmistakable sound—followed by an equally unmistakable smell—permeated the air.

"You'll have to excuse Duchess," Free said primly. "Cocky teenage boys make Her Ladyship gassy."

"Her Ladyship?" Gabriel asked, arching an eyebrow.

"Duchess," I explained, nodding to the dog. "Also known as Her Ladyship."

"I hesitate to point this out," Gabriel said, "but the proper address for a duchess is *Her Grace*."

Free and I stared at him.

"What?" Gabriel muttered. "A former juvenile delinquent can't enjoy the occasional historical romance novel?"

Free recovered before I did. "Pretty sure that makes it official," she told me. "He's definitely Miscreant material."

An hour later, when Cady joined us at Silver's grave, Gabriel made his exit. Cady watched him go.

"I believe Ness was telling the truth about Gabriel's brother," Cady told me after a moment. "He wasn't one of her lost ones."

I wondered if Gabriel believed that. I wondered if he was headed back to his place to stare at the maps on the wall.

"Still think he's too *volatile* for us to be around?" Free asked, conveniently forgetting that Cady had only cautioned *me* to stay away from Gabriel.

Cady brushed a stray strand of blond hair out of Free's face. "I'll make you a deal," she told Free. "You agree to ask for makeup finals, and I'll forget about the hitchhiking."

"Or," Free countered, "I agree not to hitchhike again, and you forget about finals."

Free enjoyed having the last word enough that I wasn't surprised when she tossed Cady a triumphant grin and sauntered off.

I wasn't sure if I was ready to be alone with Cady yet. She knelt and laid her hand gently against the freshly turned dirt of Silver's grave. I stood, staring down at Cady, down at the place I'd buried Silver.

"She was a mess of a puppy." Cady closed her eyes, her fingers curling downward into the dirt. "Chewed everything, cried if you left her alone at night, spent the first two years of her life convinced she was a lapdog instead of a German shepherd."

"She saved me." My voice was every bit as hoarse as Cady's. "*You* saved me."

"Did you ever think," Cady said, still looking down, "even once, Kira, that maybe you saved us? Me. Jude. Silver."

My throat stung. "You should have told me the truth." I struggled to find the words. My lips felt clumsy forming them. "Maybe not at first, but later, when I was older . . ." I swallowed. "I could have handled it. If you'd been the one who told me, I could have been strong."

Cady turned to look at me, incredulous. "You've always been strong, Kira." When I didn't reply, she stood. "Do you think Saskia's weak? Because of her scars, because of what she's survived?"

"No." I thought my girl was beautiful and wild and strong, and if I could have spent five minutes alone with the person who'd left marks on her, I would have showed *him* what weakness was.

"Yesterday, when Ness turned that gun on you . . ." Cady shook her head, her lips pressed into a thin white line. "I just kept thinking that it should have been me." She paused, then repeated herself. "It should have been me, Kira, and not just then. When you were a kid, growing up in that house, fighting for your life in the forest, the years afterward when you had to fight *so hard* just to look people in the eye . . . it should have been me." Cady's voice shook. "There should be a way for a parent to do that for their child, to go through the things that no kid should have to go through, to feel every ounce of that pain so that you feel none." She let out a ragged breath. "But there's not. There are things that I can't protect you from and things that I can't undo, and it breaks me. It breaks me in ways that I hope you never understand, but I have never—not once, not even for a moment—wanted to protect you because I thought you *couldn't* handle something. I just . . ." Cady lost her grip on her emotions then. I'd never seen her cry before, and I thought of Jude, deciding that he didn't need to know about his father if asking hurt her so badly. "I thought you shouldn't *have* to," Cady said finally. "I thought that maybe once—just once—I could be strong for you."

"Once?" I asked, the muscles in my chest constricting. "Cady, you've been there every day—"

"I'm your mom." Cady reached out and laid a hand gently against my cheek. "It's my job."

I leaned into her touch and thought about Jude saying that she would have taken a bullet for either of us. I thought about how close we'd come to losing each other the day before.

"And speaking of a mother's job," Cady said, pulling it together and fixing me with a capital-L *Look*. "If you *ever* literally step into the line of fire again, I will—"

She cut off abruptly, and I realized we had company. Bales came to stand on my other side. "Don't mind me," he told Cady mildly. "By all means, try to find an effective way of threatening a fearless child."

Cady snorted. She wasn't fearless. Neither was I, but it was clear from her father's tone that he saw himself as having been in her position more than once.

"I expect you'll be leaving soon." There was no judgment whatsoever in Bales Bennett's tone.

"We will," Cady said. "Mac is going to come back with us—at least for a little while." She paused, and the silence stretched out like a canyon between them, until Cady muttered three little words. "You could, too."

The edges of Bales's mouth crept upward. Cady's did the same. She didn't wait for a verbal response, and her father didn't offer one as she turned and walked back toward the house.

"You got something to add?" Bales asked me when he noticed me staring at him.

I stuffed my hands into my pockets. "Not a thing."

He'd spent half a lifetime here, with Ness. Whatever the last months of his life held for her, it wasn't going to be pretty. He *could* come home with us, but as I took in the overwhelming view of the mountain and breathed in the summer air, I wasn't sure that he would.

"There's an election coming up," Bales said after a long moment. "For sheriff."

I thought of Gabriel, of the way his stepfather had approached Bella's case, of the thing's he'd said to me.

"You have a candidate in mind?" I asked Bales.

"One of the FBI agents has family here. Seems to me he's a bit burned out on the bureau."

I felt the edges of my lips curve slightly upward. A gentle wind lifted my hair off my shoulders. For several minutes, Bales and I stood there in silence, and then he reached into his back pocket and pulled something out.

A photograph, folded and creased.

"I heard what you said to Ness yesterday—about Ash." Bales unfolded the picture. He stared at it for a moment, then held it out to me. "Figured you were bluffing."

I took the picture from him and recognized it as the one Ness had left for us the day before—Cady and Mac and Ash, in their early twenties.

"Funny thing," Bales continued. "Ash did have a scar that ran from his jaw to his chin—but he didn't get it until after the three of them started working hand in hand with the military."

I didn't follow what the implication of that statement was until I looked down at the photograph in my hand. *Cady. Mac. Ash.* Looking at it now, I could hear every confession that had crossed Cady's lips the day before. I could *see* John Ashby reaching the extraction point and turning back.

What I *couldn't* see was a scar in the photograph. No white line slashed across Ash's jaw.

That's not possible.

"How did you know?" Bales asked me. "About the scar?"

Suddenly, I was back in the forest, caught in a trap. *Girl sees Man. Man helps her. Man always helps her—*

In the span between one breath and the next, the memory was gone, and no matter how hard I fought to get it back, I saw nothing but the forest, the wolf, the dark-haired woman's body on the kitchen floor.

I was bluffing, I thought, my head spinning. *I was just trying to distract Ness. I made it up.*

So why was it suddenly so hard to breathe?

"Maybe I will take Cady up on that offer," Bales said, studying my expression. "I'd like to see more of this town of yours—more of your forest."

Something wet and warm nudged my hand, and I jumped. I looked down to Saskia—*loyal* and *wild* and *strong-willed* and *scarred*. I'd never questioned how she'd come to us, who had dumped her on Cady's property, why her previous owner had finally let her go.

As I sank down next to her, my fingers curling into her fur, her heart beating in tune with mine—I wondered. Wondered who had saved her. Wondered who had delivered her to Cady.

To me.

ACKNOWLEDGMENTS

The writing, revising, and copyediting of this book spanned two and a half years, two pregnancies, two babies, and the most hectic period of my life to date, and I could not have done it without a wealth of support from people to whom I am incredibly grateful. First and foremost, my editor, Kieran Viola, is incredible—all of the characters (but especially Kira, Gabriel, and Free) became so much more themselves with her guidance. I could not ask for a more supportive, thoughtful, hardworking editor, and I am so grateful for the way she worked with me to give me some time off when my babies were small. I am also incredibly thankful for my agent, Elizabeth Harding, and the rest of my team at Curtis Brown (especially Ginger Clark, Holly Frederick, and Sarah Perillo), who fight for my books and bring me so many smiles along the way. I am also blessed to have an amazing publishing team and would like to thank Emily Meehan, Mary Mudd, Marci Senders,

Dina Sherman, and Cassie McGinty for all of their hard work on my behalf.

I am also so thankful for all of the support I have received (and continue to receive) from family and friends. I've been an author since I was nineteen, but the transition to being a writer *and* a mom is not one I could have made without such an incredible support system, full of people who are always there to help when I need them. I am particularly grateful to my husband, Anthony, who is the most incredible partner I could ask for; to my parents, who are never more than a call away; to our wonderful babysitters and daycare providers; to my colleagues and students at the University of Oklahoma; and to Rachel Vincent, who in addition to being my partner-in-crime for all things writing, was also one of the first people to come visit me after each of my babies was born.

Finally, thanks go out to all of the readers, librarians, teachers, and booksellers who have supported my books for more than a decade. The ongoing support for my Naturals series in particular was one of the things that inspired me to ask myself, "What would I get if I mixed *The Naturals* with *Raised by Wolves* and threw in three generations of family drama?" This book was the result.

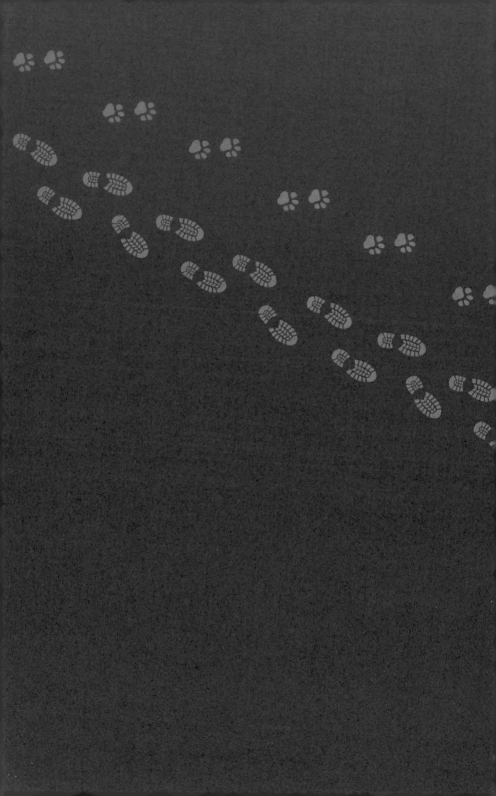